# Faithful

## LOUISE BAY

Love
Louise Bay

Love
Lois & Gary

Published by Louise Bay 2014
Copyright © 2014 Louise Bay. All rights reserved

Without prejudice to the generality of the foregoing, no part of this publication maybe reproduced, stored in or introduced into a retrieval system, or transmitted, in any form, or by any means (electronic, mechanical, photocopying, recording or otherwise) without the prior written permission of the author of this book.

This is a work of fiction. Names, characters, businesses, places, events and incidents are either the products of the author's imagination or used in a fictitious manner. Any resemblance to actual persons, living or dead, or actual events is purely coincidental. The author acknowledges the trademarked status and trademark owners referenced in this work of fiction, which have been used without permission. The publication/use of these trademarks is not authorized, associated with or sponsored by the trademark owners.

ISBN - 978-1-910747-00-1

# Chapter One

**You girls up for a glass or four of wine tonight?**

I didn't need to ask twice. There were advantages to having single girlfriends. We were all set for 7 p.m. at the Chancery Bar.

"Leah, can you pop into my office when you have five minutes?" David was a senior partner. He was a good guy, generally, maybe a bit handsy at work functions, but you couldn't take that personally—that was life at a City law firm. Compared to most of the partners, he was generally fair. He never threw anything at me or swore at me, and so I was a step ahead of most of my girlfriends who were lawyers. But of course, he didn't mean when I 'had five minutes.' He meant 'drop what you are doing.'

I grabbed a notebook and headed toward David's office. "How can I help?"

"Take a seat, Leah." David was soft-spoken but authoritative. "I've been thinking about our conversation last week, about you developing your client relationship skills. Clients like you, Leah. You're a good listener. You seem to understand their concerns. I want to use that and get you involved when we pitch for new clients. Speak to marketing and let's get some time in the schedule in the next few days to see what you can contribute."

I'd been waiting for this opportunity. I'd worked hard for six years at this firm and finally I was getting some recognition. It would mean more work for me, but I could be good at this stuff. If only I could be as successful in my personal life.

7 p.m. came around quickly and I emailed Anna and Fran to say I would be running a bit late. When I arrived, they seemed very excited. Fran got laid on the weekend and Anna was living vicariously.

Fran was gorgeous but couldn't keep a guy for longer than two weeks. Her relationships seemed to involve her spotting someone she liked, followed by three months of stalking him to find out everything about him—where he liked to hang out, what he did, who his friends were, etc. etc.—followed by a 'chance' encounter that ended in a couple of great shags, after which he never called her and she moved on to the next one.

My best friend Anna had a different approach to men. She would date a guy for three to six months, and when he was besotted with her, she got bored and dumped him.

I was by far the most conservative of the three of us. Charlie and I had been together six years.

"So, what's your news, Leah?" Anna asked.

"Well, David wants me to get involved in client relationships. Going out to clients on pitches and stuff. I'm so thrilled he asked me. Not many associates get that opportunity."

"That's so great! Finally, all that hard work is paying off! I hope it's not just a chance to spend more time with you though, Leah. He gives me the creeps."

"Ugh, that's so gross. He's old enough be my fath—well, much older brother." We all laughed so loudly that others at adjoining tables turned to look. "He's happily married. Oh, and as of Saturday night, I'm engaged."

"WHAT!" Anna and Fran screamed in unison.

"Yeah, he asked me. Finally." Saying it aloud made me feel sick.

"Well, you sound excited," Anna said.

"Hmm, you're right. I'm not. But I guess that's just because it's a bit anticlimactic, right?"

"Er, I guess it could be. I thought you'd been waiting for this for years," Fran said.

"Well, yes, that's what we've been leading up to for all this time, and the timing is good. I'm established at work and Charlie just made junior partner, and if we want to start a family we need to start sooner rather than later." Hardly romantic and passionate, but after six years, was that what a relationship was about?

"Let's change the subject. Fran, tell me about the sex. Was he worth the wait?"

"You have no idea," she said. "I came five times in two hours. He was unbelievable, despite alarmingly small equipment." We collapsed into giggles again and ordered another bottle of wine.

On the tube home, I wondered if I would feel differently, more excited, if any of my past boyfriends had just asked me to marry them. Probably not. I was still in touch with my only serious boyfriend before Charlie, and as much as I was still fond of him, I knew I didn't want to be married to him.

Charlie was a good guy—solid. We met when I was interviewing for his firm while I was at law school. I went travelling for a couple of years after Uni, but was finally convinced by my parents that I couldn't travel forever and that real life had to kick in at some point.

I didn't get the job with Charlie's firm, but I did get a Charlie as a boyfriend. After that, life just seemed to take over and had gone by in a bit of a blur. I started my training with the law firm where I did get the job, one of the best in the City. I didn't *not* enjoy my job—I was good at it and it paid well. Charlie's career went from strength to strength.

We worked hard and we played hard. We moved in together after a couple of years together. It made sense, as it meant I didn't have to pay rent—his flat was a birthday gift from his wealthy parents for his 21st.

Charlie was hopeless at any kind of life admin, so I made sure all the bills were paid. On top of that, both our jobs were very demanding; if we wanted to see each other, living together seemed the best option. It wasn't particularly romantic, but it worked. We rarely argued and life just rumbled on. Our sex life also just rumbled on. We occasionally had sex during the week but mainly it was restricted to weekends, and then not every weekend. That's how it was when you'd been together a long time, though.

I expected Charlie to propose soon after we moved in together, but he didn't, so from time to time I brought up marriage and children and he skillfully changed the subject. That was the next step, wasn't it? I didn't understand what he was waiting for. Just after I turned thirty, I gave him an ultimatum: Either we got married or we split up. I had given him six months to decide. I needed something more from him. I felt relieved after I gave him the deadline, but increasingly I was beginning to think that the 'more' I needed wasn't his hand in marriage.

When I got home, I ran a bath. Charlie wasn't home; he sent a text to say he might have to work through the night. I knew first-hand what the demands were of being a City lawyer.

My skin felt wonderful after my bath, soft and smooth. With Charlie at work so much recently, I had been spending more time at the gym. My skin always improved after regular workouts. I slipped on a silk robe and climbed into bed with my iPad to check my email. Along with the usual sales promotions and news alerts, I had had three LinkedIn invitations. I logged in to my account and accepted them, and then I typed 'Daniel Armitage' into the search box.

He was my first high school crush. We were only at the same school together for a couple of years; he moved away and we hadn't stayed in touch. We were 15 when he left, and my crush always remained unspoken. I suspected he had liked my best friend, so if I said anything I figured it would have only ended in heartache.

Four results came back from my search. Two with photos, two without. Well, he certainly wasn't either of the Daniels in the photos. Looking at the other two profiles, one was the right age. He had gone to Oxford University the same year as I had gone to Warwick. I had nothing to lose. I sent Daniel Number Two an invitation to connect. I didn't add anything personal to the message; if it wasn't the right Daniel, it would be less embarrassing.

I must have fallen asleep shortly after. I woke up when Charlie climbed into bed, reeking of alcohol. It was 3 a.m.

I had an early meeting the next day. We were leading up to a closing on a big transaction, the sale of a well-known high street chain of restaurants. I was up and out before Charlie woke up, and in the office by 7:30 a.m., prepared for the meeting. I wanted to impress David. I dressed carefully and conservatively in a black trouser suit, a nude silk camisole, and killer nude heels. I felt great.

The meeting went until lunchtime, and when we finished the clients seemed happy. Everything was on track. David praised me on my contribution to the meeting and the deal team in general. Work was going well.

When I got back to my desk, I listened to my voicemails while scrolling through the emails that had come through since this morning. My second voicemail was from Charlie, saying he would be working late again. I didn't hear the end of his voicemail as I was distracted by a LinkedIn notification: Daniel Armitage had accepted my invitation and sent me a message.

**Hey, stranger. What have you been up to? D**

My heartbeat seemed embarrassingly loud—so loud I got self-conscious and had to go to the bathroom. What was my problem? It was just some email from a high school crush who I hadn't seen for 15 years. I needed to stop being so dramatic. After returning to my desk, I forwarded the message to my personal email account and went on with my day. I didn't need any distractions.

I left the office at a decent time. I couldn't get home quickly enough; I wanted to email Daniel back. I picked up a bottle of wine on the way and, before I changed or even kicked off my heels, I found my iPad.

**Hey stranger, yourself. I take it I am talking to the person I went to school with in the late nineties? What have I been up to in the last 15 years? Oh, you know, this and that. Keeping myself busy doing the London lawyer thing. You? L**

I changed into my comfy clothes and poured a glass of wine. My email beeped as I was closing the fridge. My heart skipped. Would he reply straight away?

**Yes, I believe so—I've not had many Leahs in my life. I started a business just after Uni and have been keeping busy doing that since. I'm in the US at the moment meeting a potential business partner. I'm only halfway through my day, but with my jet lag, I might not make it through this next meeting. I'm based in London but seem to spend too much time in New York. Are you home for the day now? What are your evening plans? D**

He emailed like we had been in touch all these years. It was so familiar. If I emailed back straight away, would that look desperate? No, I hadn't replied to him all day.

**Yes, I'm home for the evening now. I'm enjoying a glass of wine. Jealous? No particular plans this evening. I may watch a trashy rom-com movie and have an early night. I have an early start tomorrow. Where in London are you based? What's your business? L**

I barely had time to exhale and he'd replied again.

**Jealous? Absolutely. Can I join you for a glass remotely? I'll just have to use my imagination... I have a place in W1. A comedy sounds good. I have a really vivid memory of your laugh. D**

It was so cute that he was asking to have a drink with me remotely. Was he flirting? I'd been in a relationship for six years; I had forgotten what flirting looked like. No, I was imagining it. He was always super-confident, sure of himself, particularly with women. Daniel always seemed a couple of years older than the other boys at school. I'm sure any flirting was imagined on my part.

**Would you like red or white? I'm having a glass of Rioja. My laugh is memorable? In a good way? I remember your freckles. L**

What was I doing? I was engaged!

**Rioja sounds perfect. Yes, your laugh was memorable in a good way. Stop fishing for compliments. Particularly if you are going to remind me of my freckles. D**

He saw right through me and set me straight. I liked that.

**Busted. Sorry, but they were cute freckles. L**

I was certain he wouldn't reply now. He was going into a meeting and the conversation was at a natural close. I poured myself another glass of wine and went to run a bath. I was grinning hopelessly and feeling a bit giggly after the wine. I took my iPad into the bathroom and put on some music. I quickly changed my mind about Jill Scott—too sexy, and I needed to cool down. I got into the warm water and reached for my wine. My email pinged again. Really?

**Cute? I don't hear that adjective a lot when people describe me. Can I get a top-up? D**

I bit back my grin.

**Now you're fishing for compliments. I'm in the bath. Can you help yourself? L**

Now I was flirting—I couldn't deny that.

**Is it a real or virtual bath? D**

**No, it's a real bath. Help yourself to the Rioja, though. L**

**Wow. I'm meant to be concentrating in this meeting. I don't like to mix business with pleasure. D**

I shivered, my nipples tightened, and I felt a rush of warmth between my legs. What did I say to that? I took a deep breath and tried to keep it light.

**So if not cute, how do people describe you? L**

God, what if he was bald and fat with bad teeth and three wives? I had an image in my head of some tall, dark, handsome, single man, still confident and sure of himself. I didn't even know what he did for a living. He could be a cab driver, although I doubt that required international travel and provided him with a place in

W1, one of the most desirable postcodes in London. I needed Fran's help to do some cyberstalking—she was the expert. Who was this guy I was flirting with?

In the absence of Fran, I Googled 'Daniel Armitage.' A technology wunderkind I was not, but I could manage Google. Some videos popped up along with some news articles.

No email ping. Had I pushed things too far?

I clicked on one of the videos; it was obviously him. He had the same dark, soulful eyes, but everything else was different. When I had last seen him, he was a tall, dark-haired, lanky, cute boy. The man who was addressing his audience on the video was not that boy. His voice was deep and powerful. He seemed to choose each word carefully. He was tall, at least six feet, and my god he was beautiful. Maybe beautiful wasn't quite the word, but those familiar dark eyes were hypnotizing, and he had such a presence—the sort that comes with confidence and success. His hair was still the same almost-black color, but it was longer than how he wore it as a teenager, and his skin seemed darker. His suit was expensive. He went without a tie and there was a glimmer of hair poking out at his neck. My crush was back after 15 years. I had to get some clothes on. I felt inappropriate watching the video naked, like he could see me through the screen.

I let the video run as I got out of the bath and

wrapped myself in a towel. He was talking to an audience of entrepreneurs about how he started his business. He spoke passionately about his journey, the mistakes he made along the way, and his eventual success.

So what did he do that meant he was giving talks about his successes? Impatiently, I stopped the video, clicked on one of the news items, and wandered over to the bed. So his title was CEO of Gematria Enterprises. I'd never heard of it. Gematria Enterprises seemed to be a holding company for a number of other businesses that had different names. Hotels, restaurants, medical supplies, technology companies, commercial real estate investments; that was an eclectic mix.

I clicked on one of the other videos. There he was again. My heart rate quickened as he walked onto the stage, this time with his hair shorter and an unmistakable circle of gold on his left ring finger. I slumped back onto the bed. Well, of course he was married. He was young, gorgeous, and successful. And anyway, it wasn't like I was hoping to date him. I was happily engaged.

Back to the first video. No ring in that video. Maybe he was recently married ... or recently divorced?

I'd not had another email, which was probably a good thing. I was with Charlie and shouldn't be flirting with devastatingly handsome and potentially married men. *Move on, Leah*, I scolded myself.

At that moment, I heard Charlie's keys in the door. It

was nearly midnight. All at once, I wished I were asleep. I slipped a nightdress on and got under the covers.

"Hi babe," I called. He replied but didn't come into the bedroom. I turned off the light.

My email pinged. My iPad was right next to my bed. I should have been thinking about sleep or Charlie but I couldn't resist quickly checking it.

**Get some sleep. D**

I *had* embarrassed myself. I felt stupid. I quickly closed the email and tried to put Daniel out of my head. Eventually I drifted off. I didn't hear Charlie come to bed.

The next morning I resolved not to respond to Daniel, to stop cyberstalking him, and to make more effort with Charlie.

When I got up, Charlie was in the kitchen leaning against the breakfast bar reading the paper and drinking his juice. I came up behind him, put my arms around him, and rested my head on his back. He patted my hands. "Remember, we have dinner with my parents tonight. They are going to freak out when we tell them we are engaged."

What did he mean they were going to freak out?

"Yes, I hadn't forgotten. Freak out?"

"Well, you know they always saw me with an heiress. They thought you were just for fun."

"Oh, really."

"Yes, I've told you that before. They think it's weird that I'm with a working girl."

"I'm not a *prostitute*, Charlie. I have the same job as you!" I removed my arms from his waist and headed back into the bedroom for a shower.

"I'll pick you up at seven. Can you try to wear something feminine?"

I took a deep breath. He must just be nervous about telling his parents. I had no room to judge. I'd not told my parents yet. The only people I had told were Anna and Fran. And I didn't have a ring yet, so it didn't feel real.

The day passed in a blur. I was so busy I didn't have time to think about anything, including Daniel. Anna emailed me at lunchtime.

**Are you around tonight? A**

**Tonight is dinner with Charlie's parents. We are telling them about the engagement. Charlie told me this morning that they might freak out when we tell them, because they wanted him to marry an heiress and thought I was just for fun! Was he joking? And he told me to wear something feminine. Do I dress like a man? L**

I probably shouldn't have said that to Anna. She wasn't Charlie's biggest fan and didn't need more reasons not to like him.

Anna replied.

**He said *what*? He must have been joking. Otherwise, he's a total dick. You are kind, funny, gorgeous, and have a bod that screams *bow chicka wow wow*. Can we get married instead? Don't listen to a word he says. Can we get together this week, just the two of us? I want to hear about the proposal—you didn't seem to want to talk about it yesterday. And now I want to hear how dinner goes! A**

We agreed to meet on Thursday night. Charlie had a partners' meeting followed by a partners' dinner, so I knew he would be late.

I had taken a change of clothes to work so I could wear something 'feminine' to dinner. Charlie had never asked me to dress in a particular way before. Whenever he commented on what I wore, it was normally to say how sexy I looked.

Charlie called last minute to say he would meet me at the restaurant. We were going to Murano in Mayfair. It was a favorite of his parents. Now I was nervous. I had always thought his parents liked me, but perhaps they simply tolerated me as a fling. I hoped Charlie was there before I was.

In the cab home, Charlie and I didn't say much to each other. Dinner had been awkward. Charlie had leaned into me at one point and whispered, "Your dress is very appropriate. Thank you." He was being nice, or at least trying to be, but the comment really irritated me. I was irritated with him because he had asked me to dress a certain way, irritated with myself because I had complied, and now I was irritated because I'd let him pat me on the head like a dog.

Charlie's parents' reaction to our engagement was muted. But their reaction to most things was muted. They were very old-school and kept their emotions in check and their upper lip stiff. They congratulated us and asked about dates and the ring. Of course, neither had been sorted out. We'd not discussed dates and Charlie said that we were going ring shopping this weekend.

As I stared out of the cab on the way home, I looked up at the magnificent buildings that towered over us. It was cold, dark, and raining, but that just added to the romance of London for me. Especially around Mayfair, with the little streets weaving between beautiful squares, lined with wrought iron railings. We were heading back east. I briefly wondered if maybe Daniel lived around here. He had said W1. I could imagine him in one of these grand houses, staring out into the rain while sipping a glass of Rioja.

"Are you OK?" Charlie put his hand on my leg.

"Yes, of course. Just thinking about work. How do think your parents took our news?" I asked.

"I thought it went very well, considering. Well done, sweetheart."

*Considering what?* I pondered. I wasn't sure I cared.

Tonight's dinner meant that Charlie and I actually got into bed at the same time. I was lying on my side facing away from him; he came up behind me and reached around to my breast, then stroked my nipple until it hardened. It had been a couple of weeks since we had had sex. Even on the night of our engagement, Charlie had passed out drunk by the time I came out of the bathroom. I missed it, the physical contact. I found myself thinking about sex more and more in the office, and increasingly Daniel was the face of my fantasy.

I let out a small groan of pleasure and reached behind me for his thigh, pulled his body closer to mine. I wanted to feel his desire for me. Charlie pecked me on the shoulder. "I have an early start tomorrow. We should get some sleep."

*Really?*

# Chapter Two

Wednesday came and went. Charlie arrived home just after I did. I made us some dinner, we swapped work stories over our stir-fry, and then he went into the office to work. I went to bed early. Something clearly wasn't right between us, but I didn't know if it was him, me, or both of us. We should have talked about it, but I didn't have the energy or inclination. Thinking about Daniel seemed to take up my energy over the last couple of days. He hadn't emailed me again. He probably realized we'd been a bit too flirtatious and was feeling guilty. He was married, but that didn't stop me thinking about him.

As I hit my desk late at 9:30 a.m. on Thursday, I got an email from Anna.

**Can you try to get out of the office at a decent hour tonight? Can you do 6 p.m.? A**

As usual, Anna was already thinking about the end of the day before it started.

I finally got to sit down with Patricia from marketing and David. Patricia was enthusiastic about my involvement. She said that clients were increasingly asking associates to be involved with tender processes, as they would be the ones who would be putting in the most hours. This is where she said I could be of most assistance.

When Patricia described the pitch process, it sounded quite straightforward. We would submit a proposal for a piece of legal work according to the criteria specified. I wouldn't really assist with putting the proposal together, but I would study it and then go along to any client presentations where we would talk about the work, our credentials, and then the potential client would get to question us. It sounded fun and so different from what I was used to. I was proud of what we did as a firm and was keen to talk about it to anyone who would listen. It would also be a great step to creating my own client base, which I would need if I decided I wanted to go for partner. It was so nice of David to come through for me like this.

Anna and I agreed to meet at 6 p.m. but not at our usual place—we wanted a proper catch-up and didn't want to run into anyone we knew. Was I going to tell her about the awkwardness between Charlie and me? Should I tell her that I was having a crazy fantasy about some school crush from decades ago? We told each other everything and I imagined tonight would be no exception.

"So, out with it Leah," Anna said. "You don't seem at all excited about the engagement. What's going on?"

I had barely sat down. So we were definitely going to get into it; there was no avoiding her question. She was on a mission. Anna was nothing if not direct.

"I don't know, Anna. Things between Charlie and me are weird. Sometimes I'm just not sure Charlie likes me that much."

"Well, of course he likes you. He's asked you to marry him, hasn't he?"

"Yes, after six years he has finally asked me. But I'm not sure he really likes me anymore, and I'm not sure if he ever did. And I'm not sure I like *him* much anymore. He can be so insensitive. And I thought the sex would liven up at least for a bit after the engagement, but we've not slept together in weeks." It all kind of spilled out, and putting it into words made it sound awful. "But maybe we are just going through a rough patch. No couple is perfect. And maybe I'm afraid of commitment on some level and this engagement thing is getting me worked up." All that stuff about him marrying an heiress who didn't work hadn't helped either. I wasn't sure I was what he really wanted.

Anna interrupted my thoughts. "Well, if you've not set a date yet, you can see how things go in the next few months. You'll probably get back to normal. But you know what they say—the time before you get married is the best it's ever going to get. Don't marry him just because that's what everyone, including you, has been expecting. You owe it to yourself to think about what you really want."

Anna was right. I needed to make a conscious decision. "So ... when you are getting married to someone, are you supposed to be having fantasies about the one that got away?" I asked.

We both collapsed into giggles.

"I feel we need a round of tequilas before we get into this."

Anna came back with the tequilas and slices of orange.

"So who is the one that got away? Have I heard about this one? Not Matthew?"

"God, no not Matt," I said. "It's nothing, really. The other day I just LinkedIn with a guy who I had a crush on when I was 15. We had a bit of a chat over email. I just can't stop thinking about him. It doesn't help that I Googled him and he's totally hot. He's just a fantasy, though. It will pass soon enough, I'm sure."

After much cajoling, I brought up his photo on Google so Anna could pass judgment on his hot factor.

"Wow, he *is* hot. Talk, dark, handsome, successful. He's definitely fantasy worthy. So, is he gay, married, or both?"

I threw my head back and laughed and then blushed as I remembered what Daniel had said about my laugh. "I think he's married. I've been doing some Fran-like cyberstalking and he seems to be wearing a wedding ring in some pictures. Anyway, like you say, it's just a fantasy. It will have worn off by the end of the week." I wanted to get off the subject. I felt silly for feeling as caught up with him as I did. He was married, I was engaged, and we had just exchanged a few emails. "So, speaking of Fran, how is she? I emailed her earlier in the week but I've not heard back from her."

Anna and Fran worked at the same law firm around the corner from my mine, so they saw each other every day. I knew Fran through Anna, and although I would consider her a good friend because I spent a lot of time with her, I rarely saw her unless Anna was with us.

"Well, I've not really seen much of her this week, and really other than Monday I've not seen her for a few weeks. I think that she's been totally into that DJ that she shagged over the weekend. Maybe he's still hanging around, wanting something more than a one-night stand. Who knows with Fran."

"Maybe she's just moved on to her next stalkee and she's wrapped up in that?" I asked.

"Probably. She just seemed a bit odd. She called in sick on Tuesday, which is so unlike her, and she seems really subdued."

Fran was a really pretty girl: tall, very thin with curly blond hair. She had had a tough upbringing. Her alcoholic father died when she was a teenager, and her mother hadn't coped well with being on her own and seemed to let Fran and her brother run riot. Being a lawyer was an escape for her. She had loads of friends as she was so easy to get along with and was always up for a party. Relationships were her Achilles' heel: She always had one in her sights, but she was never with a man for very long.

"Why don't the three of us do a shopping and lunch day this weekend to cheer ourselves up? We can indulge in a man-free zone!" I suggested.

"Oh my god, I'm totally up for that. Saturday? Let me text Fran to check if she's free."

"Oh, Anna, you won't mention my doubts about Charlie and me to Fran will you? I would hate anything to get back to him. And please don't mention Daniel. I'd die of embarrassment."

"Of course not. But is that what you're having? Doubts, I mean?"

"I guess." I'd not labeled any of my feelings up to that point. But doubts seemed to cover what I was feeling.

My phone buzzed—an email. From Daniel. I wasn't expecting that! I'd not heard from him since Monday. I thought I'd made such an idiot of myself that I'd never hear from him again.

**I'm at JFK and drinking Rioja before my flight. Care to join me for a glass remotely? D**

I drew in a sharp breath.

"What is it?" Anna asked.

"Oh nothing. I forgot I had a training session at the gym tomorrow morning, and I just got a reminder. In fact, I should get going. It's getting late."

I couldn't wait to get home and reply to Daniel. I wanted to be able to concentrate on my reply and didn't want Anna asking questions. After dashing out of the bar, I kissed Anna goodbye on the street and waved down a cab. When I'd given the driver my address, I fished out my phone from my pocket and typed a reply.

**I've had one or two glasses already. I'm not sure I should. I'm happy to keep you company while you wait for your flight though. How was your day? L**

Daniel came back straight away.

**My day has been grueling. I need to be distracted. Are you in the bath again? D**

The flirtatious tone of his emails had escalated quickly. My nipples tightened against the lace of my bra; my heart quickened. He wanted to be distracted by me in the bath. I wish he were here with me now; I would be happy to distract him in the flesh. What was I going to say? Was I imagining his flirtation? I couldn't think straight. I was suddenly aware I was not alone and the cab driver was looking at me strangely in his mirror. We pulled up to the flat and told him to keep the change as I handed him a twenty. As soon as I got through the front door, I replied.

**No bath for me this evening, I had a shower this morning. I'm just getting ready for bed. Do baths distract you? L**

I wandered into the bedroom and started to change. I should be asleep already. I smoothed my favorite Chanel lotion over my legs. My body seemed to be on full alert and just my hands gently sliding over my skin while about Daniel caused a throbbing between my legs. God, I missed having someone touch me, make love to me.

**The thought of you in the bath distracts me. The thought of you in bed distracts me. D**

No, I wasn't imagining it. He was being very clear. I slipped into bed and replied.

**Well, you are quite the distraction to me this evening, Mr. Armitage. L**

Again, he replied straight away.

**It's nice to know I have the power to distract you, too. D**

I wish I knew what he was thinking. He was probably married. So was this some harmless flirtation to ease a seven-year itch?

**I think you have enough power already, if the results of my Google search are anything to go by. L**

**You've been Googling me? D**

Yikes, I'd just given away my cyberstalking.

**Well, I don't normally have remote drinks with complete strangers. I had to know who I was sharing my Rioja with. L**

That seemed reasonable enough, didn't it?

**They've just called my flight. Let's discuss this over dinner. D**

Holy crap. What had I gotten myself into? I couldn't have dinner with this *married* man. But I didn't want the flirting to stop.

**Have a good flight. L**

And my email fell silent. Was he angry at me for Googling him? Surely he couldn't be. Had he guessed that I knew he was married? Would he email me again? Eventually I fell asleep.

The first thing I did was check my email when I woke. Nothing. Would he have landed yet? Should I check the Heathrow arrivals website and work out if he had landed? I was starting to lose my mind.

*Calm down, Leah,* I told myself in my head as Charlie stirred beside me. *You are 30 years old, and you need to get a grip.*

I headed into the shower and resolved not to obsess. Charlie and I barely exchanged two words. I told him I was going shopping with the girls the following day. He said he'd already arranged golf for the day. I thought we were going ring shopping, but he didn't mention it and neither did I.

My morning seemed to drag. I was on a conference call for most of it. Sitting at my desk, I kept peering at my personal phone to check my emails and then remembering I should be concentrating. There were about 16 people on this call. It was completely unmanageable. Luckily, I had a trainee on the same call taking notes. I emailed her.

**Deb, can you make sure you keep a separate list of the action points that we are responsible for? Thanks, Leah.**

Hopefully, between us we wouldn't miss anything—my brain was not in gear today. I was always so composed and on top of things at work, no matter what was going on in my personal life. Apparently today was the exception.

Just as the call wrapped up, Brendan, the PA I shared with David, threw a courier delivery on my desk. Brendan was lucky he was funny because he was a terrible PA. Because he kept us all entertained with his colorful stories of London's gay nightlife, and his sarcastic comments about the more challenging partners at the firm, we were willing to overlook his lack of skills—like the fact he threw my mail at me. Humor was the most effective stress relief.

Deb wandered over to my desk so we could formulate a plan after the call as I opened the package. Inside was a rich cream envelope in thick paper. This wasn't a work delivery. A wedding invitation? I ignored the envelope and took Deb through the action points and broke them down into smaller tasks, but my focus was diverted by the delivery and I quickly gave up. I told her just to write up the list and then let me see it. I wanted to know who was getting married. As Deb scurried away, I opened the envelope. Inside was a card in the same rich cream.

You didn't answer my question. Dinner? Saturday?
D

I flushed. He knew where I worked. I felt like his eyes were on me. He hadn't just emailed me, he had written to me. This had taken a bit of organization and effort. There was no doubt that he was asking me a question now. I needed to clear my head, so I volunteered to do a coffee run.

I took my phone with me and replied in the ridiculously long queue for lattes. I wondered how many working hours were spent in line for coffee. We could probably end the recession by just closing down Starbucks.

**I got your note. I didn't realize you had asked me a question. I can't have dinner with you on Saturday, I'm sorry. I have plans. L**

It was true, I did have plans, but it wasn't entirely honest, either. This was an opportunity to tell him I was engaged, to say that I had plans with my fiancé this Saturday night. But he hadn't mentioned that he was married, and maybe I had read the situation wrong and he wasn't interested in me like that. I didn't want to jump to conclusions.

*Ping.*

**We *will* have dinner now that I'm back in London. Pick a day. D**

He wasn't making a request. That decisiveness meant I wasn't going to say no. OK, so I would meet him for a quick supper, catch up on old times, and drop my engagement into conversation. Yes, that would bring things to a close.

**OK. Tuesday. L**

**I'll pick you up outside your office at 7 p.m. I look forward to it. D**

On Saturday morning, I was sitting at my dressing table getting ready for my girls' day out when Charlie came out of the shower.

"You look beautiful, Leah."

"Don't be silly," I said without turning around.

"I mean it. You look beautiful. You are beautiful. I don't say it enough."

He was looking at me intensely.

"Thank you."

He came over to me, swept my hair aside, and kissed my neck and then my shoulder.

"I'm so sorry I've been so busy at work the last few weeks. Things have been really intense."

I reached around his neck and pulled him closer. He turned me around on the stool, took my face in his hands, bent over, and kissed me deeply and passionately.

I found Anna and Fran in the shoe department at Harvey Nics.

"I'm so sorry I'm late girls. What did I miss?" I was right on schedule this morning until Charlie's libido had woken up. My legs still felt a little wobbly.

"No problem, we know Charlie likes his sex on the weekends!" Anna was so cheeky. I smacked her on the arm.

Fran ignored her, fully engrossed in a bright red patent pair of Louboutins that we were now going to have to spend the rest of the day talking her out of buying.

"Let's talk about Fran's sex life instead, hmm? Have you seen him again?" I asked.

"Nope, I've decided to get serious about dating. No more boys. I need a man. At some point, I want to get married and have a family, and it's not going to happen with the idiots that I've spent the last few years chasing."

Anna and I exchanged a look. "In the words of the Spice Girls, you 'want a man not, a boy who thinks he can'." Anna was singing her quote at the top of her voice, oblivious to the stares she was getting from her fellow shoppers. "So what's brought on this change of heart?" She got straight to the point, as ever.

"I'm sick of having my heart broken. It's the same every time: The guys I'm with don't see me as marriage material. Hell, they don't see me as someone they want to take to dinner. I've reached my limit."

"Well, I think we should toast to that. Let's go and find some champagne and some lunch to go with it," I suggested.

As we toasted Fran's new approach to dating, Anna grabbed my wrist and spilled my champagne all over my hand.

"Oh my god, are you trying to be nonchalant about that rock on your hand?"

"This old thing?" Charlie had presented me with my engagement ring in bed after our morning sex. I had thought that we were going to go ring shopping together, but it seemed Charlie had had other ideas. Apparently, the ring was a copy of his mother's engagement ring. It had taken a bit longer than expected to finish, which is why Charlie hadn't presented it to me when he proposed. It wasn't exactly what I would have chosen. It was a bit big and a bit fussy. But you couldn't deny that it was beautiful.

"Wow, that's huge," Anna screeched.

"You must be pleased," Fran said, a bit more subdued.

"It needs resizing, really, but I wanted you girls to be the first to see it before it went back to the jewelers."

The rest of the day seemed to be spent with the emphasis on talking rather than shopping, but I picked up a new skirt for work and Anna bought a beautiful dress for an upcoming wedding she was going to. Fran did much better than us and spent a fortune. In fact, Anna and I spent most of the day gossiping while waiting outside changing rooms and by cash registers for Fran to continue her sartorial reinvention.

While Fran was trying on a jumpsuit in Armani Exchange, Anna brought up the subject of Thursday evening's conversation. "So, things seem better between you and Charlie? The sex? The ring?"

"Yeah, he said things had been intense at work and he apologized. Perhaps it was just the tension around the engagement that was getting to us both. He seems to want to make things better."

"But do you?"

Anna found the heart of the matter, as usual. I didn't know what to say.

Anna prompted me. "Sorry, I'm not trying to interfere."

"No, I know you're not. I just don't know how to answer you. All I can say is that I'm not ready to walk away. But I'm not ready to marry him, either."

I didn't tell her about dinner with Daniel. I didn't know if I could go through with it after this morning. It seemed like Charlie really wanted things to work between us, and I owed him that, didn't I? I loved him didn't I?

Charlie initiated sex again on Sunday. Maybe things between us were really turning a corner. I guess maybe we both were affected by taking such a big step in our relationship after so long and now things would level out. After my gym session on Sunday morning and Charlie's extended nap, we spent the day doing chores and getting ready for the week ahead. Well, I did. Charlie spent most of the day in the office. I wasn't sure what he was doing, but we were together under one roof and we snuggled up on the sofa to watch TV together on Sunday night.

First thing on Monday, I grabbed Brendan and dragged him into a meeting room so I could practice my part of the Phoenix presentation that was scheduled with David and another partner on Tuesday. Brendan was doing impressions of David the whole way through and I could barely keep a straight face. My cheeks were aching from trying not to laugh, so much that by the time we'd finished I thought I might be in a state of permanent cramp. I was still nervous, but at least I felt prepared. If I could get through it while Brendan was making me giggle, I felt confident that I could deliver my part as required in front of a normal audience. I really wanted to make a good impression—it was such great experience and I didn't want it to be a one-off.

Luckily, the presentation kept me distracted from my personal life. I didn't hear from Daniel over the weekend, but when I got home on Monday evening it suddenly hit me that we were due to meet the next day. Was it too late to cancel? Did I want to cancel? I really didn't. I wanted to see him, to see if the man in my head matched the man in the flesh. I wanted to know if he was married. Was I just meeting up with an old school friend, or was I meeting up with someone I was completely attracted to?

On Tuesday morning, Charlie had already left for work when I got out of the shower. I was relieved. I had enough to think about without analyzing my interactions with my fiancé this morning. I dressed carefully. A black fitted shift dress that finished at the knee with a matching jacket, which would be great for the presentation but could be ditched for dinner tonight. I paired them with my favorite nude killer heels. I decided I would scrape my hair back into a ponytail just before the presentation and then let it down again for dinner. I wanted to look great for dinner without looking like I had made too much of an effort.

I made sure I packed up all my makeup and a change of stockings into my favorite Mulberry handbag and headed to work.

"Wow, you look amazing, babe." Brendan let out a whistle. I guess I'd failed at not looking like I'd made an effort, but at least people would think it was for the presentation and not for a clandestine after-work dinner.

"Thanks B, wish me luck for this afternoon," I replied, trying to reinforce the reason for any change in my normal work appearance.

"You won't need luck. You've worked hard and you're a natural."

We had a dress rehearsal that morning and then bundled into a cab to the client's offices at Canary Wharf at just after 1 p.m.

---

I was high on adrenaline on the cab ride back. It had all gone exceptionally well, and David and George, the other partner giving the presentation, thought we had a great shot at landing the client.

"You did an excellent job, Leah. Have a word with marketing and make sure you get another pitch lined up. We need to make the most of you. I could see they really responded when you spoke."

"Thank you so much, both of you. It's really great to have this opportunity." I wasn't sure either of them heard me; their heads were buried in their Blackberries.

I checked my personal email for any messages from Daniel, but there was nothing. Perhaps he'd forgotten.

Because of the rehearsals and preparation for the presentation, I was really behind with my work, so the rest of the afternoon sped by as I endeavored to catch

## FAITHFUL

up. At 6:45 p.m. I closed my programs, logged off, and went to the bathroom to reapply my makeup and calm my increasing nervousness.

Should I wait downstairs? Would he email me when he arrived? Perhaps he'd just forgotten. I decided to wait at my desk. At 7 p.m. exactly, my office phone rang and I jumped out of my skin.

"Leah, I have a Mr. Armitage in reception for you."

Well, this was it. I went to replace the receiver, but just before I hung up, I heard the receptionist say, "Leah?" I hadn't responded.

"Thanks, I'll be right down."

# Chapter Three

As I walked out of the elevator, I saw him ahead of me; his back—his broad back—was turned to me and he was leafing through the firm marketing materials that were set out in reception. As I came through the turnstiles, he turned around and caught me staring. His gaze bore right into me.

I vaguely heard someone on reception wish me good night, but I couldn't speak. I couldn't take my eyes off the man in front of me. The videos I watched of him didn't properly show how tall and physically imposing he was. He must be around six-foot-four. He was wearing a luxurious dark navy suit that covered his powerful body. I was semi-aware of people coming in and out of the entrance doors, but somehow our connected gaze blunted my hearing and vision of everything else around me.

As I got nearer to him, the corners of his mouth turned up and I couldn't help but smile right back at him. When he was close enough to touch, I stopped and just stared at him. His eyes were still as I remembered, hypnotizing, but there was something behind them now that there wasn't when he was younger. Strength and power, for sure. But a hint of sadness, also. His jaw was achingly strong; I fought my instinct to reach up and stroke it, to run my finger over his beautiful lips.

"Hey, stranger," he whispered without taking his eyes off me. I felt a current of desire go through me and I closed my eyes in a long blink.

"Hey stranger, yourself," I whispered back.

We stood there for what seemed like hours, smiling and staring at each other. I lost any concept of time and place. I just wanted to stand there and drink him in; he was intoxicating.

"I have a car waiting outside. Let's go," he said. He rested his hand in the small of my back and I felt that current of desire go through me again like an electric charge and I gasped, my lips parted and I looked away, breaking the gaze between us. I was embarrassed that my body gave me away so easily. I looked toward the doors and just nodded and he led me to the car.

I was in trouble.

I slid into the backseat and tried to compose myself as he came around to the opposite side and slid in beside me.

"How was your day?" he asked. I looked down and away from his intense stare, thinking I might be able to form a sentence if I wasn't looking into those eyes. But he reached out toward me and tilted my chin back up. "Look at me."

I took a deep breath and my eyes met his again. My skin was vibrating where he touched me and I wasn't sure if I was going to be able to answer.

"It was great actually. Really great. What about yours?" I needed him to do the talking. I needed to concentrate on breathing in and out.

When he spoke, unlike me, he seemed to be able to form a full sentence without any difficulty at all. His eyes never left me. Even when I looked away, I could feel them on me, exploring me.

"It has been going quite well, but it just got a whole lot better." The corners of his mouth turned up again and I just sighed and relaxed back in my seat. Good god, I was a mess.

When we arrived at our destination, Daniel's driver opened my door, and as I got out of the car I turned my head to see where Daniel was. He was right there, and before I knew it, he had taken my hand in his and was leading me between two buildings down an unlit alley. Nervous, I instinctively reached my free hand across to our joined hands. It seemed natural that we were joined like this, even though we had only just met after so long. Daniel increased the pressure in his clasped hand reassuringly. No wedding ring. I was relieved and my stomach clenched—the guilt pushing through. Where was he taking me?

# FAITHFUL

After about 30 feet, we came to a heavy black Georgian door on the right hand side that opened as we approached it.

"I wanted to bring you to my favorite place in London," he said, leaning into me, his mouth just an inch from my neck, his breath on my skin.

We were met in the entrance hall by a hostess who should have been gracing the pages of *Vogue*, not showing people to their seats at … wherever we were. She was tall, lithe, beautiful, and beaming at Daniel. A surge of jealousy coursed through me. Maybe this was his favorite place because of her.

"Mr. Armitage, so lovely to see you again."

Daniel didn't seem to hear her. He was looking at me with that half-grin on his face.

"Can I take your coat?" the goddess next to me asked. I shrugged off my coat and gave it to her. Daniel grabbed my hand again and I exhaled in relief at his touch as we headed downstairs to what the discrete sign promised was the Coltrane Club.

As we got to our table, I felt completely overwhelmed. Why had I never heard of this phenomenal place? It felt secretive and intimate. The room we were in had a bar at one end and a small stage at the other. The ceiling was tented in deep red silk and down each side; there were about four little booths, made up of oxblood leather semi-circular bench seats with high backs, each with its own little tented ceiling. There were also a smattering of tables in front of the stage, but we were ensconced in one of the booths. Someone was playing the piano, and there were other instruments on stage, which seemed to suggest there was more to come. Daniel sat almost at a right angle to me. We were no longer holding hands, but the air between us was thick and I realized I wanted—I needed—a part of his body to be touching mine.

When the waiter came over, Daniel ordered for the both of us without any reference to me. We both knew he was entirely in control of this evening. I tried to make conversation.

"So, this is—"

"Intense?"

I threw my head back and laughed. "Yes, intense, that's exactly what it is. I'm not imagining it, then?"

"No, it's real." He reached up and trailed the back of his index finger across my cheekbone.

Our champagne arrived.

"To a wonderful evening." Daniel raised his glass. I smiled and, mirroring him, I raised my glass.

The band came out on stage and started playing 'I've Got You Under My Skin.' It was a welcome distraction; I was able to focus on something else. I could feel Daniel's eyes on me and then I felt his hand rest on my thigh. I felt myself moisten and I slumped forward and put my head in my hands. I couldn't do this; I had to tell him about Charlie. Daniel moved his hand from my thigh and rubbed my back.

"Hey, what's the matter? Are you OK?"

This was it—this was my opening. I had to tell him. "Daniel, I— I need ..."

"Take a deep breath, Leah. Look at me. What is it?" He continued to rub my back.

"Daniel, I'm in a relationship."

"I know. You're engaged." He hadn't taken his eyes from mine.

"What? My parents don't even know I'm engaged! How do you know, and if you know, what are we doing here?"

"Leah, I want you to take a breath and then have a sip of champagne." I sat back and I did as I was told.

"Look at me, Leah." I turned my head. "I don't have any kind of meeting, business or pleasure, without knowing exactly who I'm meeting. I'm thorough, Leah. I have to be. I don't like surprises. I require complete transparency in my life. I've been caught out before and it will never happen again."

"How long have you known?"

"Since before I emailed you from JFK."

Oh, he'd known all along.

"Are you married?" I blurted out.

He smiled. "No, Leah, I'm not married. I was married; we divorced."

"I'm sorry. When? What happened?"

"I'm happy to tell you everything about my marriage and my divorce, but not now, not tonight. I want tonight to be about us."

"But Daniel, I'm engaged. You said it yourself."

"Yes, but as you said, you've not even told your parents ... Why is that, Leah?" It was a question I'd been asking myself a lot lately. "And as you also said, this is intense."

"So, what is this tonight?"

"I have no master plan. Let's just take a time-out, put everything else out of our heads, and enjoy this evening together. We are, after all, old school friends." he added and grinned wickedly.

I didn't respond for a few minutes.

"OK, time-out, just for tonight."

I relaxed a bit; the intensity was still there but with less discomfort than I felt before. We talked properly and we didn't stop talking: about the band on stage, about our jobs, the music we liked listening to, what we had been doing since we last saw each other, what we enjoyed about our lives. We both skirted around our romantic relationships—we were on a time-out, after all. We talked and laughed, sat in comfortable silence as we listened to the band play some amazing music. It was like we had known each other our whole lives.

Some hours later, I dragged my eyes away from

Daniel and scanned the room. We were the last ones left. Holy hell, it was past 1 a.m.

"I need to go."

Daniel's smile faltered almost imperceptibly and I saw that sadness again in his eyes. He nodded and he asked for the bill.

"I'm sorry; I'm having a lovely time." I reached over and grabbed his hand and he interlaced his fingers with mine. The driver was waiting for us when we got into the street.

"I really want to see you home, but given the circumstances, I've asked my driver to take you from here and I'll get a cab." I was a bit shocked. I thought we would have the car journey back together.

"Oh, thank you, but I can take a cab," I said, trying to cover my disappointment.

"My driver will take you, Leah. I don't want you in a cab at this time of night."

"Thank you for everything tonight. It's been a wonderful evening."

He trailed his fingers up my spine and cupped my face, then placed a chaste kiss on my lips that set a fire racing through my body. My legs collapsed a little and I stumbled. Daniel steadied me and helped me into the car without saying another word.

I went to say goodbye and he raised his index finger to his lips, as if he were willing me not to end the evening.

The car pulled away and left him on the sidewalk, staring at the sky.

The tears came from nowhere. I'd had such an amazing evening, but quite suddenly I felt that something inside me had died. I knew our time-out was over and I couldn't see him again. I knew that before the evening began, but now the thought scorched through my head and I desperately wanted to pull it out and stop the pain.

I arrived back at the flat exhausted by my sobbing. Daniel's driver didn't say a word about my inexplicable tears. He didn't even glance in his rearview mirror, for which I was very grateful. How would I explain my state to Charlie? Hopefully he would be fast asleep. I crept into the flat, trying to navigate the dark in order to avoid waking him by switching on the lights.

When I reached the bedroom, Charlie wasn't there. I checked my phone, no message. All I could think was how relieved I was that I wasn't confronted by his physical presence. I could delay the full extent of my feelings of guilt. Then it occurred to me that maybe something had happened to him. I checked my email and he'd sent me a message that he would be working very late and might not make it home. God, he was working his behind off at the moment, and for what? To provide for our future together. And there it was: The guilt poured over me.

I think I must have drifted off at some point, although I couldn't be sure. I certainly didn't feel rested

# FAITHFUL

when the alarm went off. Charlie hadn't been home all night. I texted him and asked him if he needed me to bring a change of clothes into the office for him. He normally kept a clean shirt there but he'd done a couple of overnighters recently, so I thought he might be have used them up. When I came out of the shower, he'd texted back to say that he was coming home for a shower shortly.

I ran around getting ready as quickly as I could. I wanted to get out of the flat before he arrived, I couldn't bear to face him. I left him a note saying I would cook dinner for him this evening if he was going to be home. I would begin to make amends.

When I got to my desk, I was confronted by a bouquet of white roses sitting in a vase. Brendan came waltzing over.

"Roses after six years. He's either cheating or working too hard—or both!"

I laughed as convincingly as I could. They weren't from Charlie. I knew that without looking at the card. White roses had always held a bit of fascination for me, something I associated with true love and fairytales since I was a child. But I'd never received them, and it wasn't a fascination that I'd ever shared with anyone. How did he know? And how had he even gotten flowers to me by 8 a.m.?

Apart from Brendan there weren't many people in

the office, and I reached for the card without fear of anyone sneaking a peek over my shoulder.

Thank you ... for an intense evening.

Dx

I hid the card in my handbag and took a deep breath. This had to be over. Whatever this was, it couldn't continue. Not even the email flirting. It was all too dangerous, too frightening, too intense. And I was engaged.

I threw myself into work and by the time people began to arrive, my was head lost in the job. During the course of the day, I managed to catch up on the work that had built while I was absorbed in the presentation pitch.

I jumped three feet out of my chair when Patricia came over that afternoon.

"Sorry, I didn't mean to frighten you!" We both laughed. "I hear you did a fabulous job yesterday."

"Did you? That's so nice, thanks. To be honest, I really enjoyed it more than I expected to. I'd love to get involved again if and when the need arises."

"I'm so pleased to hear you say that, because I have a bit of an ulterior motive. David had a potential new client call in earlier today about representing them through a sale process. It's a small chain of boutique hotels. Palmerston—have you heard of them?"

I shook my head.

"David said you acted on the Daleton sale, so you have some good industry experience. And because you did so well yesterday, you seem to be the perfect candidate for this pitch and presentation. What do you think?"

"Wow, that's great. I'd love to help! How do we get started?" This was just what I needed: an overload at work so I didn't have to think about anything going on at home.

"Well, that's the only catch. We only have until next Tuesday to prepare. They aren't doing a two-stage process; they've just invited three firms to present and take questions next Tuesday afternoon. There's a lot to do, but this would be phenomenal for the firm, it would really cement our expertise in this sector."

"Sounds good. When's the kickoff meeting?"

"Tomorrow at 8 a.m. I'll send you some background reading in the meantime. Beautiful flowers, by the way."

Great, I was going to be too busy to think!

I took Patricia's reading home with me, so I left the office at a decent hour and stopped by the supermarket on the way home to pick up some food and a bottle of merlot—no Rioja—for dinner tonight. It was a fresh start, a new day.

I just needed to email Daniel to say thank you for the flowers, and I needed to ensure he was clear there would be no more time-outs and then that would be the end of things. I would start my amends-making by preparing and enjoying dinner with my fiancé.

Every time I started to write my goodbye email to Daniel, I managed to distract myself. I told myself I had to give Deb some comments on her note from yesterday's call before I wrote the email. I had to book a hair appointment. I had to give Brendan my filing and go through my schedule for next week with him—by 3 p.m. I realized that I was just rude for not thanking him for the flowers and dinner last night. There was no way around it: I had to email him, and I had to do it then. I volunteered to do a coffee run again and started typing in the queue.

**Thank you so much for the flowers. They are quite beautiful. You seem to have access to my most private thoughts; white roses are a particular favorite of mine, but I've never received them from anyone until now.**

**You said last night that you require transparency in your life, so I want to be completely clear with you—I had a truly wonderful evening last night. Thank you, but I'm back in reality now and I realize that we can't pursue whatever there is between us. I hope that doesn't sound presumptuous of me; I have no idea if you think there is something between us and no idea if you want to pursue it, but I know how I feel. I feel something and if circumstances were different ... but they're not and I can't get in deeper than I already am.**

# *F*AITHFUL

**I'm so thankful we had last night.**

**Lx**

That was the end of it. I logged out of my email and went to shower and change before starting on dinner. There was a finality about the tears that ran down my face during my shower that was reassuring. I just let them out, knowing they were for Daniel and therefore couldn't be a part of me anymore.

When I came out of the shower, I had received a text from Charlie saying he would make it home tonight but not before dinner and for me to go ahead without him. Oh well, that gave me time for me to do the reading I guess.

I was starting to feel a bit more settled when Anna called later that evening. I didn't tell her about meeting Daniel. I probably would at some point soon, when I felt a bit less raw.

"Can you do drinks on Friday?"

"I think so, yes. I have to go into work this weekend, though, so I can't have a late night. Is Fran up for it as well?"

"No, I'm not inviting her. There's something not right with that girl. I've barely seen her, and when I have she's so moody. And to top it all she says she isn't drinking this month. Now, you can't tell me that's normal behavior from Fran."

"Well, abstinence from alcohol is bound to cause moodiness." I tried to lighten her mood.

"Agreed, let's change the subject. How are things with Charlie?"

"Better, I think. I've not really seen him since Sunday. He's been working so hard, but things seem to be on the right track."

"Well, that's good, Leah, but remember that you need to know this is right for you for the rest of your life."

"I know, I know."

"Have you told your parents yet?"

"No, not yet."

"Leah, how come?" Wasn't that the sixty-four-thousand-dollar question.

"I will, when it's right." I wasn't quite sure what I meant by "right," but Anna took the hint and we spent the rest of our call gossiping about news of intra-law firm indiscretions. There was more than enough material to keep us busy for a lifetime. Anna was always good at cheering me up and vice versa—tonight was no exception.

As I was finishing off my reading, my email pinged and my stomach lurched. He wouldn't have replied would he? Apparently, he would.

**It's not presumptuous. I feel it, too. I'm fully aware of your situation and I understand it would be easier if I stayed away, but it's not an option. I'm not going anywhere, Leah. X**

I was in deep trouble.

# Chapter Four

His mouth was on my neck, licking and sucking and groaning my name. My back arched as he slowly and frustratingly trailed his tongue from my throat to my stomach. It was almost too much. I felt on the edge of consciousness, as if I were about to pass out from the ecstasy of it. I was so desperate for him. I pushed my hands through his hair and he groaned again as he dragged his thumbs across my nipples, again and again. He kissed and licked further and further down my body. His hands reached under me and pulled me closer to his mouth; his tongue reached my clit and I moaned, "Oh, please, yes."

And I sat bolt upright at the same moment Charlie came out of our bathroom.

"Leah, are you OK?"

"Yes, I just saw the time—I'm so late." I jumped out of bed and ran past Charlie and straight into the shower. Had I said that aloud?

Daniel was right: He wasn't going anywhere. He was front and center of my mind all day and every day and now he seemed to be invading my nights as well. There must be a way to block him out, to shut down my desire for him.

I hadn't responded to his last email. What could I possibly say that wasn't some kind of lie to Daniel or betrayal of Charlie? I had already said that I felt something for him but I couldn't act on it; there was nothing to add. He hadn't emailed since.

Thankfully, it was Friday. I was distracted this week at work, which wasn't like me at all. I needed to get my head together this weekend and start next week fresh. I was meeting Anna tonight and I was going to tell her about meeting Daniel for dinner. After all, it was history, and so I could try to pass it off as just a catch-up with an old friend … which it was.

After a day working on the Palmerston presentation and trying to fend off urgent emails, I walked into the Chancery Bar. Anna was there with Brendan, of all people. This town could be so small at times.

"Hey, you two, are we having a threesome?" I quipped.

"Darling, you couldn't handle that. No I'm just waiting for a date and passing the time gossiping. Unfortunately, now that you are engaged we have no gossip about you. It's dull now that you are official. No will-they, won't-they. It's all white roses and wedding planning." Brendan was rolling his eyes.

# FAITHFUL

"Why white roses?" My stomach turned at Anna's question. Of course she would pick up on that.

"Ugh, Charlie sent a huge bouquet of white roses to the office this week. Makes me want to heave," Brendan said.

Anna looked at me and I looked away and Brendan kept rattling on about how boring my love life was and how awful weddings were. I just smiled and let him get on with it while I contemplated the awkward questions I would get from Anna when Brendan's date finally arrived. After about ten minutes, Brendan dropped us like stones and I braced myself for Anna's questions.

Once he was out of earshot, Anna turned to me. "So, I'm going to order another bottle of wine and while I'm gone you can decide whether I'm going to have to interrogate you or if you are going to explain willingly what is going on, Leah."

"No waterboarding will be necessary. Get some wine." There was no point in trying to pretend the flowers were from Charlie. Anna knew him better than that.

In the end, I told Anna that Daniel and I had met for a drink to reminisce about old times and that Daniel had indicated he was interested but I had been clear that I was engaged. I didn't mention the subsequent email exchange. She seemed satisfied and didn't push things further. I think it helped that she had other news.

"So, you know how Fran has been really moody recently and not drinking?" I was only half-listening while wondering whether Anna had really dropped her questioning of Daniel and me.

"Leah, are you listening? Fran is *pregnant*."

"Are you serious?" I whispered loudly.

"Totally and completely serious. She's about three months apparently. She told me last night because I confronted her about her weird behavior."

"Is it the DJ's? Or that barman's? Does she know?"

"She said she was pretty sure that it was some random guy she met in a club one night. I don't think she's holding out much hope that he's going to make an honest woman of her. I don't think she's even planning to tell him. I don't know. It's a lot to take in for her, I guess."

Fran didn't want anyone knowing, so I was instructed by Anna to pretend I didn't know until she was ready to tell me.

Discussions over Fran's situation took the rest of the bottle of wine, and, as selfish as it was, it was a welcome distraction to the Daniel drama that was going on in my head. Not that that would last for long.

I checked my personal email in the cab on the way home. There it was: another message from Daniel, and the end of my distraction. I felt relief knowing he hadn't given up. Would he want us to meet again?

**I dreamt of you last night. I dreamt of you in my bed, of the taste of your skin, the sounds you made as I touched you and your beautiful face as I made you come. x**

My stomach flipped and my cheeks blushed. I'd never had a man be that direct with me before and it was, well, hot. We were dreaming of each other now. I felt like he was running at me at 100 miles an hour and I wasn't sure whether to get out of the way or stand here while he crashed into me.

Charlie was in front of the TV when I got in, his feet up on the coffee table and a beer in his hand.

"Hey, there. Did you have a good night with Anna?"

I couldn't look at him. I was convinced the he would be able to read my expression and see that I was thinking about someone else. I needed to pull his focus from me. I needed to think about something else.

"Yes, it was great. But oh my goodness, Charlie, you will never believe it. Fran has gone and got herself pregnant."

He actually turned to look at me. "What do you mean? No she hasn't."

I really shouldn't have told Charlie, I wasn't supposed to tell anyone. I was just desperate for us to be talking about anything other than us.

"So whose baby is it? Is she going to keep it?" Charlie went on.

"I don't know, and I think so. She wants to do it on her own, apparently. Anyway, I'm tired. I'm going to bed. Are you coming?" I really hoped he said no.

"No, I'm going to finish watching this. I'll be in in a bit."

I went into the bathroom, locked the door, and took out my phone to read that email again.

---

The weekend passed without me replying to Daniel and without him emailing again. Other than going to a birthday dinner for a friend of Charlie's on Saturday night, Charlie and I didn't spend much time together. I went to the gym. Charlie seemed to spend most of Saturday in the office and then in bed on Sunday.

Things were strained between us on Saturday night, but maybe I was making more of it than was actually there. Maybe things were always like this and I hadn't noticed before. But would I be thinking like this, questioning like this, if I wasn't getting this attention from Daniel? I was just imagining the grass on the other side of the fence. I was being immature. I'd been happy for six years and suddenly, because someone else was interested, I was starting to question what I'd previously been happy with.

Maybe.

But I think Anna had a point when I had said the same thing to her on Friday night. I'd had these thoughts before Daniel came along. I hadn't told my parents about the engagement before Daniel. Charlie and I had stopped talking, stopped connecting, before Daniel.

I was relieved to get back to work on Monday. I wanted to be out of the flat. It seemed everywhere I was, I wanted to be somewhere else. Nowhere was comfortable.

I redoubled my efforts to throw myself into work. I was so busy on the Palmerston presentation that I didn't have time to think. Monday whizzed by. Charlie didn't come home until after I was asleep on Monday, and I couldn't wait to get to work on Tuesday. I had a bigger part of the presentation to deliver this time; I'd prepared well and was feeling confident. It was just David and me presenting today, so more pressure, but I had done this before.

When we arrived at the Palmerston offices, David and I were herded into a huge meeting room with views of St Paul's. It was awesome, despite the gray drizzle. I could just make out Lady Justice on top of the Old Bailey. London was distractingly beautiful. Finally our audience arrived: the General Counsel and his assistant, Jim, and Emily. Jim was one of those men who looked friendly; he was chubby and wearing a tie that probably hadn't been on sale since 1987, but it suited him. He couldn't stop smiling. It was comforting; I liked him and felt more at ease. We all swapped business cards—I noticed

Jim's title was General Counsel of Gematria Enterprises. I'd heard of them, but couldn't think where. I thought this was Palmerston?

Jim gave us a brief introduction to the Palmerston Hotels.

"The hotels were the beginning of this business and we are very proud of them, a bit emotionally attached to them. Even the CEO—he might join us. He wants our advisors to understand this is not just a business deal for Gematria. It's more than that; it's personal."

Realization crept up my body. Oh god. This was Daniel's company. I was sitting in his meeting room. I wanted to run. Did he know I was here?

"Excuse me. I just need to use the ladies room."

I just reached the bathroom when the floor started to move beneath me. I crashed into one of the stalls and sat down with my head in my hands.

What was going on? Did Daniel know I was here? Had he planned this or was it fate? He couldn't have known I would be involved. There were over 500 lawyers at my firm. It was surely just a coincidence. I needed to man-up and get back in that room before I threw away my career.

I splashed some water on my face and tried to steady my breathing. This was work and nothing else. I reapplied some makeup and took another deep breath and strutted back to the meeting room.

Something was different when I entered the room; the air was heavier than it was before.

Jim smiled at me. "Leah, this is Daniel Armitage, our CEO. I said he might be joining us. This is a very personal project for all of us." My mouth dropped open as my eyes followed Jim's line of vision.

"Leah." Daniel extended his hand looking right at me. The room fell away and I found myself staring at his hand. Covering for me, he grabbed my right hand with his. His hands felt soft and enveloped mine and I closed my eyes. He abruptly pulled away and invited me to take a seat.

I sat down and refocused. I could do this. He didn't mention that we knew each other, so I followed his lead and pretended he was a stranger.

Oh god, had he invited my firm to pitch because of me? Was this meeting to see me? He took his seat at the head of the table and addressed David. His hair was glossy and the perfect length for running my fingers through—

*Focus, Leah.*

He completely commanded the table. No one was able to take their eyes from him, especially not me. I found myself studying his lips and absentmindedly reached for my own as I imagined what his would feel like on mine. My eyes moved down to his broad chest covered in his expensive suit and tie.

And that's when I noticed. That distinct band of gold on his left ring finger. I looked from his left hand up to his eyes for the first time since we shook hands and he caught my eye and I looked down again to check I wasn't imagining what I'd seen. He must have realized what I was looking at and he instinctively covered his left hand with his right and shifted uncomfortably in his seat. My breath caught in my chest.

I caught him in his lie.

The rest of the meeting was a blur. I was on autopilot—I spoke at all the right points and in the same way as we had rehearsed, but I didn't have any conscious control over anything. It just happened. I addressed everything I said to Jim and Emily. I could feel Daniel watching me, but I couldn't look at him. I was worried I would blurt out, "You're married! You told me you were divorced! I've been questioning my relationship because of you!" Of course I didn't. And then we were packing up our papers and being seen to reception. Daniel was called away before we said goodbye.

"Good job, Leah." David said on the walk back to the office.

"Really? I was so nervous that I wasn't sure what I said."

"No, really excellent  Even better than last time. I think they liked us."

*Thank goodness. That's what good preparation*

*rewarded you with*, I thought. I was right to throw myself into work. And now I had no reason to be distracted. Daniel was married, I was engaged. That was the end of that.

Back at my desk, David came over. "Leah, I've just had a message from Daniel Armitage's office. He'd like another copy of our presentation. Can you walk it over?"

"Sure, I can get Deb to go."

"I think you should go in case he has other questions. Stop on your way home. Thanks, Leah."

Great. He's going to think I want to see him. I couldn't say anything to David now, though. I had left it too late. Oh god, I hadn't even thought of what would happen if we actually won the pitch. I'd have to see him all the time!

I finished what I was doing, logged off my computer, grabbed another copy of the presentation, and headed out the door. I would just leave it at reception and run like the wind.

"Hi. Is that the additional copy of the presentation?" The bubbly receptionist smiled at me.

"Yes, can I leave it with you?"

"Actually, Mr. Armitage has a couple of questions for you. I'll see you to his office."

I wasn't sure how this day could get much worse.

The receptionist put her head into an office. "Daniel, I have Leah from Wilkins & Watkins for you." She beamed at me. "Do go in, Leah."

I stepped just inside the door, my eyes fixed on the ground. I left it open. Hopefully this would be strictly professional.

Daniel got up and reached behind me to close the door. He was close enough for me to breathe in his masculine scent, and my god, he smelled delicious. He held both my shoulders in his firm grip.

"Look at me, Leah." I couldn't stop myself; I brought my eyes up to meet his. "I need to explain all this to you. I realize this afternoon could have felt like an ambush—"

"I need to go," I interrupted.

"Not before I've explained. Sit down, Leah."

I didn't argue—I couldn't argue. His hands, still on my shoulders, guided me to one of the sofas and pushed me gently to sit down. He sat next to me, his body positioned toward me. I was hyper-aware of every inch of him and his proximity to me. I stared at his hands covering mine. His body heat was overwhelming. I wanted to melt into him, have his hands all over me.

I jumped to my feet. "It's so hot in here. Don't you have air conditioning?" I started grabbing at my jacket buttons and pushing my jacket from my body.

"Leah, it's not hot in here. Sit down and look at me." He reached his hand up to my arm and pulled me down toward him.

"Where's your wedding ring?" Had I imagined it?

"I've taken it off."

"So it wasn't my imagination. I can't believe you lied to me. Why? I was telling you no. You had no reason to lie."

"I didn't lie, Leah. I'm not married."

"So you just wear a ring for fun?" Sarcasm was a core skill of mine.

"No, I wear the ring because I don't like people gossiping about me and my private life. I've never discussed my divorce in the office. It just stops questions and speculation." It sounded like bullshit. He smelled so good.

"I know it's stupid. I've taken it off now. I won't put it back on. I'm sorry, but I didn't lie to you."

"I don't believe you. I think you're married," I hissed.

Daniel sighed and stood up abruptly and walked over to his desk and dialed a number. It was on speaker; I could hear the ringing. How inappropriate for him to make a call! I stood up.

"Leah, please sit. I want you to hear this."

"What is it, Daniel? I'm really busy," the speakerphone squawked.

"George, you're on speaker. Leah, Georgina is my ex-wife. George, how long have we been divorced?"

"Well, clearly not long enough if you still think you can interrupt my day to play bloody stupid games. What is this? What do you want?"

"George, look, I've still be wearing my wedding ring

in the office to avoid awkward questions, and I need to explain to Leah I'm no longer married."

"No, Daniel, you are no longer married. We've been divorced five years because you are an intimacy-avoiding workaholic. Take the ring off, you idiot, and stop being a coward. I'm hanging up." The line went dead.

Daniel laughed affectionately. "So, that was my ex-wife."

He came sat opposite me on the coffee table with his legs on either side of mine, his hands on my knees. "I'm sorry if I upset you, I would never want to do that," he whispered. He rubbed his hands up and down my thighs. "Please, Leah. Tell me you know that."

"I don't know anything anymore, Daniel. You wandered back into my life just a few weeks ago and I don't know anything anymore." My eyes watered; Daniel wiped away the tears with his thumbs.

"Leah, I'm so sorry. Tell me why you are crying. What can I do to make it better? Please talk to me, I need to know."

I sighed, resigned to telling him anything he wanted to know. I seemed to lose all self-control around him. "A month ago, everything in my life was so neatly packaged and in its place, safe and contained. My work, my relationship ... And now I feel like everything has been tipped out of its neatly packaged box and into the middle of the floor and you ..." I paused. My emotions were overtaking me, but I couldn't stop. "You are standing over all of it. You are everywhere. In my thoughts when I'm at home, in meetings at work, even in my dreams." Daniel started to pull me onto his lap.

"Daniel, no. What if someone walks in?"

"No one would dare. Anyway, the door is locked." And he drew me onto his lap, onto his tight muscular thighs and against his body. This was not helping. One arm was around my waist and the other brought my head to his chest and pushed my hair from my face. His touch calmed me and my tears stopped, but I didn't move.

"I know."

"What do you mean you know?"

"I know what you are feeling."

"You don't know. How can you know? You don't know me well enough to know how I feel."

"It's the same for me; that's how I know. This is not what I expected, either, but it's real."

I didn't answer him; there was nothing I could say.

He stroked my back rhythmically for what felt like hours. I was cocooned by him and his delicious scent. I felt safe and warm and increasingly aroused. His hand moved down to the small of my back and I gasped—I was so sensitive to his hands. I turned my body toward him and trailed my hands up and down the contours of his chest.

He felt amazing. It was difficult not to imagine what

he looked like without his shirt on. In response, Daniel made a deep guttural sound deep in his throat and tilted his head back. Hearing him respond to my touch like that was so arousing; I felt a throb between my legs, and I moved my hands up over his shoulders to push off his jacket. He released me for a second and quickly resumed his stroking of my body, more urgently now, my back and my thighs over my skirt, and then trailing the skin just under the hem of my skirt, just grazing the lace of my stockings.

I felt myself moisten; I was desperate for his fingers to reach higher up my stockings, up my thighs, and for a second I felt resentful at his power over my body.

My resentment didn't last for long as I buried my face into his neck and breathed him in. He ran his lips over my jaw and I pulled him closer to me. He trailed his tongue from my jaw to my neck. My breath quickened. I tried to stop myself, but couldn't help but moan at the sensation of his tongue on my skin. He met my eyes, leaned his forehead on mine, and brought his hand from underneath my skirt as he slowed his hands over my body. Our lips were almost touching.

"I want you, Leah. I want to kiss you."

He didn't wait for a response before crashing his lips to mine with such intensity that I inhaled sharply. He pulled back slightly and ran his tongue across the inside of my top lip, tantalizing me until I couldn't take any more. I pushed my tongue to meet his. He clasped my head in his hands and I couldn't stop myself from making insistent moans into his mouth; it felt so urgent and so necessary.

I shifted my weight and, without breaking our kiss, he took the opportunity to pick me up and lay me back on the sofa. He positioned himself above me, pushed his tongue deeper and deeper, and slid his hand up from my waist to my breast. I wanted him closer—I wrapped my legs around him. He responded by circling his hips. Through the layers of fabric between us, he was hard as stone. He clearly wanted me as much as I wanted him. He ground against me, pulled his lips from mine, and looked into my eyes.

"What do you do to me, Leah?"

I reached my hands around his backside and I pulled him harder toward me. He tongue dived into my mouth again.

A shrill ringing from his desk and sharply reminded me of where we were. I pushed him away.

"Daniel, your phone."

"Seriously, do you care?"

"Yes! You should get that, we should stop this. What are we doing?" I kept pushing on his chest.

Daniel moved off me and slumped into the couch. "Jesus, I feel like a teenager." He started laughing.

"Are you going to get that?"

"No. There's not enough blood left in my brain to allow me to take calls." He laughed again.

"This is not funny, Daniel."

"No, you are right, this is anything but funny. This is—you are—sexy, passionate, consuming, thrilling, and all I want. But no, it's not funny."

I couldn't respond. The outside world began to seep into my thoughts. *What time was it?*

"I need to leave."

"Stay."

"It must be getting late. I should get home."

"I don't want you going back to that wanker."

"What? Charlie?"

"Yes, Charlie. He's an idiot, Leah. I don't want you near him."

I stood up and grabbed my jacket. "You don't get to tell me who I go near. He's my *fiancé*. He's done nothing wrong. I'm the one who's being an idiot—I'm betraying him."

Daniel grabbed my arm. "I'm sorry. I just don't like the guy, and I want you to have what you deserve. And you deserve better than him."

"And you are what I deserve? How dare you! Let me go!" I stormed out of the office without waiting for a reply.

Talk about whiplash. I had gone from not being able to resist this man to wanting to physically hurt him.

What I had done to Charlie was bad enough without the man that I had done it with telling me he was an idiot.

I couldn't get out of the building fast enough. I needed to get back to reality.

# Chapter Five

My handbag was vibrating as I stormed up the street. Work was probably trying to call me. I put my best telephone voice on, trying to keep a lid on my anger: "Hello, Leah speaking."

"Leah, please come back. You're ri—"

"How did you get this number, Daniel? Are you a professional stalker? Leave. Me. Alone." I hung up and turned my phone off.

As I got home, I braced myself for seeing Charlie—my lovely, dependable Charlie. My lover for the last six years, the man who wanted to spend the rest of his life with me. I was so lucky to have him. I just needed to remember that and be more attentive to him. I hoped he hadn't noticed how distracted I had been. But Charlie wasn't home. I changed into my robe and ran a bath. I needed to wash Daniel's scent off of me. I needed to rid myself of Daniel. I stretched out in the bath and tried not to remember all the parts of my body that had been touched by someone else.

"Hey, Leah, are you in there?" Charlie's voice came through the door.

"Yes, come in—I'm just about to get out."

"It's OK. I'll pour us a glass of wine."

Charlie sounded odd, subdued. So I climbed out of the bath, relieved I'd had the chance to cleanse myself of Daniel's smell. Charlie was on the sofa with his head in his hands and two glasses of wine in front of him. I sat next to him.

"Hey, are you OK?" I gently stroked his arm.

"Well, not really. I think we need to talk." My vision blurred and I was suddenly nauseated. Oh my god, oh my god. He knows. Someone saw me. Oh my god.

"We've not seen much of each other recently and I feel like we are drifting—"

"I'm so sorry, Charlie. I know I have been distant."

"No, it's me. I've had my mind on other things. Work and stuff. But I do love you, and I want us to be right again."

"And I love you. I feel like I've not been giving you enough attention."

Tears ran down Charlie's cheeks—I'd never seen him cry before.

"Don't ever blame yourself, Leah. It's not you. I'm a prick. I don't deserve you."

Did he know about Daniel and me? Was he scared of losing me? Had he realized he'd been a bit insensitive about his parents' reaction to our engagement? I couldn't make sense of what he was saying. I reached my arms around his shoulders and brought his head to my chest.

"Hey, don't say that. We just need to make a bit more of an effort with each other sometimes. We've been together a long time and we are figuring out how to be together forever."

"You are too lovely, Leah. I really don't deserve you."

I felt so ashamed. If only he knew. I really didn't deserve *him*. I may not have had sex with another man, but I couldn't fool myself: I had been fooling around behind Charlie's back. I was also having serious doubts about our relationship and hadn't discussed them with him like he deserved. Maybe I should tell him that I had doubts, tell him I caught up with an old school friend. Clear the air properly.

Something about his reaction, his tears, made me think that maybe he wanted to say something, too. If he knew about Daniel, surely he would say something. In any event, it wasn't like Daniel and I had fully consummated our feelings for each other. We had come pretty close, but now that we were done, I had no intention of seeing him again. I would have to make some excuse to not work on the Palmerston deal if our pitch ended up winning. What would I say to David?

"Leah?" Charlie pulled out of my arms.

"Yes?"

He didn't respond.

"Charlie, what? Talk to me." He rubbed his face with both hands and then pecked me on the cheek.

"Nothing, I love you. Let's get in our jammies and order takeout and watch a comedy on TV."

I giggled. "That sounds perfect." I was relieved he didn't want to have sex to reconnect. Not tonight.

---

As I opened my eyes the following morning, I smiled. Last evening was lovely, making each other laugh and talking. Talking about the minutiae of work colleagues and deals we were working on. He told me how last week he found one of the trainees drunk in the office leaving offensive voicemails for all the partners. He arranged for them to be deleted and sent the guy home and covered for him. I told him how I was getting more involved with pitches and presentations for work.

For the first time in a long time. I remembered why I loved him and why I said 'yes' when he asked me to marry him. Why I had waited and wanted for so long for him to ask me. I felt like a weight was lifted from me. I thought we would never get back here.

I turned over and reached out to him, cupped his face. With his eyes closed, he pulled me toward him and pushed my nightdress up my body.

I was late for work.

I arrived at the office beaming. I felt fantastic. I was wearing my favorite work outfit—an electric-blue wrap dress that clung in all the right places and patent black platforms. The sun was out in full force, which always improved my mood, and London's skyline was beautiful against its clear blue backdrop.

"What the hell happened to you?" Brendan barked as I logged on to my desk.

"What?"

"Oh my god. You look like you just had sex with Ryan Gosling, which I presume you didn't, so why are you so bloody happy?"

"Brendan, you are outrageous. I can categorically confess that I have not had sex with Ryan Gosling. I'm just in a good mood! Shoot me!"

"I may well do that unless you tone it down. You're at work! Don't make me feel worse about being stuck in the office on this beautiful day."

I swiped him 'round the head and went to talk to Deb. I avoided turning on my phone and checking my Gmail. I hoped that Daniel hadn't contacted me, but I was doubtful. And I wasn't quite willing to break the spell of my good mood just yet—denial felt like the best option for now.

My desk phone seemed to be ringing non-stop all morning, but I was juggling it all and still managed to make progress on the contract I was working on, so things felt good. The phone rang again and I answered absentmindedly, trying to proofread the email I had just typed at the same time.

"Hello, Leah speaking."

"So, you are still alive, that's good to know."

I was caught unprepared and didn't know what to say. I was at work; I had to control my emotions in a way I hadn't done in Daniel's office yesterday. Like a deer in the headlights, I just froze.

"I need to explain, Leah. Please meet me tonight. Let me take you to dinner."

"No, I'm having dinner with my fiancé."

"OK, I get it, Leah. But I need to explain. Over the phone with you in the office is not appropriate. Please, come to my office after work tonight before you go home?"

"What do you need to explain? There's nothing to say. Nothing." I leant into the phone, my voice a whisper. I didn't need the whole office gossiping about me.

"Leah, I completely understand you are upset with me and you never have to see me again after tonight. I promise I will never contact you again after today if you don't want me to. But you need to listen to my explanation. I have your best interests at heart, believe me. Just give me thirty minutes this evening."

"I have no interest in your explanation. There is no need for any explanation—but to stop you contacting me again you can have twenty minutes. I'll be there at seven. After that, I never want to hear from you again. Agreed?"

"Agreed. I'll see you then, Leah." Was I being a complete bitch? I put the phone down and grabbed my wallet and jacket. I needed some fresh air and a caffeine hit.

I didn't understand what he needed to explain so badly. I didn't really hold anything against him. He had been rude about Charlie, but that was fairly understandable in the circumstances. I had been leading him on and I hadn't been fair on him. I owed *him* an apology, really. He wasn't committed to someone else like I was. Well, at least I would have the opportunity to apologize, and hopefully we would be able to part amicably.

---

I was nervous entering the reception area at Gematria Enterprises, partly because I was worried what people in his office must think about me and why I would need so much of the CEO's time. But also, I was fully aware of the effect Daniel's physical presence had on me. I needed to be in control, to ignore my undeniable attraction to him. I was quickly shown to his office by the receptionist.

"He's on the phone, but he said for you to go in. He won't be long."

"Oh, OK." I looked at my watch. I had told him 20 minutes. It was just past 7. I took a deep breath and pushed open the heavy walnut door. Before I even saw

Daniel at his desk I felt him—that thickness in the air was still there despite things being difficult between us.

He looked up from his desk and smiled. He was so incredibly handsome, there was no denying that. His inky black hair looked a bit less sleek than usual, but no less sexy, and that masculine smell seemed to cling to every molecule in the room. His jacket hung on the back of the door and his shirt sleeves were rolled up, displaying his muscular arms.

I shouldn't have agreed to meet him like this. It was too dangerous. I should have suggested going for coffee, but I didn't want to run into anyone I knew and have to explain myself. I grabbed one of the chairs at the conference table in the middle of the room to avoid the sofa. Good. We would have a desk between us.

"Look, I'll leave it up to you. I have another meeting now and I can't spend any more time on this," Daniel barked into the phone and hung up.

Daniel took a deep breath and ran his fingers through his hair, creating more order in the inky blackness. He pushed himself away from his desk and stood. His body seemed to be taking up the entire room; it was the only thing I could see. As he brought his eyes to meet mine, I looked at the floor.

"I'm sorry to keep you waiting, Leah. Thank you for coming."

Without waiting for me to respond he took some keys out of his pocket and crossed the room to unlock a cabinet. I watched in silence. He removed a large envelope and carefully locked the cabinet, then came across to the conference table. He took a seat across from me, placed the envelope on the table, and laid both hands over the top of it. I was grateful for the distance.

"Leah, you were upset yesterday and I took advantage of you, and I am sorry for that. I seem to lose control of myself around you. And I know that you were annoyed at me for what I said about your boyfriend."

"My fiancé," I mumbled

"I know we have only been reacquainted recently, but the depths of my feelings for you are something I've never experienced before—"

"Daniel."

"Please let me finish. What I want to say, and am not saying very well, is that what I feel for you is so different from anything else I've ever felt in my life—I want to possess you, know every inch of you, body and soul. I need to have you permanently naked in my bed. This feeling makes me lose all control. But more than that, I have to have you safe, and I have to have you happy with someone you love and you deserve ..."

No man had been so open about his feelings about me. In fact, I wasn't sure any man had ever *had* such feelings for me. It took every ounce of control to stop myself from going to him and cupping his face in my hands.

"... and I understand, although I can't bear it, that that person might not be me."

So he had been listening to what I was saying.

"I want you to know that this is not about me having you, despite me wanting you."

"What are you saying, Daniel? I don't understand."

"I also understand that, after I show you what I'm going to show you, you may hate me, and although I can't bear that thought, I believe that leaving you ignorant would be worse for you. You are more important."

"You're scaring me, Daniel. What are you saying?" My heart thumped in my chest.

Daniel took another deep breath. "You know I told you I did my due diligence on people that I have dinner with?"

"Err, yes, you go professional stalker on people. Where are you going with this, Daniel? Please, just tell me what you want to tell me."

"Well, my due diligence on you extended to Charlie." He pushed the envelope in front of him toward me.

I jumped to my feet as if the envelope was on fire. "What is it? What's in there?"

"You need to see, Leah. Open it."

Time shifted into slow motion as I picked up the envelope and slid my fingers underneath the seal. I pulled out the contents: photographs.

Daniel looked pained when I caught him glancing at me. He put his head in his hands.

I didn't understand what I was looking at at first. The pictures were of Charlie going to and from work. They looked like they had been taken with a zoom lens: close-up photos, but he was clearly unaware that he was being captured.

Then I saw similar pictures of Fran leaving her office. Was Daniel carrying out surveillance on all my friends? What was going on? The next was of Fran and Charlie. That was odd. They didn't know each other that well. Had they bumped into each other in the park they were sitting in? Her hand was on his arm and his hand was on her back and ... oh god, surely not.

I skipped to the next picture. It was taken at night. A professional couple, both in dark suits—but what they were doing was far from professional. He had pinned her against a wall with his body and they were kissing passionately. The next one was the same scene but from a different angle, and again, and another and another.

Unmistakably, the couple I was looking at was Fran and Charlie. I tried to rationalize it: Maybe it was before I met them. But Charlie's tie was one his mother bought him last Christmas. I didn't need to see more. The photos spilled out onto the floor and sprinkled like confetti.

I stared after them as the extent of my fiancé's affair surrounded me. I couldn't pull my eyes away; the pictures seemed endless, taken on different days, in various points in their passion, all over the city. There were several of the two of them going into her flat at night and coming out during daylight hours.

I was going to fall. My arms, like lead, refused to steady me and I gave into it, almost wanting the pain of hitting the floor to wake me from this slow-motion nightmare.

The pain never came. And then there were arms around me, and I was upright though I made no effort to try to stand. My whole body was just limp, and Daniel scooped me from my half-standing, half-falling position and carried me to the sofa. He went to move away and I grabbed his hand and pulled him back.

"Don't leave me," I whispered.

"I'm not going anywhere," he said quietly.

I didn't understand what I was feeling—numb, I suppose, like I wasn't really there, like I was just watching myself. My cheeks were dry, I wasn't crying. I just found out my fiancé was cheating on me with a close friend of mine and I wasn't crying. I felt no pain, no loss. Maybe this was what shock felt like. All I was aware of were Daniel's arms around me. His strong hand stroking my shoulder, his mouth pressed to my temple, and that delicious scent of his enveloping me.

My numbness made way for the beginnings of my arousal. The feeling was unmistakable, but I tried to ignore it. It seemed so inappropriate. But it wasn't anymore, was it? There was no longer any reason for me to deny what I felt for Daniel. I was free to give in to it, to give in to him.

I placed my hand just above his knee. The hand stroking my shoulder paused for a second and then continued its rhythm. I moved my hand up his thigh and up to his waist and his powerful chest and he exhaled. His hand continued its rhythm and he pulled me closer. I trailed my fingers down his chest, tracing the hard outline of his muscular chest down to the waist of his trousers and I ran my hands across the top of the waistband. I could see his desire for me increase as his trousers became more taut, and I was suddenly desperate to uncover him.

Charlie might not want me, but I was in the arms of a man who did. He'd told me so. Emboldened, I brought my hand to his face and turned my head so our foreheads were touching. He closed his eyes and sighed but made no move to kiss me. His hand moved down, circling the dip in my lower back. My nipples strained against the confines of my bra and my breath came in shallow bursts.

I was aware of the slickness between my legs. I was ready for him so quickly; he had such an unrelenting impact on me. I wanted to him to feel it, feel the effect he had on me. I brought his hand from around my back between us and placed it over my breast, rubbing it over my hardened nipple and he buried his head in my neck.

"You feel so good, Leah. You are such a sexy girl. You get me hard just looking at me."

I reached my hand down to his hardness. "It feels so good that I do that to you." I never felt comfortable saying what I was feeling during intimate moments, but now it was like I didn't have a choice. I wanted him and I wanted him to know it.

"Are you wet for me, baby?" he growled. The coarseness of his words combined with the sweetness of him calling me baby sent a jolt of desire through me and, unable to contain myself, I moaned and pushed myself against his mouth, delving into him with my tongue. He returned my enthusiasm as we devoured each other, pushing harder and deeper, exploring every part of each other's mouths. His slight stubble from the day grazed my chin over and over, like he was marking his territory. It felt so masculine, so virile, so *him*. My clit was throbbing. I was desperate for his touch to relieve the ache. Without breaking our kiss I drew myself up and straddled him.

He cried out, "Oh god, Leah, I want you so much." He grasped my buttocks and pulled me into him as I reached behind his head and tangled my fingers into the inky smoothness of his hair. I reached down to his zipper, and, my hands shaking with anticipation, I fumbled to find the opening.

Sharply he brought his arms around, clasped my

shoulders, and pushed me away. "No, Leah, no. Not here. Not like this." He moved me off him and stood up.

I was left stunned as he stalked over to his desk.

Facing away from me he shouted, "Fuck!" in a deep, angry voice. "Fuck, fuck, fuck!" He kicked the desk, sending papers flying onto the floor as he thrust his hands through his hair.

Then my tears started falling. I wasn't sure if it was the shock of finding out that Charlie had cheated with Fran or the humiliation of being rejected by the beautiful man I had just thrown myself at, but the floodgates opened and saltwater was streaming down my face.

"Fuck, I am such an asshole. What the fuck is the matter with me!" Daniel howled at the moon but he had stopped kicking the furniture.

I stood up, desperate to get out of that room, to be away from my embarrassment. Why did I assume he still wanted me when I couldn't keep a man interested even a few weeks into our engagement? I forced myself to halt my tears and gathered up my jacket and handbag, then looked around to see if there was anything I had forgotten. I didn't want to have to return.

"What are you doing?" Daniel stood up and came toward me.

"I've got to go. I've embarrassed myself. I need to leave."

"What do you mean you've embarrassed yourself?

Why would you feel that? Leah, look at me." He reached out for my arm but I twisted my body away from his.

Without looking at him, I repeated, "I need to go."

"I'm so sorry for being such an asshole, Leah. Look at m—"

"Please, enough," I interrupted. I turned to the door just as I felt my heart rip in two. I forced myself onward and fled for the elevator.

Thankfully the reception area was deserted and there was no one to witness my physical and emotional disarray. Exiting the elevator, I made toward the exit when I heard my name called.

"Leah, Mr. Armitage has asked me to drive you to your destination. Would you please follow me?"

Disoriented and with no energy left to argue, I followed the smartly dressed man outside. The fresh air hit my lungs and nausea hit me like a truck. Where was I going? I couldn't face Charlie. I mumbled Anna's address at the driver and collapsed into the back seat.

The drive to Anna's takes forty minutes at least, but I had no memory of the journey and suddenly we arrived. Did I sleep? Anna was in her doorway as we pulled up. Had I called her to tell her I was coming? My head was spinning and the nausea hadn't lessened. Anna came over to the car and opened the door.

"Hey, lucky for you I just opened a bottle of wine," she said gently as she poked her head into the car. "Come here." And she took my arm and led me up the path to her flat.

# Chapter Six

I watched the man in his luminous overall frantically waving and managed to raise the corners of my mouth at his furious baton waving. Nudging Anna next to me I pointed at him and she smiled and went back to her gossip magazine.

"Have you heard this about Tom Cruise? It's crazy, look. Read this."

Anna had a weird fascination with Mr. Cruise and his various ex-wives. I think she seriously thought at some point in her life she was destined to be one of them. I smiled and started to read the article she pointed to despite my complete lack of interest. Anything to distract me from the roar of the engines and the impending take off.

Anna had been quite simply fantastic. Last night, during intermittent sobbing and slurring of words caused by the consumption of copious amounts of sauvignon blanc, I gave Anna every last detail of the previous 24 hours. Her initial reaction was total shock and incredulity. I realized I was relieved at her response.

She hadn't known. Her reaction was my confirmation of that and I garnered some strength from the fact that not everyone in my life had betrayed me. She didn't know about Charlie and Fran; she didn't lie, cover anything up, or turn a blind eye. She was as stunned as I was.

After the initial shock wore off she went into survivor mode. She was fantastically patient and sympathetic, but also incredibly practical. The following morning she called my work and persuaded them to let me take a week off and did the same with her boss. She then booked us a last-minute vacation and twelve hours later we were hurtling down the runway.

In those twelve hours, Anna arranged to have movers at Charlie's flat for when Anna and I arrived later that day, and while I locked myself in the bathroom trying to stem the flow of my tears, Anna and the movers carried me out of my old life piece by piece.

By the time Charlie was home from work, I would most certainly be at the airport, if not in the air. It was what I needed to happen. I didn't want to—couldn't—deal with the inevitable confrontation of him: the tears, the shouting, his excuses, the blame I would see in his eyes that I would hang onto for an indeterminable period of time. Most of all I couldn't bear the thought of him seeing how much he had wounded me.

I just wanted to escape.

Apparently he texted me to see where I was while Anna was booking the trip. She confiscated my phone so there would be no drunk-dialing, no room for his excuses, no more pain. He assumed I'd worked through the night at work.

Panic washed through me. All those nights I assumed he was working, he was with her, in her bed. All the guilt I felt at him working so hard for our future and he was fucking around on me. Was he in love with her? Or was it just the sex? Fran was experienced, that was for sure. She was probably much more adventurous than I ever was. I tried to push images of them together out of my mind, but they kept creeping back in—Fran's hands in Charlie's hair, Charlie's tongue over Fran's neck. Christ, I needed a drink.

"Excuse me, can I get a glass of wine?" I asked the stewardess. Thankfully, Anna had managed to get seats in business class on my miles, and the crew in business were always much more accepting of women getting drunk before noon than they were at the back of the plane. Or at least they faked their acceptance better.

"Certainly madam."

I turned to Anna. "When did I stop being 'miss' and become 'madam'?"

"The day you hit 30, sweetheart," Anna replied without missing a beat, engrossed in another magazine. She seemed to have a never-ending supply. "There's some kind of invisible sign women start to hold the day they turn 30. It's genetic, or a pheromone or something."

Oh my god, I was 30 and single. I felt I'd been punched in the stomach. My life was not meant to turn out like this. I handed the magazine back to Anna and started to sob again.

"The baby, Fran's baby. Charlie's the father, isn't he?" Anna and I had skirted around Fran's pregnancy, neither of us mentioning it since I dropped the bomb of Charlie and Fran's affair 24 hours ago. Anna finally put down her magazine and turned to me.

"Honestly? I don't know. Maybe."

"What about that DJ? It could be his, couldn't it?" I was desperate to somehow make the situation less dire that it really was.

"It could be, Leah. But, realistically, the DJ may have not existed. If you think about it, Fran didn't juggle men. She slept with lots of people, but they didn't overlap. At least I never thought they did. I'm not sure I really know who she was or is."

"How long do you think it has been going on? Since before the engagement, I guess," I answered myself. "I thought she seemed a bit subdued when I told you guys, but I thought she was just disappointed that she wasn't at the same point in her life—I suppose I was right, she wanted to be at the exact same point in her life, with the same guy ... Jesus!"

"Look, babe, I don't think there's any point in torturing yourself about it. Whether the baby is his or not shouldn't matter to you anymore. They have both betrayed you, whatever the genetic code of that poor child. At least you know now and you didn't end up marrying him and finding out later that he'd cheated with your friend—not that I would ever touch him with a bargepole, you know that."

I did know that. Anna had never liked Charlie. Not that she was pleased with what he had done—I believed wholeheartedly that she would never want me to feel like this—but I think she was relieved that her instincts about him had been right and she no longer had to worry about what was going to come. It was here. And she was right, there was no point in torturing myself about him and Fran and the baby. But it wasn't that easy. It was all I could think about.

How long had it been going on?

What had I done to send him off looking for something more than me?

What was it about Fran that attracted him?

Well, I suppose the attraction bit was obvious. She was tall and thin with curly blond hair and a wide smile. I'm sure she could model if she wanted to; she was gorgeous. In comparison, my figure with hips and waist and my barely containable breasts must seem dumpy, perhaps too obvious for his taste, although I never heard him complain. He took the opportunity to trade up, simple as that.

Somehow, though, I just couldn't see them together. Charlie was a bit of a snob, to be honest, and from what he had said about his parents thinking I was "for fun," it ran in the family. What would they say about Fran? She was so far from the other side of the tracks she was on a different continent.

Fran's family, which consisted of her mother and a younger brother, certainly didn't have money or status. She had been the first in her family to go to University. Her brother had had his share of problems with drugs but was now working in a factory just outside of her hometown of Coventry; he was married with two children, in his mid-twenties.

I couldn't imagine Charlie spending Christmases in a two-bedroom flat over a convenience store in Coventry. His idea of an idyllic Christmas was with his parents, at their country house in Scotland, spending his time huntin', shootin', and fishin'.

Perhaps she had changed him. Maybe it was just physical, her beauty combined with sexual prowess. Maybe it was just a fling, a final sowing of his oats before he settled down to one woman for the rest of his life.

Images from the last time Charlie and I had sex flickered through my head and I cringed. He must have been comparing us. Oh god, how horrible. She would have been so much more forthcoming than I was, more confident, more ... creative. I had thought we were finally reconnecting after a few months of me being distant and doubtful. I hadn't realized I was being scored, and if I didn't rate highly enough I would lose my fiancé. But the distance I created in the first place must have started it, pushed him away, forced him into Fran's bed because he wasn't getting the attention he needed—the attention he *deserved*—from me. Maybe I had done this.

Tears started to flow again and, embarrassed about feeling so sorry for myself, I pretended to sneeze, wiped them away, and waved at the stewardess for a top-up. I wanted to drift off into unconsciousness and not think about this anymore. At some point the alcohol must have its desired effect because the next thing I knew we thudded to the ground at Cancun International Airport.

"Hey, sleepyhead. I was beginning to think you were never going to wake up. You've been passed out like the dead. Come on, brush your hair. Try not to look like a homeless person. This is a really nice hotel we're going to." Anna smiled. If you didn't know her, you could be easily offended. But I knew she was trying to cheer me up, get me to see the future and not wallow in Charlie's betrayal.

In all the drama, I managed to push to one side my embarrassment about what happened between Daniel and me. I was so taken up in my grief over Charlie that finally descended on me like a cloud as I had relayed the situation to Anna that I managed to relegate what happened with Daniel to the separate part of my brain that stored up fuel for my neurosis for when I next needed it. There was always plenty of fuel slushing around in there and I was used to keeping a lid on it. God, I really hope we didn't get the Palmerston job. I could never face him again.

The hotel was all Anna promised it would be. We had a beautiful two-bedroom suite with a balcony off the living area that opened out onto the beach and a hot tub. The bed was huge and canopied. *Very romantic*, I thought wistfully.

I quickly changed into my bikini and raced down to the pool to meet Anna. Some vitamin D would improve my mood, I was sure of it. I found Anna at the bar flirting up a storm with the very handsome, topless, barman.

"Fast work!" I teased as we headed to our loungers.

"Yes, a little work up front and hopefully our drinks will be constantly refreshed without another word all week. Besides, did you see the bod on him?"

I threw my head back and laughed. I realized it was the first time I'd laughed since I'd seen the photos. The vitamin D was working already. It was a relief to see the first evidence that I wouldn't feel as wretched as I currently did forever.

I slept on and off again on the lounger; the sun mixed with the alcohol was like the most effective sleeping tablet ever. It seemed like days passed, but it could only have been hours. Anna was engrossed in her magazines every time I summoned the energy to turn my head in her direction, and then sleep pulled me under again.

When the sun completely disappeared from view, Anna ordered us back to shower and change for dinner. If I had my choice, I would just crawl into bed, but this was Anna's holiday, too, and I felt I should make an effort.

---

When I came out of my room Anna was waiting for me. "Oh, dear God!" She looked at me and rolled her eyes. "You look like an Amish person."

Before I could respond she marched me back into her room, barked at me to remove my pastel linen shirt and drawstring trousers. "That shirt and trousers should never be put together and shouldn't be worn at all unless we are sightseeing, do you understand me?" She dressed me like I was three years old in a strapless maxi dress, a bold tribal style necklace and applied some tinted moisturizer, lip gloss, and mascara to my bare face.

"There. Slightly less Amish, slightly more like you." She was right; I did feel more feminine, more attractive.

At dinner we were surrounded by a lot of couples. The pain it caused was a constant tightness across my chest and I found it difficult to look up and around and kept my head focused on the menu, my plate, my hands. Anything so I didn't have to witness other people's loving relationships.

"Do you think he ever took her away? Like, for a break? What about the weekend he went fishing with his brother last November? Was he with her?"

"I don't know, Leah," Anna said honestly and she patted my hand.

"Have you spoken to Fran? Have you had a text or email from her?"

"No, I don't want to speak to her, I don't want someone who would do what she's done anywhere near me. She did text me to see what I had done at the weekend but I didn't reply and I won't reply."

"Don't feel you don't have to speak to her on my account. We don't know who instigated what. Maybe Charlie started this whole thing and maybe he's not to blame so much either."

"What do you mean?"

"I have to be honest with myself, I pushed him away. I was having doubts and wasn't making time for him so it's not surprising he found someone else." Tears started to pool in my eyes, threatening to make a run for it down my cheeks.

"Just stop right there. Charlie and Fran have both been completely shitty to you. I don't care if you were having doubts or whatever. You were together six years.

It's not all going to be fair sailing. And even if he did want out, sneaking around with your close friend wasn't the way to go about it. Fran always wants what everyone else has and even if Charlie did come on to her, she should have kneed him in the bollocks and run screaming. She was meant to be your friend."

"I think it's more complicated than that. Look, I was flirting with Daniel, I've kissed another man. That was a betrayal of Charlie."

"Jesus, Leah, you and Daniel was or is a mild flirtation. Fran's pregnant, and she's a close friend. You get that, don't you?" I didn't respond—the wound felt fresh again. She was going to have the life I was meant to have.

"In the words of Barbara Streisand and Donna Summer, 'enough is enough.' No more tears. Not tonight, anyway." I did manage a half-chuckle at that. "Let's fully embrace denial this evening and then tomorrow morning between 10 and 11:30 I will allow you to wallow again, and then it's back to that river in Egypt—Denial—for the rest of the day. We've got to at least fake-enjoy ourselves in this beautiful hotel with this beautiful weather. Not to mention the beautiful barman! Deal?"

"Deal." I responded. That sounded fair.

---

The next morning, I was awake early and managed to go to yoga and then run on the treadmill in the gym.

I actually could feel myself beginning to feel a bit more normal. Anna was very patient with me during my allotted wallowing time.

She didn't know if they were in love.

She agreed that Charlie's family would hate Fran.

She thought that Charlie would get bored with her within six months.

We decided that even if they did end up trying to have a normal relationship together they would definitely cheat on each other and maybe eventually just become swingers. Finally, we agreed that they might give each other a disease and debated for some time which particular STD that would be. I felt a lot better getting all that out. It felt like I had at least bought my ticket for the healing train and it was about to depart.

The rest of the day consisted of the complex juggling of naps, reapplication of sunscreen, discussions of who would likely be Tom Cruise's next wife together with the stop start of the cerebral novel Anna had packed for me followed by the inevitably more lengthy study of US Weekly.

My next period of slumber brought a dream of Daniel, that beautiful scent of his, his powerful hands down my back and over my breasts, his tongue digging insistently into my mouth while he pressed himself up against me, hard as stone … I felt myself slide back into consciousness as a cloud created a shadow over me and a shiver ran through me, my nipples beading. Even out of my dream I could almost smell that delicious masculinity that enveloped him. I needed to cool off in more ways than one – a dip in the pool seemed the obvious solution.

I opened my eyes and realized Anna wasn't next to me. I forced myself to sit upright, to seek her out, but my view was blocked by a silhouette, which was also shielding me from the sun.

"She's at the bar," a familiar voice informed me. I blinked a couple of times, my eyes blurred from sleep and the bright sun, trying to make sense of the voice ... and the smell.

"Oh my god!" I jumped up from my lounger and pulled my beach towel in front of me. "Daniel, what on earth ...? Are you crazy?" I shrieked.

He just looked at me but didn't say anything. I wrapped the towel around myself and grabbed a t-shirt from my beach bag. I couldn't understand what he was doing here, but he looked so great in a crumpled white linen shirt and khaki cargo shorts, and his aviator sunglasses pushed back into his inky black hair. I'd never seen him in casual clothes, I realized. He looked younger. He looked wonderful. His muscular frame was much more pronounced without the structure of a suit. I pulled myself out of my perusal of his body and brought my eyes to his. He was just looking at me, patiently, and

I looked away and blushed, embarrassed at the memory of his rejection of my advances.

Very calmly, he simply said, "Do you want to have this conversation here in front of your fellow guests or shall we go somewhere more private?"

"What conversation? Why do we need to have a conversation?"

"Come on, Leah, not here." And he took my elbow and guided us toward our suite. I shrugged him off, unable to bear the scorching heat I felt when his hand touched me.

Apparently he knew which room we were staying in as we arrived back at the suite without having exchanged a single word. Once inside I pushed open the balcony doors and stood against the balustrade facing the sea.

"I was worried. I didn't know where you were, and I needed to see for myself that you were OK," he said simply.

"So you flew to Mexico?"

"Leah, I told you I have to have you safe. I have to have you happy."

"So you flew to Mexico?" I repeated.

"You ran off when I last saw you and then wouldn't answer your phone or emails, and you weren't at work."

"*So you flew to Mexico?* Don't you think that's a slight overreaction?"

"Well, given your reaction to my being here, I

understand that you think it might be an overreaction. But come on, give me a break. I don't know how to deal with this. I'm doing my best."

"What? What are you dealing with?"

"These feelings that I have. The fact that your happiness and safety seem to have become my priority over anything else in my life."

I tried to process what he was saying. Were his feelings romantic? Well, no clearly not after his clear rejection of me in his office. I suppose we had a history of sorts and so he felt protective of me.

"Oh."

"So, you're alive, which I'm relieved about. How are you feeling? Are you having a good time?"

"Erm, I am actually. And I'm healing. I just need some time to pass and I will be OK." I actually meant was I was saying. I was actually much more OK than I expected.

"I'm so sorry that I had to tell you …"

"Don't be. It's better that I found out when I did."

"Why did you run off, out of my office, if you're not angry with me for showing you those photos?"

Oh god, I inwardly groaned at being brought back to that humiliating scene. Was he really going to make me relive it?

"I'm sorry. I get it. I really do," I mumbled. "Why would you want me? I was just feeling emotional. I'm sorry."

"You think I don't *want* you? You think I stopped things escalating between us because I didn't *want* you?" He laughed and flung his hands into his hair. "It took every ounce of self-control I had not to rip your underwear off you and fuck you into next year. I've told you this. I get hard whenever you look at me."

I couldn't resist: I lifted my eyes to look at him. He grabbed my hand and pushed it over his thickening erection. There was no mistake over what I was feeling. I felt wanton, standing there with my hand on him. He removed his hand from over mine but I stayed where he left me, looking directly at him. He groaned, stepped away, and turned his head out toward the sea. He hadn't rejected me in his office; he had wanted me. But he had pulled away, just like now. But why? He answered my question before I asked it.

"I feel so raw around you, Leah, like you could rip my heart out without really trying. I was trying to protect myself *and* you. I can't have you want me because you want to get revenge on Charlie, or because you want to drown out your pain. And I couldn't bear to think I was taking advantage of you at such a vulnerable time. But make no mistake: There is no minute of my day that I don't want you."

Daniel was leaning on the balustrade, looking out to sea. I brought my hand to his back and smoothed his crumpled linen shirt.

# ƑAITHFUL

"Thank you." It was all I could think to say. I was thankful that he had stopped things in his office. I would have hated myself if I had ended up having sex with him after just finding out about Charlie. He was right, I would have been partly—mostly—using him. I was thankful that he was so open, so vulnerable with me. No man had ever talked about his feelings for me like Daniel did.

I was thankful that he cared so much he had *flown to freaking Mexico* to make sure I was OK.

I was thankful he was in my life.

Daniel stood up and pulled me into his chest. I snaked my arms around his waist, and we stayed there for what seemed like hours, both looking out to the sea. Eventually, he sighed and kissed me on top of my head. I looked up at him and smiled.

"I need to go. My flight leaves soon."

"You're going back? You're not staying?"

"No, I have to get back. You need this time; you need to heal. I can be patient, for a short while at least," he said with a grin. Hand in hand, we made our way to the reception area and were told that his car was waiting. He kissed me on the forehead and then slid into the car.

Just before the car sped away, he brought down the window and looked at me. "When you get back, be ready, Leah, because I'm coming for you."

# Chapter Seven

I couldn't wipe the grin off my face as I wandered back to the pool and bounced back onto my lounger. Anna looked over. "Are you OK?"

"Yes, actually."

"Have you been off flirting with Brad the buff barman?"

"His name's not Brad—it's Carlos, and no, I just saw Daniel off to the airport."

After considering all her options (stalkerish, mentally unstable, serial killer-like, possessive, etc. etc.) Anna finally settled on Daniel's flying to Mexico to make sure I was OK as being romantic, but a bit over the top.

I could live with that. To me it felt lovely, caring, and yes, romantic. Apart from anything else, I no longer worried about him pushing me away in his office or about working on the Palmerston deal. Two things less to worry about in less than an hour sounded good to me. Perhaps if I was listening to it happening to someone else it would have been different and I would have thought it was a bit weird, but Daniel seemed to lay himself bare for me. I couldn't do anything but take his explanation and accept it.

My mood improved no end after that. I still had my 10 a.m. to 11:30 a.m. moping period of going over and over what had happened with Anna, both speculating about how long things had been going on and whether they would stay together, get married, and raise the baby together, or if they would split up and Fran would end up as a single mother on benefits and if Charlie would be disinherited and forced to live on just the six figures that he got in salary each year.

It was painful and awful and horrifying, but outside of those times my denial didn't seem like denial so much. I found myself genuinely enjoying myself—it wasn't hard with all that sunshine and all inclusive alcohol.

Daniel had given me a phone before he had left. *A new number, a new start*, he had said. His number was the only one programmed in. He texted me twice a day: once when he woke up and once before he went to sleep. Just little messages about his day, about him thinking of me, asking about my day. It wasn't too much; it was just what I needed.

Three days before we were due to leave and a little over a week after Charlie and Fran's affair had been exposed, I decided I was going to use the lobby computer to email Charlie. From a practical point of view, I would have to contact him at some point and I'd rather do it when I was 5000 miles away, without the black cloud of dread of having to do it when I got back to London. I wanted to return to a new life, not to the remnants of my old one. Anna came with me and sat on the next terminal, checking her email. I had no idea what I would find in my inbox.

There were 12 emails from Charlie in total. I laughed in resignation. That was the best he could do. No dramatic flight out to come and find me, not even a phone call to the hotel. If he'd even called my parents, they would have emailed me to find out what was going on, but he hadn't even done that. I guess his ego wouldn't let him. So there it was, just 12 emails. Now I knew exactly how much I was worth to him.

They started with him confused about where I was and then when he realized I'd moved out he was angry. It dawned on him the following day that I had discovered his affair. That's when the apologies started. Then the excuses flowed, followed by copious amounts of blame.

I was relieved I'd not read these until now. I couldn't say I didn't care and wasn't wounded by his words, but now I was resigned to it. It occurred to me that I didn't really need to read the emails to know what they would say. It was no shock that he wouldn't really cop to it, wouldn't take responsibility. For the first time I understood how weak that was, how unattractive he was to me. How had I not realized before? He didn't care about me or my feelings. It was Charlie's world and I just lived in it.

I typed out a response to him. Ignoring everything he had said I simply talked about practicalities: the joint account, the household bills in my name that needed to be changed, etc., etc. There was nothing else to say. I didn't care anymore why he had done what he had done. It had happened and it told me all I needed to know about him and our relationship. I was right to have had my doubts about our engagement—about him—and I began to realize that those doubts hadn't forced Charlie to sleep with Fran.

---

Anna insisted I move in with her when we got back to London, and I was grateful. The thought of flat-hunting and then living on my own for the first time ever seemed like too much change for me at the moment. And she had a great place within walking distance of work. I put some of my stuff in storage before we went on vacation, but my room was big enough to have enough around me that made me feel at home and there were some bits of mine scattered throughout the kitchen and living areas.

Daniel was in New York for the few days after we got back. We had agreed to have our first official date on the following Saturday. My jetlag would be gone, but hopefully my tan wouldn't have faded—the perfect combination!

Going back to work was easier than I expected. Going in on the first day was helped by my tan, that glossy sheen sun kissed hair takes on and a killer new outfit that was as tight as, the neckline as low as, was possible while still being professional. I looked great, even if I did say so myself. I took Brendan out for a coffee and explained what had happened. I knew by doing that I wouldn't have to repeat the story to people asking about my sudden and unexpected holiday—Brendan would do that, which suited me.

My drama was overtaken by lunchtime by the fact that an email was circulated by one of the partners in another department announcing he was gay. He had been married 25 years. Of course Brendan couldn't wait to tell me that he had suspected all along. It really put Charlie cheating on me, albeit with a close friend of mine, into perspective.

I hadn't spoken to Daniel since he left Mexico, but our texts were becoming more regular, particularly since being back in London. It was just friendly, inconsequential stuff, not pushy, not sexy, just light and nice.

When Saturday arrived, after feeling serene for the week, my anxiety kicked in. I was suddenly terrified. I didn't think I could see him. He probably had a girlfriend in New York. He seemed to be there all the time. I'd heard about pilots leading double lives, having two families living on separate continents. Daniel might not be married to his English wife anymore but what about his life in New York? I didn't want to open myself up to potential new heartache. It would be so much easier just to cancel our date. A Chinese takeaway and The Vow on DVD seemed like a much safer option.

I lay in bed, staring at the ceiling, thinking up excuses to give to Daniel.

Anna wandered in. "So, are you excited? What are you going to wear?"

"I don't think I can do it. I'm going to cancel. It's too soon." Anna got into bed beside me but didn't say a word. We both lay there. "Anyway, it was a bit too much that he flew to Mexico to see me. For goodness sake, who does that? No one, that's who. I think he might have a problem and I don't need another man with a problem. I just got rid of one. And he bought me a phone. That was weird. I think it's all a bit weird. A bit too much. And he probably has a wife in New York. And he's too good-looking. I could never trust a man that good-looking. His face is offensive it's so handsome. He must have women throwing themselves at him. I just can't do it."

"Have you finished?" Anna asked after I stopped rambling and my breathing returned to normal. "Daniel is not Charlie, Leah. He seems to genuinely care for you. And he's not going to kidnap you and whisk you off to Vegas and force you to marry him—it's just dinner. You enjoy his company, so why wouldn't you have dinner with him? But, if you feel it's too soon, then maybe it's too soon. Only you know for certain."

"When did you get so grown-up and wise?"

"It's a curse. I'm great at talking sense to other people, it's just I don't always follow my own advice."

So I decided the best plan was to try and push through my anxiety and at least start to prepare for the evening. I could always cancel later but I could at least try. So after a trip to the gym, a body scrub, and long hot soak in the tub I went and got a mani-pedi and a blow dry.

When I got back to the flat Anna was on the phone to her man of the moment Greg, the paramedic. I suddenly felt bad; she must have been neglecting him because she had been spending so much time with me. What was I doing, thinking of dating some new guy when my best friend was still having to coddle me like a five year old? I grabbed my phone from inside my bag and went into my bedroom to text Daniel to cancel.

**Hey, I seem to have a really bad headache coming on, Maybe we should reschedule?**

I changed into my favorite raspberry silk robe, and I slumped back onto my bed. Was I doing the right thing?

Within a minute I heard the familiar ping of a new text.

**Is this a real 'I'm sick so bad I can't have dinner with an old friend' headache, or is it an**

**'I'm freaking out and making myself sick by overthinking things' headache?**

He completely called me out, in the nicest possible way. God, that was sexy.

**... the second option I think. L**

**OK, well I have a cure for that. Are you at Anna's flat? D**

**... what do you mean, cure? L**

I got no response. I didn't quite know what to do at that point. I guess dinner wasn't cancelled but my anxiety was alive and kicking. I went into my ensuite bathroom and started putting on my makeup. Anna came strolling in in her running clothes, an iPod strapped to her upper arm. "I'm off for a run. Are you going to cancel dinner or get over Charlie by getting under Daniel?" I play-slapped her on her arm but couldn't help but giggle.

"I'm not getting under anyone, Anna! I've texted to say that I might have to cancel but I've not decided properly yet."

"In the words of Charlie Brown, good grief." Anna headed out for her run.

About two seconds later I heard her scream at the top of her voice. "Leah! Can you come here a sec?"

Jesus, it was only a small flat, I'm sure a number of Parisians would have heard that. "Coming."

As I entered the living room I saw Anna escape just before the door closed, and then I became aware of a very tall, handsome, delicious-smelling man coming toward me.

What was Daniel doing here? He wasn't meant to pick me up for an hour. As he came closer I started backing away from him, but he just kept on moving closer and closer toward me and I kept moving backward. The next thing I knew, my bottom met the wall and there was nowhere to go. Daniel didn't stop until his whole body was pressed against mine, his hands resting on my shoulders, his index fingers stroking my neck. I was pinned to the wall, unable to move.

"Hey, stranger," he said.

"Hey stranger, yourself," I said, filling my lungs with that beautiful scent.

"You look perfect. I'm clearly not too early."

"Daniel, I'm not even dressed yet."

"Like I said, perfect." And he trailed one hand down from my neck, down my décolletage, and back up to my chin.

"So, talk to me. What are you overthinking?"

I couldn't speak. Daniel's other hand moved from my neck and trailed down the outside of my robe, past my waist, behind me, over and down to the back of thigh, then up to my waist again. A path of fire seemed to follow his fingers, and every part of my body became hypersensitive to his touch. His growing hard-on pressed into my stomach and I gasped.

# FAITHFUL

This man was like a snake charmer. I was hypnotized by him. I brought my arms around his neck but he pulled them off and pinned me to the wall with just his hips. He brought my arms above my head and held them there with one hand, trailing his other tantalizingly down my body. In a quick movement he parted the robe at my waist, his eyes not leaving mine as he trailed his index finger from my navel lower and lower until he reached between my thighs and trailed his finger along my slit forward and backward, deliciously slowly, I gasped and turned my head, blushing.

"Look at me, Leah," he commanded. "And talk to me. Tell me what you are feeling now."

He pushed his thumb against my clitoris, and started to circle my nub in an unrelenting rhythm. Not daring to break his gaze, I bit my lip and simply moaned, unable to form words.

"You don't feel like you are freaking out," he whispered. "You feel hot ...and wet around my fingers."

I felt the pleasure intensifying and before I lost the last vestiges of control, I tried to twist my body to dislodge his thumb.

"No, you don't." He pushed me harder into the wall with his hips and his thumb increased its pressure, circling again and again. "You are going to stay right there, baby, looking straight at me while you come. I've been dreaming of what you would look like when I touched you like this: fighting against pleasure because you are so desperate to keep control, keep a lid on yourself. You just need to accept that you will give yourself up to me." His thumb sharply changed direction.

My breath became deeper and shorter and I couldn't help myself as I cried out, "Please. Don't. Stop."

My words seemed to give him pleasure. He moaned, "Baby, come for me." His command was my final undoing. My orgasm crashed over me as I screamed out his name. "That's it, that's what I wanted to see. You're so beautiful. No thinking." His pressure on my nub lessened slightly as the last spasms shuddered out of me, and finally he withdrew his hand.

He brought his lips briefly to mine and then to my chin, his soft mouth working its way down between my breasts and over my belly. My hands finally free, I grasped his hair and savored the sensation of his breath on my skin. Looking down at him, I saw him kneel before me as he grasped my bottom with both hands and brought his tongue to the place recently vacated by his thumb. Oh my god, was he not going to stop? I could feel renewed wetness pool inside me at the sight of this beautiful man's face buried in my sex. Alternating in rhythm and pressure, his tongue was relentless; he wasn't giving up.

I felt a second orgasm begin to build. He slipped his thumb into me and began to pulse in and out, around and around. The sensation was just overwhelming. The most incredible waves of desire ran through my entire body, and I couldn't hold back anymore as I confessed, "Daniel, please, you feel so good. I'm so ready for you." I felt my entire sex throb and convulse around his thumb and tongue. Losing my ability to stand, I slumped down the wall, but Daniel was there to catch me.

He scooped me up and kicked the door to my bedroom open and placed me on the bed. I couldn't look at him. I was too embarrassed. I had never talked ... well ... dirty during sex, but the way Daniel made me feel left me with no choice, the words just tumbled out.

Daniel sat on the bed next to me and swept the hair from my face, stroked my cheek. My hazy mind cleared enough for me to remember that he hadn't yet climaxed and I reached across and put my hand on his thigh to initiate his pleasure. He must have read my mind as he took my hand in his and whispered, "No, Leah, not now. This is about you. Sex should never be *quid pro quo*." It was a sharp reminder of Charlie; that's what our sex life had been about, him giving to me so I would give to him. With Daniel it was different already.

"But I want to please you." I was telling the truth. I wanted his pleasure in the way he wanted mine. I didn't want to please him because he had pleased me.

"And you do, and you will." He kissed me gently, running his tongue under my top lip from side to side.

I moaned and he pulled back. "You're right. You are ready for me, in every way. But for now, we have dinner plans. And I can't fuck you properly worrying that your flatmate is listening." Daniel grinned, then kissed me on the forehead. He morphed from Sex God Daniel to Playful Daniel in less than a second.

"What, now you worry about my flatmate?" I teased.

"She went out for a run. She told me she'd be about 45 minutes. When I get to fuck you properly, we are going to need a whole lot longer than that, believe me."

"Is that a threat or a promise?"

"It just is what's going to happen." He looked at me seriously; back to Sex God Daniel.

---

Daniel's driver was waiting for us when we got outside Anna's building and we slipped into the black Mercedes hand in hand. "Where are we going?"

Daniel was wearing soft, faded jeans and a long-sleeved, midnight blue t-shirt. It was a sexy, comfortable vibe, so when I dressed I followed his lead in tight, dark blue jeans and a shocking pink casual shirt, teamed with platform, studded ankle boots—it wasn't a choice for people going to a private members' club in Mayfair, that's for sure. "I thought we could keep it casual and local tonight, if that's OK with you? I know a place, just around the corner from me." He grinned at me.

"Sounds perfect." I grinned back.

Dinner was delicious. The place was very authentically Italian and the owner greeted Daniel like a son, with a big bear hug that Daniel returned with enthusiasm.

As we sat down, Daniel pouted. "This table is too big, I need to be closer to you."

"I think they need to have somewhere to put the food," I teased in response. He placed his fingers over mine, stroking my skin up toward my elbow. The now-familiar heat of my desire for Daniel's touch started to increase my body temperature. I quickly withdrew my hand and broke our eye contact as I fanned myself with the specials menu.

"Have some control, Leah. We are in *public*," Daniel teased.

"Then stop touching me!" I exclaimed in a whisper.

"Hmm, nope. Not ever."

Thankfully our waiter interrupted. "Mr. Daniel, so good to see you with a lady tonight!" The waiter turned to me when he said "Mr. Daniel, he works so hard he says he has no time for a lady, no time for love, and always eats alone. So I am very pleased to see you tonight." Daniel laughed good-naturedly at the indiscretions of his host.

"I pay him to say that to all the girls I bring here!" He looked at me. "I'm kidding!" he responded at my scowl.

Daniel went on to order for us, checking a couple of

times about my preferences, but choosing what I was going to eat. How sexy was that?

I couldn't stop myself from staring at him throughout our meal. His eyes barely left mine. It was very easy between us; it didn't seem like a first date and wasn't as awkward as I expected—not awkward at all—but I guess that was the point of Daniel's anti-anxiety master class which I participated in earlier. I flushed with the memory of my words to him and the images of him buried between my thighs caused a rush of liquid to my sex.

"We need to leave, baby. Seeing that look that just ran across your face has made me as hard as steel. I need you naked right now."

We tripped over ourselves trying to get out of the restaurant as quickly as was humanly possible. Bursting out onto the street I looked around for the car.

Daniel grabbed me. "My place is less than a block up." He put his arm around my shoulders and I snaked an arm around his waist and leant into him, breathing in his masculine scent that was increasingly familiar to me.

I was excited to see where he lived; I wanted to know everything about him. When we stopped outside a three-story Georgian mansion, I looked at him curiously. Surely the whole house wasn't his. It must be converted into flats. A flat around here would run into millions.

No, apparently the whole house was his. What the

what? Who had I just had dinner with? He had had it remodeled when his ex-wife moved out—it looked like it had just been done. The colors were pale beiges and rich chocolates, like Kelly Hoppen lived in it. Of course, that was because apparently Kelly Hoppen had designed the remodel and redecoration.

He seemed so comfortable and at home there, which I guess made sense, but I had expected more of a bachelor pad, something less warm and inviting, less comfortable The entire ground floor was open plan; we wandered into the kitchen area and Daniel kicked off his shoes and padded to the fridge in his socks. Cute.

He brought out a bottle of wine, poured us two glasses, and handed one to me, brushing my fingers as he did. I blinked slowly in response to the touch.

"You are so sexy when you do your slow-motion blink." And his lips were on mine in an instant and he grabbed my wine and placed it on the counter behind me; my bottom quickly followed as he lifted me up and placed me on the counter in front of the wine.

The desire that had inflamed me back in the restaurant returned. I buried my hands in his hair, pulled him deeper into me. He undid the buttons on my shirt pulled at my lace-covered nipples with his thumb and forefinger. Was it possible to climax like this, just from his kiss and his hands on my breasts? I was about to find out.

"Why ... what ... why did you stop?" I stuttered.

He steadied himself using the counter as a support, avoiding my eyes. After what seemed like three days, his breathing returned to normal and he looked at me.

"Leah, are you sure about this? I don't want to push you into anything. I want this—I need this—to be about you and me, and not you and Charlie."

I laughed and threw my head back and he pouted and crossed his arms across his body. He was so cute when he was sulking. I reached up and stroked his face and his hand covered mine

"Charlie who? If you don't think I want you right now from your hair follicles to the tips of your toes, then we have been on different dates this evening. All I want to know is why we are both fully clothed and in your kitchen. I thought you were going to fuck me into next week. I'm beginning to think you are all talk, Mr. Armitage."

# Chapter Eight

Daniel pulled me into a bedroom. His urgent hands were all over me, pulling off my clothes until I was down to my underwear. Thank goodness I had thought ahead and pulled something half-decent out my drawer. Cornflower blue lace, it was my favorite: girly and sexy at the same time. Daniel was still fully clothed and he ran his tongue over my bra as he reached behind me and unclasped it. My breasts tumbled out and he pulled back, drew breath, and looked over my body as if deciding where to go next.

I used the opportunity to reach down and unbutton him, desperate to feel his physical need for me. And there it was, I reached beneath his boxer briefs and he shuddered as I stroked his hardness using my whole hand, wrapped around him. I held his gaze and wet my lips at the thought of getting to feel him in me any minute now.

"Jesus, I need to be inside you right now or it's going to be too late."

Daniel moved off the bed and hurriedly stripped

himself naked before he hooked his thumbs under my panties, and pulled them off. Climbing on the bed tearing a condom wrapper open with his teeth, he said, "Baby, this going to be quick and it's going to be hard. I can't hold myself back much longer."

He looked at me for confirmation. Desperate for his hardness and overcome by his directness, I reached down for him again, but before I found him he covered my body with his and plunged into me.

My back arched in response and I threw my head back. It was if he was climbing inside me. Very slowly he pulled completely out and rubbed himself up and down my sex and then plunged again. "You are so ready and wet for me."

I was lost in him. He picked up speed and I felt as if I were being pushed into the bed, deeper and deeper each time. I tried to catch my breath between thrusts but I couldn't get enough and I swung my hips toward him. He took the opportunity to find my clitoris with his thumb and I cried out, "Daniel, please harder. I need you."

He grunted and increased the pressure to my nub and I came undone, my whole body pulsating into orgasm. In between each thrust he bellowed "You. Are. So. Beautiful." I saw his climax in his eyes overlap with mine and as he emptied himself into me.

Collapsing beside me he put his arm under my neck

and pulled me into him kissing the top of my head and I rolled my body toward his and put my hand on his chest. "Jesus, Leah, I've not come like that since I was a teenager. You might well be the death of me."

"What a way to go," I said breathily and we both giggled.

"I'm sorry, I couldn't hold off for longer. You are just too damn sexy."

"Daniel, I've had three orgasms today. You have nothing to apologize for."

"I'll take that," he replied and kissed me again on the top of my head, and then brought his hand down between my breasts, stroking, feeling me, reassuring me. He cupped my sex and whispered, "This here, it feels like home." His fingers slid backward and forward, slick with my arousal, and I felt the familiar heat build in my stomach.

"Daniel."

"Yes, baby. Tell me. Talk to me."

He pushed one finger into me and I twisted my hips away from him.

"You're not going anywhere, Leah, give in to it." He maneuvered me so my back was to his front and delved inside with another finger. "Oh, that's it. Open up for me, Leah. You are so wet." He pushed rhythmically into me.

"I feel it," I gasped. I could feel nothing else, nothing

but his body, his breath, his heartbeat racing across his skin.

"How does it feel?" I could hardly catch my breath now as he pushed into me. His cock growing against my back.

"It feels too good." His thumb was circling my nipple now and the mixture of sensations was too much. He was everywhere, touching every part of my body. My thoughts fell away and I just gave in as I felt my orgasm deep in my stomach, building and then as he pulled my nipple it pounded through me. "Daniel," I cried out.

He pulled his hand from my sex and without him behind me I fell lifeless onto my back. I was vaguely aware of the mattress moving beneath me and then I felt him between my legs.

"I can't waste a drop." His tongue prolonged the pulses coursing through my body and then soothed me as my heartbeat started to return to normal.

Daniel licked, kissed, and nipped his way up my body. When his eyes reached mine they were hungry. I reached between us and squeezed his thickness and he moaned my name. He was hard and ready and I loved that I did that to him. I stroked my clit with the tip of him and then positioned him at my entrance.

"Leah," he said softly again and started to slide into me, slowly, teasingly.

"More, Daniel. Deeper."

Instead of giving into my begging, he pulled out. "Say it again, baby."

"More, Daniel, please. I want you inside me."

"You do, baby?"

My hands found my way around to his bottom to urge him forward but I couldn't move him. "Please," I begged again.

"Louder."

"Please. Daniel. Please fuck me," I screamed.

He slammed into me, taking my breath with him, pushing me up the bed with the force of his movement and then pulled almost all the way out and slammed into me again.

"Look at me, Leah, don't close your eyes." My focus was blurred but I found his eyes concentrating on my face, on the pleasure streaked across it. "Don't close your eyes." And without breaking eye contact he moved above me, so close that I could feel him against my clit, against my nipples, against my whole body as if his body was molded perfected into mine to become one. It was an intimacy I'd never felt before, my mind, body and soul connected to his. I felt every movement more acutely because of what I saw in Daniel's eyes; they darkened and filled with lust. Lust for me. And something more.

He pushed up my knee and the change in angle was all I needed to feel the beginnings of my orgasm in my spine. It couldn't be possible. Sex like this couldn't be possible. Everything was magnified, every feeling, every movement. Every inch of my body had been kissed and licked and covered with him. And I never wanted it to stop.

I looked between us at where he was moving into me.

"You like that?"

I looked back up at him.

"You like seeing where I'm moving into you?"

His words took me over the edge and I felt myself tighten around him and could see in his eyes that he felt every movement. He grunted and increased his rhythm and seconds later he stiffened, his climax crawling up his body and across his face. He slumped over me and sleep took us both.

The next morning I awoke with a start. The bed beside me was empty and I felt a pang of insecurity. The sex had been amazing. Well, for me anyway. Maybe last night was par for the course for Daniel. With Charlie I rarely climaxed, but reconciled myself to the fact that was the case for a lot of women and put it down to my biology. But my body seemed to work differently with Daniel.

Maybe that sexual connection was all that was between us and now that would be it. Maybe for Daniel, I was unfinished business from high school and after yesterday I would be crossed off his task list. I shouldn't have fallen asleep last night. I should have jumped in a cab. I quickly gathered up my clothes from the floor and dressed.

I popped into the bathroom and washed my face, tried to tame my recently fucked hair. Eurgh, my teeth needed a brush and I needed a shower. I couldn't wait to get home. I wondered whether Daniel was downstairs or if he'd left me in the house hoping I'd be gone by the time he got back. I had to get out of here now. I was driving myself mad.

I tiptoed down the stairs and saw Daniel sitting at the counter, reading the weekend *FT* and eating breakfast in his underwear with damp hair—he must have had a shower already. His body was so amazing it was ridiculous. What must he have thought of my wobbly bits when every inch of him was hard muscle?

I breezily said, "Morning," and I turned my attention to looking for my bag.

"Hey, baby, what are you looking for? Come here."

I found my bag and tentatively headed toward Daniel, avoiding his eyes. He grabbed me and pulled me in to him, but I twisted my face away. No morning toothbrushing, no morning kissing. That was a strict policy of mine. He rubbed his stubble up against my cheek and breathed me in as he ran his hands around my back and up under my shirt.

"You're wearing far too many clothes. Wanna take a shower with me?"

I patted his back briefly and pulled away. "I need to get going. I don't have a toothbrush and I don't want Anna to wonder if I'm OK."

His hands dropped from me and he slid off his stool. "Well, I have a spare toothbrush, but if you want to go, I'll take you back to Anna's." He seemed a bit cool.

"No need, I can get the tube."

"Leah, you're not getting the tube. Let me throw on some clothes. I'll be two seconds."

He was only slightly longer than two seconds and without exchanging any further words or eye contact. The awkwardness level was rising by the minute when we finally left his beautiful house and he guided me toward a silver sporty Jag.

Once in the car, we drove silently through the almost-deserted streets of London. I wasn't sure if he couldn't wait to get rid of me or was angry, but the atmosphere was unbearable. I shifted in my seat, desperate to break the tension. Should I try and make polite conversation—show him that I didn't care if it was just sex for him. I could handle that, couldn't I?

Finally we pulled up outside Anna's flat.

As I gathered my things he said softly, "Please don't go without telling me what happened. Did I push you into sleeping with me?"

My tummy flipped over. Is that what he thought? That he did something? My eyes welled. I threw my head back on the headrest. "I am just so exceptionally bad at this." He turned his head and our eyes met properly for the first time that morning and a tear trickled from each eye, how humiliating, now I was crying.

"Leah," he looked panicked. "Please don't, what's the matter?" He took my face in his hands and kissed my forehead. "What is going on in that head of yours, baby? I can't deal with not knowing what you are thinking."

I took a deep breath and confessed to the thoughts that had been running through my head that morning: I followed his lead and laid myself bare to him.

I told him I was worried our connection that I felt so strongly was just sexual and that I might just be another notch on his bedpost, that I felt I should have gone home and I maybe I'd outstayed my welcome, that I would be overtaken by my feelings for him, fall too deep too quick for him and that I was worried that my neurosis would push him away. I even told him I was worried I wasn't good enough in bed, that he wouldn't like me now he'd seen me naked.

Once I started I couldn't stop.

At some point during my confession he pulled me onto his lap and I was curled into his chest drinking in his smell. When I finally finished he started chuckling. Great, just the reaction I was looking for.

"What part of 'wanna take a shower with me' left you feeling so insecure? I need to ratchet up the quality of my come-on." I started to laugh with him. I was clearly being ridiculous.

"You're right, but I had created a problem in my head by that point." I tried to explain.

After our laughs subsided he kissed the top of my head. "I love making love with you. I love how much you seem to enjoy it, how much it feels like you want me as much as I want you, which is a lot in case you were wondering. I love that you let go and give yourself up to me. But it's more than that for me. I feel you in my heart, Leah." I pushed closer toward him.

"It's true, I do," I whispered

"You do what, baby?"

"Want you. A lot," I said to his chest, embarrassed by my revelation outside the heat of the moment. Daniel shifted underneath me uncomfortably.

"I'm sorry, but having you on my lap, saying things like that to me is making my dick twitch."

"Daniel!"

"What?" he sounded a bit offended.

"It gets me hot when you talk like that."

"That's it. You need to get off my lap or I'm done for." I giggled and he opened his car door and slid me out to the pavement.

He led me upstairs to Anna's first-floor flat, holding

my hand all the way. As I rummaged in my bag for my keys, Daniel nuzzled my neck and pulled me against him. I finally found my keys and we went inside.

Anna was under a blanket lying on the sofa facing away from the door, watching a rom com. A definite sign of a hangover.

"Hey, hangover girl."

She didn't move. "I feel horrible. But what about you, how is your vagina? All used up? Has the neurosis kicked in yet?"

"Daniel, you've met Anna." Anna sat up and laughed when she saw him.

"So Daniel, did you use up my friend's vagina?"

"Anna, knock it off, will you?" I said.

"Well that's a yes if ever I heard one. There's no need to be so uptight. You'll tell me later, anyway, and you know you will." I couldn't argue.

Daniel reached out to shake Anna's hand. "Nice to meet you again, Anna," he purred.

"Well, he's just lovely. And you're right, he smells delicious!"

"Anna, are you quite done embarrassing me?"

"Sweetie, it's not hard, is it? Not about stuff like this. Daniel, you need to sort this girl out. By day she's a confident, ball-busting super lawyer, but by night, in her personal life, she transforms into a neurotic headcase who puts up with assholes because she doesn't think she deserves any better. That's not you, by the way."

"Yes, thanks, I got that," Daniel smiled and put his arms around my waist.

After the events of this morning, I couldn't help but muse on the fact that he "got" her interpretation of my double life—not just that she was taking pot shots at Charlie rather than him. It was a nice feeling that he had had first-hand experience of it and hadn't yet run for the hills.

"Right, before this gets any worse for me, I'm going for a shower. And Daniel, you're coming with me."

"That's more like it!" Anna said.

"No, he's going to sit and watch TV in my room while I shower. I just don't trust you not to corrupt him if I leave him in here with you!"

As I pulled Daniel into my bedroom he started unbuttoning my blouse. I fought him off and pushed him onto my bed and turned on the TV. "Stay here. I need to shower—alone!"

I emerged from my bathroom fully clothed with my makeup done, hair damp. Daniel pulled me on top of him. In an effort to inject a little of my work self into my personal self, I asked tentatively, "So, do you want to do something together today or do you have plans?"

"I have plans to hang out with you all day." And he kissed the base of my throat where the collarbones meet—oh, I loved that.

I threw caution to the wind and told him so. "I love it when you kiss me there." I sighed.

"You do?" He pulled back and looked at me as if to check if I was joking.

"I really do."

He smiled and rolled me to my back where he continued his kissing. Just the bits of me not covered by my clothes. It felt lovely and intimate and relaxing. I threaded my fingers through his hair, encouraging him every step of the way.

I pulled his lips to mine and, building on my renewed confidence, ran my tongue across the entrance to his mouth until he parted his lips. He dove in, explored every spot, skimmed the roof my mouth, pushed against my tongue. Our breathing became more urgent; he ground his pelvis into mine and I moaned. He pushed off me and stood up.

"We need to get out of here or we'll never leave."

I looked at him and grinned. It was so sexy seeing to see him try to regain control of himself.

"Let's go to the zoo. There's nothing remotely sexy about a zoo. I think that's the best place for us," he said.

I laughed and nodded my head and tried to tame my just-kissed-into-next-week hair.

"But will you bring your toothbrush?"

"To the zoo?"

"Yeah, I'd really like you to stay with me tonight and maybe not freak out tomorrow morning. I'd like a do-over." He seemed pleased at the prospect of getting to rerun what had happened this morning and I felt guilty. I had upset him by being so insecure and it made my heart ache a little.

"OK, but I'll need a bit more than a toothbrush."

After putting some stuff together in a bag, including the bits I needed for work tomorrow we left Anna on the sofa ogling Ryan Reynolds. Daniel took my overnight bag in one hand and clasped his other in mine.

---

Daniel didn't let us lose body contact for one second as we were going around the zoo. Even as he was struggling to get money out of his wallet or drinking his coffee and trying to read the map to find the peacocks that I requested we visit.

I loved the way that he insisted we plan our route beforehand and not just idly wander about: he liked to do things in an orderly way. I loved the way he made excuses to kiss me (to warm me up, to test whether various animals would be jealous, to see if my lips still worked).

He was so playful and relaxed and that relaxed me. He wasn't hiding anything or wanting me to be anything but me.

Finally Daniel announced we'd seen everything and we could finally leave. I was grateful because I was starting to get really cold.

"So where now?" he asked excitedly as he started the car.

"Somewhere warm? That maybe has wine?"

"I know somewhere perfect," he replied.

I hoped we would go back to his place and warm up, but he seemed determined to keep us out in public so we couldn't get carried away with each other. Damnit! I was desperate to get carried away with him!

We parked up in a familiar street and I realized he driven back to his house—we were definitely back on the same page now.

He got my bag from the trunk and grabbed my hand to lead me inside. As soon as he closed the door, he spun me around, grasped my head in his hands and kissed me, long, slow, deep, and never-ending.

When he finally pulled away, without moving his hands, he looked at me and said so softly, "I've been thinking about doing that for hours. The reality was better than the fantasy." I smiled and pulled him toward me. He took the opportunity to lift me up and I put my legs around him. "Let's warm you up." And he took me upstairs as I buried my face in his neck kissing every inch of exposed flesh I could find.

We entered his bedroom and he stood me down and started undressing me like I was five years old. First my jumper, then my shirt. His eyes didn't leave mine for a second. On the couple of occasions that I broke eye contact with him, he guided my eyes back to his by just quietly saying my name. I rested my hands on his shoulders as he had me step out of my jeans and then my panties.

Finally he unsnapped my bra and there I was stood there, completely naked in front of him. Just before I started to get embarrassed he began to unbutton his shirt and I reached out to help him, being careful not to pull my eyes from his. I could feel my anticipation pool between my thighs. What I wanted to do was trail my eyes down his magnificent body, but at the same time I couldn't pull my eyes from his. When he was done I let out a gasp of anticipation of what was to come.

He guided me backward toward the bed and sat me down and I couldn't help but drop my eyes to his hardened cock, I reached out but he caught my hand and stopped me.

"You can see how ready I am for you, but I need to feel you. Are you wet for me, baby?"

I groaned at his question. I was unable to control the sounds that came out of me before he even touched me. He knelt by the bed and pushed my legs apart kissing my inner thigh to the outer edge of my sex until I thought I would explode if he didn't explore further.

"Daniel, please, I need to feel you." I didn't have to ask twice, he pushed his tongue into my slit and began that rhythm that I was so desperate for. My lips parted, trying to pull more air into my lungs.

# FAITHFUL

After a few minutes, he replaced his tongue with both his thumbs. He looked up at me. "Yes, you are so wet for me, baby, aren't you? So desperate for my cock inside you."

I dug my nails into his shoulders and, looking directly at him, I contracted against him and came screaming his name.

While I was still coming he pushed me back on the bed and flipped me over onto my stomach. He crawled up the bed behind me and positioned himself between my thighs. He pushed his cock straight into me. It felt almost brutal, but it was just what I craved. His need for me overcame any politeness. I understood that.

Pulling my hips up toward him, he drove into me again and again until I felt my desire build, quicker this time, as if last time had just been the opening act. I could feel Daniel's fight for control over his climax in the tension of his touch. I gasped, "I'm going to come again, come with me." I felt my pussy contract around him and he grunted, calling out my name and forcing his come into me. We slumped forward together, him on top of me, still inside me.

He kissed me on the shoulder. "God you feel so good, baby." I literally couldn't speak, but reached for his hand and brought it up to my lips as an answer.

After we readjusted ourselves, Daniel said, "You requested somewhere warm with wine. Are you warm enough? Shall we do the wine bit now?"

"I'm plenty warm enough. Wine would be great." I smiled lazily, finally regaining the power of speech.

In the kitchen he pulled a bottle of Rioja from his wine fridge and poured two glasses. "Not too much for me. Red wine makes my head fuzzy and I've got work tomorrow."

The evening was spent sharing stories of our school and University days and the music we liked and still liked. We ordered takeout and I drank too much wine. When Daniel opened a second bottle, I refused a further top-up. I had to try and keep a clear head, for work and also because I was conscious that our do-over tomorrow morning should go without a hitch.

When I yawned for a second time, Daniel dragged me by the hand to bed. He lay on his back and pulled my head onto his muscular chest which I couldn't help but snake my fingers over. I could feel my hunger for him return. I don't know if it was because the sex was so good or whether I just needed to be as close as possible to him but I wanted him again. It seemed that he wanted to talk.

"So, headcase, I think we need to have regular debriefs about what's going on in here so we don't have a rerun of today." He was stroking my temple. "I need you to tell me if you are feeling a bit insecure, if you're not sure what I'm thinking. I don't want to lose you because of a misunderstanding."

I nodded, "So ... you go first. What are you thinking?"

"So you want this to be *quid pro quo*? I told you, I don't do that."

"Not the sex, but the communication bit. Shouldn't that be both ways?"

"I can tell you're a lawyer." He chuckled. "OK, well for the last half an hour I've been thinking about tomorrow." I knew it, he was worried I'd mess up our do-over. I behaved like such an idiot this morning. I kept quiet to hear what in particular he was concerned about. "I can't bear the thought of all those men at your work ogling you, getting to spend their day with you."

*I wasn't expecting that.*

"I don't get ogled at work," I replied, genuinely trying to set him straight.

"I can guarantee you that you do. You probably just don't notice it because you don't know how sexy and beautiful you are."

*I wasn't expecting that, either.*

"I don't, but let's not argue. How can I make it better for you?"

"I don't think you can. I will just have to learn to live with it I guess. The thing you can do is tell me what's on your mind."

"Honestly?"

"Honestly."

"Well, I was wondering whether I had a medical

condition because I was thinking how I'd like to feel you inside me again."

"Well, that I can help you with." And he rolled me to my back and began his quest for my pleasure. I don't know how much time passed in his exploration of every inch of me, but as he slid into me my body was completely ready for him. On his first thrust he pushed out my orgasm tearing it from the deepest part of me.

I could barely breathe from the pleasure of it, but his thrusting didn't stop. Without breaking his rhythm he kept rocking in and out. "I want you to feel the effects of my cock inside you every time you sit down tomorrow. I want you to smell of me so they won't go near you. I want you to look like you've been fucked all weekend long." Reaching down to my clit he started to rub and I came undone again. Through the sound of the blood rushing through my ears I heard his climax overtake him.

# Chapter Nine

I arrived at work trying to contain my grin. I made a promise to myself that I would really try and block out what was going on at home from my thoughts while I was working. I'd been clearly distracted before going to Mexico and I didn't want to undo all the hard work that I'd been putting in for the last six years by bringing my personal life to the office.

Brendan slunk over to my desk when he arrived wearing dark glasses and the most miserable expression I'd ever seen. Brendan found it perfectly acceptable to bring his personal life to the office and positively enjoyed involving as many people as possible in his drama. The guy who he had met the night he told Anna about Daniel's roses had dumped him for someone who worked at Burberry and had an employee discount. Apparently in his gay world such a reason was completely understandable and they had parted as friends but had left Brendan feeling a little sorry for himself and a lot hungover. Great, I wouldn't get any work out of him today.

I managed to get him off my desk by handing him a pile of filing to do and promising to critique his online dating profile later in the day.

When I returned to my desk from getting a bottle of water from the machine, Anna had emailed.

**How is your vajayjay this morning? Wanna meet for lunch? A**

**If you promise not to say vajayjay. 1 p.m. at Eat? L**

**Done.**

My mind wandered to Anna's comment and I smiled to myself. I was still very ... aware of our do-over this morning.

I woke again to an empty bed, but next to me this morning was a note from Daniel saying he'd been awake since 5 a.m. and didn't want to wake me, so he'd gone downstairs. He asked me to find him before heading for a shower. I looked at the clock. It was 6:30 a.m., so I had plenty of time. I didn't have to leave for nearly two hours—hmm, plenty of time for a do-over.

I picked up the t-shirt Daniel had worn yesterday, slipped it on, brushed my teeth, and headed downstairs.

"Hey, beautiful girl." Daniel was sitting at the dining room table hunched over his laptop, dressed in just his jogging bottoms. I sighed, taking in his beautiful chest. He caught me ogling him and he chuckled and reached out his arm for me. I slunk into him and kissed him on the neck. He closed his laptop and pulled me down onto his lap and covered my mouth with his. My lips responded, my senses waking up as his tongue pushed against mine, my body relaxing into him.

We pulled apart and Daniel grinned at me. "This morning is already going so much better than yesterday."

"Really? In what way?" I teased, and slipped off his lap turning toward him and sitting back down facing him, my legs on either side of his. He reached under my borrowed t-shirt and cupped my bare bottom.

I hadn't slipped on any panties.

"Hmm, I think you just answered your own question."

I moved my hips slowly, grinding into him, and I felt him quickly harden.

"Yes, you seem pleased to see me, but maybe it's worth closer inspection," I said as I looked down at the gap between our bodies as I pulled the waist of his jogging bottoms out and reached inside grasping his penis.

"Yes, all the signs are encouraging so far," I said as I moved my hands up and down his shaft, very slowly milking him. Changing my tone I looked directly at him and whispered, "I want you nice and hard when you slide into me."

He groaned and his head rolled back, revealing his beautiful, lickable neck. "Leah, you are so sexy."

I watched my fingers tighten around him, gradually

picking up speed until a drop of moisture pearled on his tip. I rose to my feet and mounted him, pushing him all the way in as I cried out, "You are so hard." I lifted myself up and crashed back onto him.

He pulled my t-shirt off in one swift movement and grabbed my breasts with both hands and kneaded them together. He brought his tongue to my nipple and swirled around it several times until it was so hard it felt like it might burst. Then he brought it between his teeth and I cried out, not sure if I was experiencing pleasure or pain. And then he sucked, soothing the feeling. Changing approach again, his teeth nipped again.

He kept alternating between sensations, each time his teeth sunk slightly deeper, until the pleasure was too much and I pulled his mouth up to mine. Breaking free of my mouth, he replaced his teeth with his thumb and forefinger on the breast he just finished pleasuring and dove toward my other breast, his tongue and teeth starting the same routine as before.

My rhythm pushing him in and out of me faltered at the sensation of his attention on both my breasts. With both hands he reached behind me and lifted up my hips and then pulled me into him, forcing me down as hard as he could. I felt a sensation leave my throat that I'd never felt before, like a feral animal I let out my cry and let him take over. I was too consumed with the rumbling building from deep within me to try and maintain control.

I enjoyed him moving my body so it served him in the best way possible, like I was just there for his sexual fulfilment. That thought pushed me over the edge and my body spasmed against him, my muscles pulling him further into me. He growled and I felt him release himself into me and I squeezed tighter and tighter, desperate for every drop of him.

"Baby, I love it when you are so loud like that. I'm going to start getting complaints from my neighbors."

I pushed my burning face into his neck.

"Don't be embarrassed. It totally turns me on. I love that you can't hold back."

"That's what you do to me. Only you," I said.

I had never felt the need to, in his words 'be loud' with Charlie, let alone verbalize what I wanted or what felt good. In fact it had been the same with Matt, my only other lover besides Charlie.

With Daniel I just couldn't hold back, it was like a dam burst inside me each time we made love.

"It's different with you. I've never felt it like I do with you. I can't explain it, it feels new."

He pulled me close and inhaled deeply.

"That makes me so happy, Leah."

My hands threaded into his hair and I pulled his lips to mine kissing him passionately, trying to communicate to him how happy he made me, how alive I felt with him.

It was great to catch up with Anna at lunchtime. So much had happened since I had last spoken to her properly. It had been before my date with Daniel on Saturday. I wanted to know about her Saturday night and why she had had such a hangover on Sunday.

"So, you must have had a good night on Saturday to have had such a terrible hangover on Sunday?" I asked as we found a table and dumped ourselves down.

"Hmm, well not exactly. Greg and I are over. Well, we never really began, but we are definitely over."

"I'm so sorry. Why didn't you call?"

"Oh it's nothing, we went out like six times, so it's not like he broke my heart or anything. I just thought that, because he wasn't a Cityboy, there was a hope he wasn't going to be a complete dick. But apparently dicks aren't limited to the City."

"What happened?"

She sighed. "Oh god, it's humiliating. In the restaurant I came back to the table from going to the bathroom to find him getting the waitress' number."

"Wow, that's nasty." I felt embarrassed for her.

"Yup."

"So what did you do?" Knowing Anna, he would have come to understand the phrase 'a woman scorned' before she left.

"You know, I really couldn't be bothered to even

react. I just picked up my bag and left. I felt like I was kind of expecting it. Do you know what I mean? I was just waiting for it to happen. Like waiting for a bus: it arrives, you get on, and it's no big deal."

"Anna, that's horrible."

"It is, but it's made me realize something. Guys are dicks, rich or poor, so I'm only going to fuck the rich ones from now on. I might as well not have to pay for dinner if I'm going to get messed about."

"That's a profound life choice, Anna." And we giggled.

"Talking about dicks, Fran is back in the office this week." Apparently she'd been off sick the week we'd come back from Mexico.

"Oh," was all I could manage.

Part of me wanted to see her for myself, to confront her and ask her why she would want to betray me like that, why she thought it was OK to sleep with my fiancé. But I knew that no confrontation would bring me a satisfactory answer and I truly knew that I wasn't meant to be with Charlie. She was welcome to him. They would probably be a good match.

"I have seen her in corridors but I've not spoken to her. I just wanted you to know. She's not showing but it's all around the office that she's knocked up and the father is her friend's fiancé. She's not winning any popularity contests."

I sighed. I didn't know what to feel.

"Do you want to know this stuff or are you still boating down that river in Egypt?"

"Both, really. I don't want to not know, but I just wish she'd disappear off the face of the planet. I wish they both would."

"I get that. What about you and Daniel? You seem good together."

I grinned, unable to stop myself. Just hearing his name felt great.

"Well, obviously I completely freaked out after we slept together and I am constantly living on the edge of pushing him away with my neurosis, but he's really good to me and I want to be really good to him—it seems like the right start."

I knew what was coming next.

"And …? Come on … what about the sex? I bet his got a tiny penis. He's rich and gorgeous and good to you. There's got to be a catch. He's terrible in bed isn't he? Tell me he is?" She looked at me pleadingly.

I grinned again, and then sighed; she made a good point, what was the catch?

"Leah?" Anna jolted me back to her question.

"He's all in proportion and he's not terrible at anything and that's all you're getting from me, so stop."

"So why did your face just drop before you answered me?"

I couldn't get a single thing past this girl. It was exhausting.

"Just because you're probably right, there's probably a catch. I've just not found it yet. I suppose, like you with Greg, I'm waiting for the shoe to drop. No one is perfect."

"Well, in the bastardized words of Kit De Luca, the best friend of the most famous romantic heroine of modern times, it worked out for Cinder-fucking-ella, so why not you." We hooted with laughter.

The afternoon was productive, apart from the time spent on Brendan's iPad going through his online dating profile. Wow, online dating, that was a scary prospect. Gay online dating, that was simply horrifying.

It was also fascinating, a little too fascinating, going through Brendan's profile. He talked me through some of the code embedded in his stated preferences. Apparently he needed to be clear, using these accepted codes, that he wasn't into S&M but didn't mind threesomes or foursomes and didn't expect monogamy—none of which I needed or wanted to know about Brendan.

Thankfully our hushed voices probably had people thinking we were working on a big, super-confidential project that would generate loads of fees, and I suppose they would be half-right—getting Brendan a boyfriend wasn't confidential, but it would substantially improve his work output and therefore we'd all get more done and earn more money for the firm.

David interrupted our review and called me into his office. Brendan and I quickly agreed to go through it in more detail tomorrow at lunchtime.

"Great news, Leah." David's eyes were dancing about as I went into his office and sat down. "We just found out that we were successful in both pitches. The Phoenix and the Palmerston deals have both come to the firm."

"Wow, that's such great news David! Congratulations."

"This was a joint effort, Leah. You deserve part of the credit here."

"Thanks, David. I'm just so happy we got them!"

"We need to talk about resourcing these jobs. They are both going to be big, high-profile deals, and we want to make a great impression." I nodded, excited. "So, because of your sector experience I definitely want you on the Palmerston deal, and actually, Jim specifically asked you be lead associate, but we need to talk about the Phoenix deal. Do you think that you will be able to do them both?"

So Jim had specifically asked for me to be lead associate. Was that Daniel asking?

Daniel and I hadn't discussed the presentation at all. I hadn't thought about it before but that did seem pretty odd. I had sort of divorced the two people in my head. Mr. Armitage or Work Daniel, and then My Daniel.

But they were the same person. I wondered if Daniel

thought I hadn't mentioned it deliberately. And was he consciously not saying anything? I had to bring it up with him—probably at our next headcase debrief. Maybe he didn't want me working on the project. Maybe it wouldn't be good for our ... could I call it a relationship? The anxiety was really starting to kick in now and I mentally kicked myself and brought my attention back to David's excitement.

"Well, I'd like to try. I feel like I know Phoenix so well, and I think I had good rapport with the MD." I didn't mention Palmerston.

"I agree. Well, it's going to depend on the timetable of the two transactions and we don't know that yet, so let's assume you are on both and see how we go. You'll need to liaise with Brendan around my schedule, but Jim wants an all-day kick-off meeting at some point this week over at his office. But I'm not sure about Phoenix. Can you sort all that?"

I nodded, desperate to get out of his office to organize my thoughts, personal and professional.

Back at my desk I started to list out my tasks and put together a draft team sheet for each transaction. I'd asked Brendan to organize the meeting this week with Palmerston; he came back and confirmed that it would be all day Wednesday.

Then it struck me. Should I tell David about my personal connection to Daniel? Was there some kind of conduct rule about having seen your client naked? I couldn't exactly say we were together—officially we had only been dating a few days—but perhaps I could say something about him being an old school friend. Would he ask me why I hadn't mentioned it before?

I fished out my phone from my bag. Daniel and I hadn't said anything about when we would next see each other. Maybe I should ask to meet up to discuss all this. I had a missed call on my phone and I smiled when I realized it was from Daniel.

Daniel listened patiently when I explained that I needed to keep a clear head during the day and that we should limit our email and phone contact during office hours so I wasn't thinking about him all the time—I needed to keep my mind on the job. He agreed, somewhat reluctantly.

The missed call was from 5:31 p.m. He was keeping to a strict interpretation of the working day. There were also three texts: 5:31, 5:40, and 5:55 p.m. The first telling me he missed me and asking me to call him. The next telling me he missed me and asking me to dinner, and the final one telling me he missed me and was coming around to my office to see if I was still alive.

It was almost six now, so I quickly returned his call, hoping to catch him. The last thing I needed was him showing up here when I'd not told David anything and everyone was already gossiping about my personal life.

"Hey, stranger," he answered.

"Hey stranger, yourself. Tell me you haven't left your office yet?"

"No, just about. Are you ready to go? Can I pick you up?"

"I have about an hour left here. Can I meet you somewhere?"

"No, that's fine. I have plenty to do here. I'd just rather be with you." My heart melted a little.

"Me too, but I need my job, so give me an hour. But you don't need to pick me up—let me meet you somewhere."

"Are you ashamed to be seen with me?" Daniel was chuckling at his own question. Well, of course he knew he was far too beautiful for any woman to be ashamed to be seen with him.

"Very funny. I just don't want it to be difficult at work. I'll explain when I see you."

"OK, headcase, if I have my driver stop at the curb and I wait in the car, will that be acceptable?"

"Perfect, see you in an hour."

Really I needed about a day and a half, not an hour, but I was desperate to see Daniel. Just thinking about him waiting in his car for me in his expensive suit got me thinking about things I shouldn't be—I needed to focus if I was going to get out of work in an hour.

I bounced out of the elevator excited to see Daniel, and as I pushed through the turnstiles I saw the black Mercedes by the curb, right where he said it would be. I broke out into a smile and hurried out. Phil, Daniel's driver, opened the door and I peered in and found Daniel smiling back at me a little uneasily.

"Hey, are you OK?" I asked concerned.

"I was about to ask you the same thing. A whole 11 hours have passed since I last saw you. Plenty of time for you to freak out on me. Anything you want to talk about?"

"Is that what you're worried about?" I had really unnerved him on Sunday. I needed to learn to be completely honest with him.

"Not worried, I just want you to make sure you talk to me."

"So, let's talk. But can we do other stuff, too?" I leaned in and kissed him and he snaked his hands around my waist pulling me toward him and pushed his tongue through my lips. I sighed, he tasted so good.

I repositioned myself so I was closer to him and he ran a hand up my leg and inside my skirt, skimming my stocking top, I squirmed slightly, knowing that Phil was two feet away and when Daniel's hands moved further toward my panties I pushed him away and moved away from him so far my back grazed the passenger door.

Daniel just laughed at my reaction and grabbed my hand in his and squeezed.

"Dinner? Do you want to stay in or go out?" he asked.

Dinner was the last thing on my agenda. His hot body and the growling desire dampening my panties was front and center. At some point I had to talk to him about the Palmerston deal and then maybe I could think about dinner.

"Hmm, don't mind." I reached across to him and stroked his muscular thigh and inhaled deeply.

"I think we'll stay in." He grinned at me, understanding my desire. "Do you need to swing by Anna's to pick up some stuff?"

"You want me to stay tonight?"

"Leah, if I had my way, you'd be with me every night. Can we collect all your stuff and move you in with me right now?"

I laughed and poked him in the ribs. "Very funny. It would be good to have some clean underwear, though, so yes, please, can we swing by Anna's?"

"I wasn't joking." Daniel looked at me intensely. His voice changed slightly when he said, "Phil, can we stop off at the Hatton Street address before going home?"

Phil simply nodded and I tore my gaze away and looked at the darkening London streets: people rushing home to the comfort of their families. Daniel pulled me toward him and kissed the top of my head.

"I'm not freaking out. I'm just enjoying being romanced by this beautiful city of mine."

I was telling the truth. I believed Daniel wasn't joking when he said he wanted me with him every night, but it didn't scare me because I felt the same way. That's not to say I was about to move in with him—there was no way that was going to happen so soon—but it was nice to know that's how he felt and to feel it was genuine.

The journey to Anna's only took a few minutes and while Daniel took a call, I went upstairs and packed an overnight bag. He was still on the phone when I returned. Phil put my luggage in the trunk and I snuggled back into Daniel's embrace while he continued his call. It felt so easy and natural to have his arms around me while he talked into his Blackberry about financial results and their impact on the next quarter.

When we arrived at Daniel's, Phil took my case into the hallway and left. Daniel continued listening intently to whoever was on the end of the line. His brow furrowed and I shrugged off my shoes and jacket and made my way over to the refrigerator pointing as if asking him permission. He smiled and nodded and followed me into the living space, heading toward to sofas. I took a bottle of Sauvignon blanc and found some glasses.

Daniel stood with his Blackberry clamped to his ear in the living area so I slipped his jacket off. Switching his phone between his hands, I freed him from his jacket and I placed it on the back of one of the dining room chairs. Then I went back to him and slid off his tie. He bent to untie his shoe but I stopped him, knelt on the carpet in front of him, and untied them for him, slipping them off followed by his socks.

He sat down on the sofa with me on the floor at his knee and I handed him his glass of wine. I took a sip of my wine and placed my head on his thigh, breathing him in, feeling relaxed.

I must have dozed off for a few minutes, because the next thing I knew my bottom felt a bit numb. The change in Daniel's tone of voice must have woken me up. He was clearly getting stressed and the phone call had started to get a little more heated. I could sense Daniel trying to keep his temper, his free hand clenching and releasing, his head thrown back in frustration as he tried to keep his voice level.

I climbed up on the sofa next to him and stroked his muscular chest to calm him. I could almost taste the testosterone flowing from his pores; he was hot when he was angry. I started to undo his shirt buttons, very gently and between my continued stroking of his chest. I hoped he wouldn't notice.

When I reached the bottom button I found his belt and unbuckled it. The act of undressing him had started in a very non-sexual way, me wanting to make him more comfortable. It was now less about his comfort and more about my desire for him.

Daniel looked at me for the first time since he sat down as I undid the top button on his trousers and brought down his zip. The realization of what was happening appeared on Daniel's face and he tried to bring the conversation to a close, but there was clearly more to talk about and he continued to listen.

I shifted off the sofa so I was kneeling between his legs bringing my hands each side of his waist and I tugged on his trousers and boxer briefs. He briefly pushed his bottom from the sofa allowing me to pull them off him.

The sight of him bare and hard like that made me shudder. Knowing what was coming next was so thrilling that unthinkingly I looked directly at him and blinked slowly at him letting my head fall back as my eyes closed and I let out a sharp exhale. I wanted him in my mouth.

Opening my eyes I saw him twitching for me. He wanted this, too.

I leant forward taking him in both hands, gently pumping him, watching for any sign he wanted me to stop. He was just looking at me with his phone still clamped to his ear.

I held him firm at the base and brought my mouth toward him. Without losing eye contact with him and in one continuous movement I slowly licked him from his base to his tip. After my tongue circuited the top of his dick a couple of times and when I could see he had control of himself again I covered his tip with my mouth and pushed him all the way into me until I felt him hit the back of my throat.

"Fucking hell!" he cried out, hit cancel on his phone, and threw it across the room.

# Chapter Ten

I had given precisely zero blow jobs in my entire life.

Charlie constantly moaned I didn't go down on him and he made me feel that I was a sexual deviant for not begging for it. But I had held my ground and point-blank refused. It just didn't feel right somehow; the thought disgusted me. I knew most of my friends had no problem with it, but I wasn't giving in. Eventually he gave up asking.

With Daniel, I couldn't have felt more different. I desired to have him in my mouth. Yes, I wanted to please him in a way I'd never felt with Charlie. I wanted his body to respond to what I was doing to him. But it was more than that: I got wet just thinking about sucking him. I had fantasized about it.

And now he was sliding in and out of my mouth and, it felt desperately erotic. It was such a complete turn on that I could imagine climaxing just from him being in my mouth and me having my fingers around him.

I was unable to tear my eyes away from his as I sucked him. I enjoyed seeing the pleasure I was giving him. I increased the pressure of my lips each time he disappeared into me, I felt him swell and throb beneath me.

"You feel so good, baby." His voice was strained.

His face contracted and he thrust his hips forward, pushing his cock deeper into me making me gag slightly. The sound of him being too big, too much for me, seemed to undo him.

"Baby, I'm going to come." His hands on my head, he tried to pull out of me. I reached my hands over his and pushed.

I wanted him harder, deeper inside me. He cried my name and I felt him explode into me.

Watching him collapse in pleasure brought me close to the brink and I felt desperate for release. I don't know how to tell him so I stood up and wriggled out of my panties, not sure of my next move.

I didn't need to make a decision as Daniel swiftly pulled me onto his lap and brought his hands to my center. He flicked his fingers back and forward, teasing the lips of my sex. I grinded against him, his fingers pushing into me, his thumb rubbing my clitoris.

"You are so wet, Leah. Having my cock in your mouth has you so wet."

I shivered. He was right.

"I love being in your mouth, pushing myself in you so you can't speak while you swallow me whole. And you couldn't get enough, could you, Leah?"

I was helpless. I had no words.

"Leah?"

He wanted me to answer, tell him how it felt and I can't say no to him.

"No, I wanted it harder and deeper." His speed increased and the room spun as I exploded around his fingers.

He pulled my limp body toward him and stroked my hair. I couldn't move.

"You are so good at making me come, Leah." He snuggled into my neck.

Finally I managed some words. "I've never done that before."

He pulled me away from him and looked at me quizzically. "What do you mean?"

I buried my head in his chest, not able to look at him as I made my confession. "You know, the blow job thing."

"Leah, don't mess with me. You're getting me hard again."

"I'm not messing with you. I've never done that before."

Without another word, he scooped me up in his arms and carried me to his bedroom. There he undressed me, slowly and studiously.

He lay me on the bed and kissed me from my forehead to my ankles, avoiding my mouth, my breasts and my sex, first one side of my body and then the other.

Every time I tried to touch him he stopped me, firmly pushing my hands away. It was tortuous and beautiful at the same time. Eventually I sat up and pulled his face to mine and kissed him deeply on the lips grasping his bottom and bringing it toward me.

Pulling away he smiled at me. "You really can't get enough, can you?"

I shook my head, "No, I want you constantly. Every minute of every day I want you inside me, making me yours."

He groaned and said my name. I felt his re-hardened cock nudge my entrance and I exhaled, knowing what was going to happen next. I waited for the feel of him. Apparently he was not giving me what I wanted so quickly: he ran his tip up and down my sex, teasing me. I bucked beneath him, the sensations building in me.

"Please, Daniel. I want you inside me."

"I love it when you beg for me," he growled as he sunk slowly into me, inch by inch filling me up so full it caught my breath. He bent his head and nibbled and licked my neck and shoulders while he started his rhythm, the pumping in and out giving me what I was so desperate for.

I reached behind him and ran my fingers down his back and pulled him toward me, guiding him deeper and deeper. He pulled back slightly and brought my legs over his shoulders and sunk into me again. He understood exactly what I needed without me asking.

With the change in position I'd never felt anything so deep. I fisted the sheets at the feel of him right at the end of me. I moaned uncontrollably as he reached places in me I didn't know existed.

He was a part of me, mentally and physically, in a way that I'd never experienced. I clenched my muscles at the thought and his breathing increased.

"Baby, you are so tight, like a fist around me."

His words sent a ripple of desire from my core. I wanted this to continue forever, me in his bed being claimed by him, pleasured by him. We locked eyes and he saw inside me.

"You're mine, forever, Leah. This is never going to end," he said, and my orgasm shook my whole body.

Daniel didn't miss a beat and kept his rhythm exactly the same, looking at me as he kept pushing himself in and out. I was unable to give him anything in return. I lay there lifeless as he rocked in and out, aware of my wetness seeping onto my thighs.

He pulled himself out of me and took my legs from my shoulders, and rolled me to my left side and bent my right leg. I let him put my limbs where he needed them, I was barely conscious.

I was brought to life by him entering me from behind. It was somehow unexpected, and I moaned as he jolted into me. He was never going to stop, he was going to fuck me all night, until there was nothing left of me.

## FAITHFUL

"I want you to come with me, Leah."

"I can't, not again. But don't stop." I was breathless.

"I'm never going to stop fucking you, but you will come for me whenever I tell you to."

He brought his hand to my clitoris, and under his expert touch I could feel my climax start to build. I tried to pull his hand from me to stop the inevitable.

"Leah, stop fighting me. You will come for me."

His demand was my undoing and my orgasm was ripped from me like a thunderbolt. His fingers left me and his rhythm behind me increased and I felt him bite into my shoulder, prolonging my orgasm and beginning his.

When we found the energy to move, Daniel led me to the shower. With words unnecessary, he shampooed and conditioned my hair and soaped every inch of me.

When he was done, I kissed him chastely on the lips and took the shower gel from his hands and did the same for him. He bent down so I could shampoo his hair. It was such an intimate exchange and I felt closer to him than I ever thought it was possible to be to another person.

As we stepped out of the shower he pulled a towel around me and quickly dried himself and pulled on some pajama bottoms. I watched him move, so beautiful and graceful and all mine. I smiled to myself and he caught me and smiled back. Then he turned his attention to me and took care to dry every part of me before combing through my hair.

Wordlessly, he went and found my overnight bag, unzipped it, and found my silk robe. He grinned as he remembered the last time he had seen it.

He dressed me and led be back into the living room, sat us both on the sofa, clean, sated and content, our arms wrapped around each other.

"I love you, Leah," he whispered into my wet hair. I nodded. I knew he did.

"I love you," I replied, trying to keep my voice steady as tears welled in my eyes.

My tummy grumbling broke our easy silence and he laughed.

"I guess I need to organize some food for you, my love."

As we waited for the food to arrive from the local Italian that we had visited on our first official date, Daniel dived into the crazy.

"So, headcase, anything to report in here?" He tapped me lightly on the head.

"Maybe a couple of things," I said.

"Let's have it."

It was the Palmerston thing I was worried about. First, I wanted to know whether he had hired us because of me. It couldn't be complete coincidence that I ended up in a meeting with him just after we reconnected.

"Well, I had some input," he explained. "I told Jim I had heard that your firm had good experience in this area and asked him to check it out. That's all. I told him it was completely his decision who to invite in and who to hire. Ultimately, I want the best for Gematria and Jim knows better than I do when it comes to law firms."

I was relieved. I didn't want our success to have been all about Daniel inventing reasons to see me.

"To be honest, I didn't need to come into your pitch meeting, but knowing you were so close I couldn't stop myself. I'm usually so careful about keeping work and home separate, but you make everything different. You invade every part of me."

"And Jim asking me to be lead associate on the job, is that you asking?"

Daniel looked genuinely surprised. "Did he? I didn't know, honestly."

I exhaled. It was nice that Jim had asked for me without being told to by his boss.

"Will it make it difficult if I am lead associate? I don't want you to feel awkward."

"I think it will be fine. Good, I mean. I think I will have to take a leaf out of your book and try and not think about you during the day, particularly if you are in our office. People will think I'm crazy if I'm making excuses to attend meetings you're in all the time."

I chuckled. I loved that he wanted to be close to me like that.

"So, we keep ... this ... us ... between us?" I asked.

"I would prefer not to mention our relationship at work, if that's OK with you. But it's not because my feelings for you aren't everything they should be, Leah, know that. I just don't want people gossiping about my private life."

So he labeled it a relationship. I guess we had swapped I love yous, so calling what we had a relationship was no big deal. It all just seemed quick. Quick after Charlie.

"I get that. It will make it easier I think."

"Next?" he asked.

"I have nothing else. That's all for today," I said, happy that we could talk openly and honestly about these things without feeling awkward or embarrassed.

"Really?"

"Really," I reassured him. "What about you?"

"Hmm, well obviously I hate you going into work looking as hot as you always do, knowing that people think you are single. I'm sure you spend half your day being flirted with, including by that boss of yours. Sometimes it takes all my energy not to come to your offices and show up at your desk to show everyone you are taken."

I looked at him. Was he being serious? By the look on his face he was. He massaged the spot between his brows as if it hurt and I pulled his fingers away and replaced them with a light kiss.

"I'm not flirting or being flirted with at the office, I promise you. And my boss is thinking about making money, not flirting with me I can assure you."

"Don't be so sure. I've seen it in his eyes, Leah, that man wants you."

"Well it's moot—he's not having me. Like I told you I'm yours."

Daniel seemed placated by that and continued his headcase dump. "And the only other thing is I'm a little freaked by your nonchalance over the 'I love you' thing. Should I expect a delayed reaction?"

I looked up and grinned at him.

"I don't think so. I'm cool about it."

"Well, in that case, I love you, Leah."

I grinned again. "I love you, Daniel."

After dinner, Daniel topped-up our wine and we went back to the sofa to catch *Newsnight*. It was such a normal thing to do. A thing a couple would do. It felt good.

I awoke to Daniel pulling the duvet up around me. As I opened my eyes, he kissed my forehead and whispered, "Sleep." I complied.

The next morning I was zipping up my overnight bag when Daniel came back into the bedroom from the shower.

"Why don't you leave that here? There's no point in bringing your stuff over every night."

"Oh, well, I'm at home tonight so I'll need it, and it's no big deal to bring it across."

It was sweet of him to try and make me feel so welcome. Before I'd moved in with Charlie, if he ever saw anything of mine lying around, he would put on the table in the hall for me to collect on my way out.

"What do you mean you're at home tonight?"

"I'm having dinner and drinks with Anna tonight. She split with her boyfriend and I've not been around much."

"Oh." He looked crestfallen.

"It's just one night."

"I know, it's just I have to go away to New York next week and I just want to spend as much time with you as I can while I'm here."

Now it was my turn to be crestfallen. "You're going to New York? All week?"

"Yes, that's what the call was about last night. I need to go and bang some heads together. I'm flying out Sunday and hopefully on the red eye on Wednesday so will be in London on Thursday."

When I didn't respond his head spun to where I was standing.

"Will you miss me?"

His eyes were searching mine and I couldn't speak. I just nodded.

He crossed the room from where he was in two

strides and grabbed me and kissed me, with no ceremony his tongue crashed into my mouth searching for mine and pushing against it. He pushed me up against the wall hitching up my skirt, pulling my leg around his and pushing his crotch into me. Showing me how much his body wanted me.

Knowing I was running late as it was and with my hair and makeup all in place ready for a day in the office I brought my hands to his chest and tried to push him away.

"Are you saying no to me, Leah?" I could hear the lust in his voice.

"I will never say no to you. I'm just late and ready to leave."

"Then I'll be quick. I can't bear the thought of not having you today."

My arms relaxed and pulled around his waist.

"Bend over the bed, Leah."

His tone was serious and dark, and I shivered with delicious anticipation and I leaned over the bed as instructed.

"We don't have time to get you ready for me, Leah, so this might hurt."

I tensed but I could feel my wetness already. I was always ready for him. Unceremoniously, he shoved up my skirt again and just pushed my panties to one side as he entered me.

"Always so wet, Leah."

He thrust into me, pulling my shoulder and my hip. I met him with such force that I knew I would smart whenever I sat down today. Especially given yesterday's epic lovemaking.

"Is it too much?" he asked.

"Never. It's never too much," I whimpered.

His speed increased and the savagery of his need for me was overwhelming. I brought his hand from my hip to the lips of my sex, positioning his hand under mine, imploring him to grant me my release. In response, he almost violently pushed his fingers over my nub, rubbing up and down.

"Come for me, baby." He growled in my ear and that was the end for me. I arched my back against him and I felt the hot spurt of his come empty into me.

He quickly withdrew.

"Stay there one second."

He reached for some tissues by the bed. He wiped himself from my stockinged thighs, but I could feel my panties were completely soaked. I stood up and bent over my overnight bag.

"I need to change my stockings and panties."

He pulled me up to face him.

"Don't. I want you to wear me all day long."

Oh my god, this man was insatiable. I couldn't refuse him; I didn't want to.

"Can I fix my hair and makeup?" I grinned at him.

"I'll give you that. I'd prefer you went to work looking like you'd just been fucked, but I can see why that might be a problem for you."

"Thank you." I grinned and I pulled his tie to bring is face to mine and kissed him chastely on the lips before heading back to the bathroom.

Daniel, or more accurately, his driver, dropped me off at my office. I was thirty minutes late. Not too bad.

Of course Brendan was hovering by my desk as I walked in trying to be inconspicuous.

"Where've you been? You're late and you look like you've just been fucked."

Oh here we go.

"Stuck on the tube. And I should be so lucky. What is it Brendan?"

"All right, shirty, I need to go through fifteen million things with you and I'm getting very stressed about it. Can we sit down?"

Brendan wasn't onto me, he was just being Brendan. I relaxed and he took me through his list.

Just as we were coming to the end of the list I looked up as a huge bouquet of white roses came toward me. Sylvia, one of the other PA's beamed at me. These just came for you. Looks like someone's really sorry. She placed them on my desk and winked at me.

"Charlie's trying to get you back?" Brendan said

incredulously. "What does the card say?" He grabbed it from the cellophane and opened the envelope.

"Brendan! Give it to me." I snatched it back, knowing it wouldn't be an apology and the flowers weren't from Charlie.

"Come on, let's finish off this list." I said trying to pull his attention back to work.

"Err no way José. Your drama is much more interesting, I want the next installment. Open the card."

How was I going to get out of this? I had no idea what the card would say. With Daniel I could never tell; it could be sweet, loving, or toe-curlingly hot.

"Come on Brendan, give me a break?"

"Puhlease. Of course I won't. Show me the card."

He was determined and in an effort for a quiet life I gave in and he took the envelope from my fingers and gleefully slipped out the card as I slumped back into my chair defeated.

Brendan looked at the card and then looked at me and then back at the card. Then he handed me the card without uttering a word.

Brendan with nothing to say—that was never good.

I want people to know you're taken.

Dx

I smiled at his possessiveness. He really did think I spent my whole time in the office flirting. When I looked up I was still smiling and Brendan was looking at me.

"They're not from Charlie?" I shook my head. "Who then?" he pressed.

"No one you know. An old friend."

"Leah, come on. You know I need more than that. I want details!"

"That's not happening. I want to keep this to myself. Everyone knows about my love life or non-love life around here, and I can't bear it. I want this to be private."

"And that includes private from me?" Brendan looked like he'd been slapped in the face.

"This is no big deal, just a few dates. If it crashes and burns I don't want to be embarrassed again. Please don't hate me; I just can't bear the humiliation again. I've not even spoken to Anna about it."

I was lying, but I was doing it to protect his feelings so it felt worth it. I couldn't admit to myself how serious it had become with Daniel, and I was embarrassed at how quickly it had happened after Charlie. And Daniel didn't want his office to know which made life easier for me while on the Palmerston deal.

I absolutely couldn't tell Brendan the truth. He seemed to understand what I was saying, although I could tell his pride was hurt. He avoided me for most of the rest of the day and said he didn't have time to finish going through his dating profile. I was a little relieved.

I had texted Daniel to thank him for the flowers but he hadn't texted back. Which was fine, I thought. We had agreed to try and not contact each other in working hours after all. Leaving work to heading back to Anna's I stopped to pick up a bottle of wine. None of the vintage stuff that I'd had over the last few days tonight. If I couldn't buy it in Tesco Metro we weren't having it.

My mobile vibrated: it was a text from Daniel.

**Have a lovely evening with Anna. Miss you. Dx**

**What are your plans for this evening? Miss you, too. Lx**

**Just work. Dx**

Anna got in a few minutes after me clutching another bottle of wine in her hands. Great minds.

We changed into our jogging bottoms and got settled in for the night. She explained that she had still managed to avoid seeing Fran, but received an email from her asking her to meet her for a coffee this weekend. I didn't know what to say. Fran was always more her friend than mine, and I didn't want to tell her not to be friends with her, but if I said I thought they should meet I'm not sure it would sound genuine.

"How do you feel about meeting her?"

"Mixed. I feel disloyal to you. I feel she's not the sort of person that I want in my life, but I've known her a long time and I think maybe I should give her an opportunity to explain."

"I won't feel that you're being disloyal. You've been

amazing to me. I couldn't have asked for any more from you. You have known her a long time. Meeting her doesn't mean you have to be best friends with her."

"Wow, you sound really together."

"Do I? It's just an act!"

"No, I don't think it is. I think Daniel's good for you."

"I think so, too." And I bit back a grin.

Could I call him? Would that look like I couldn't cope for an evening without him? I tried to push thoughts of him to the back of my mind and concentrate on Anna.

"Have you heard from Charlie?" she asked.

I shook my head. He had replied to my email that I had sent in Mexico agreeing to my suggestions of how to divide the practicalities of the split but there had been no other contact. He had very quickly become my past, my distant past.

"You don't feel you need closure?"

"I think him getting my close friend pregnant was all the closure I needed." And I started laughing and Anna joined in.

I crawled into bed shortly before midnight with my phone for company. I'd had a text from Daniel asking me to call him before I went to sleep, so I called and he answered on the first ring.

"Hey, stranger."

"Heyyy stranger, yourself. What ya doin'?" I asked, clearly a couple of glasses of wine past sober.

"Still in the office. It sounds like you've had a nicer evening than me."

"It would have been a nicer evening with you."

"I just wanted to wish you goodnight, baby. Go to sleep now or you will have a horrible hangover. I need to get on a call with New York, so I should go. Will you stay tomorrow night?"

I was flustered. I wanted to talk to him all night, but he was distracted.

"Yes, of course, tomorrow night. Remember I'm at your office all day tomorrow."

"How could I forget? I won't get any work done thinking about you just a few feet away."

I smiled. There he was, My Daniel. I pressed cancel on the phone and collapsed into my pillow.

# Chapter Eleven

I couldn't wait to get to work the next morning. I felt like I'd been starved of oxygen. I hadn't seen Daniel for 24 hours: he hadn't touched me, hadn't kissed me, hadn't made me come for longer than I could bear. I was desperate to catch a glimpse of him, however brief. I needed to quench my thirst for him.

After a brief pre-meeting, David, Deb, and I walked over to the Gematria offices. It was a beautiful sunny day and looking up and feeling the warmth of the sun on my face felt amazing and I couldn't help but grin to myself. I'd worn another of my wrap dresses. I was going for sexy but professional. I stopped myself from doing downright slutty—which had been my initial instinct—but I knew I could never pull it off. I wanted Daniel to want me as soon as he saw me. I realized that if I was going to stop thinking about him in working hours I needed to feed my need for him in time off. I didn't want to spend another night away from him.

Before being shown into our meeting room, we were kept in reception for a few minutes. I kept looking around to see if I could see him, catch that glimpse of him that I was so desperate for. No luck. There was lots of activity, lots of gorgeous young women I noticed jealously, but no Daniel.

We were shown into our huge meeting room with an incredible view of the City right to the river and beyond, and Jim and Emily came in and greeted us warmly. Jim started to take us through a list of things he thought we should cover today and we got straight down to work.

About an hour into things, I excused myself and headed to the bathroom, still secretly hoping to see Daniel—or even better, accidently-on-purpose bump into him. But my trip was unsuccessful. No Daniel. I resigned myself to actually concentrating on what we were here to do and buried my thoughts of Daniel at the back of my head.

Shortly after we reconvened after lunch and a couple more necessary trips to the restroom had not uncovered him, the door to the meeting room swung open to reveal Daniel looking heart-stoppingly handsome. His beauty caught me by surprise, as if I were seeing it for the first time, and I could hardly believe my luck—I had been in his bed. He had on my favorite blue suit and I remembered the feel of it on that first night we had been to the Coltrane Club. I smiled and looked down at my papers, being careful not to give myself away.

"So, how are things going in here?" he addressed Jim, not looking at me. David stood up and shook his hand.

I kept my head down, pretending to read the document in front of me. His voice was slightly different: Work Daniel. He was these guys' boss—I suppose playful Daniel or sexy Daniel would be slightly inappropriate. But Work Daniel was hot—the power suited him.

"Good, we're making progress. I'll need to run through the list of names we have for the due diligence interviews to ensure you're happy with it, but I can do that with you tomorrow. I'm just about to leave for a meeting in the West End."

"I'm free at 4 p.m. Have Leah bring it to me. I don't want to lose pace." And with that he swept out.

When 4 p.m. arrived I was a little nervous. I was really trying to keep my work head on me during office hours, trying to keep Daniel in a box, ready to open and enjoy later. This meeting could open that box and blur the boundaries. But I was sure he would be busy and could only spare me a few moments and it would be fine. I was desperate to see him.

I took the list, my notepad, and pen, and found his PA sitting outside his office. His door was shut but she greeted me brightly and led me right in.

"Ah, Leah, good, come in." Gail, his PA, hovered in the doorway.

"Thank you for seeing me ... er ... Mr. Armitage." He tried to suppress a grin at our formal exchange but didn't correct me.

"Can I get you any drinks? Tea, coffee?" Gail smiled warmly, her eyes darting between the two of us. We both declined and Daniel stood up and closed the door and locked it behind her as she left. Hmm, that didn't seem very business as usual.

"Do you have your list, Leah? Please set it on my desk." Oh, he was still Work Daniel. I was a little disappointed, but I pulled the list from my papers and walked over to the desk. He came up behind me and moved me so I was standing facing the back of his desk and my flesh tingled at his touch. He didn't invite me to sit down, so I guess he wanted this meeting to be quick.

"So, the first name is?" I expected Daniel to retake his seat and inspect the list, but he didn't move from behind me.

I reached across his desk for the list to turn it around so I could read it and he took the opportunity to push me further forward so I was bent completely over the desk. He placed my forearms on the desk either side of the list. I gasped, but Daniel meant business—he splayed his hand on my back, ensuring I stayed put. My god, what was he going to do, here in his office, with people constantly walking by and his PA sitting right outside? I inhaled, and felt myself moisten with anticipation.

"The first name, Leah?"

"E-Edward Lockton," I stuttered.

Daniel pushed up my skirt to my waist and, without

missing a beat, mused, "Yes, that makes sense. The next?"

He ripped my wet panties from me and I felt a coolness as I adjusted to my lack of underwear.

I tried to focus on the next name. "Jill Elliot," I said unsteadily, trying to suppress my urge to groan as Daniel thrust two fingers straight into me without warning.

"Hmm, interesting. The next?" His fingers started a rhythmic dance in and out.

"David Green."

I couldn't hear my voice coming out as the blood was booming in my ears but my mouth seemed to move through the names.

As Daniel reached his other hand around me and found my clitoris I lost the power of speech.

"Leah, the next name," he reprimanded.

"I'm sorry ... Mr. Armitage ... it's Ben Amos."

His desire seemed heightened by words and he grunted, but his fingers left me suddenly. Before I had a chance to turn to see what was next he pushed himself hard into me, pushing me off my elbows. He repositioned me quickly, and holding my shoulders for resistance, thrust again and again.

"Yes, Ben should be on there. Who else?"

I was overwhelmed by his steady tone and the feeling of his relentless cock, slamming into me over and over, but I refocused and I tried to keep my voice steady. I kept reading out the names. He approved each one while he slid in and out of me.

My whole body was on fire. What we were doing felt so illicit. His complete control of me, of himself, was more than I could bear. I felt myself begin to contract around him and he felt it, too, as he picked up his rhythm. The proximity of my climax made me forget where I was and I finally gave in and moaned.

"Quiet, Leah. The next name?" His verbal acknowledgement of our physical act ended me.

"I'm sorry ... sir," I cried out breathlessly, unable to see the final name on the list as my orgasm crashed over me. Behind me I felt the last desperate thrusts of Daniel's climax.

We stayed silent, joined together, catching our breath. Daniel withdrew from me and I heard him zip up his trousers and tuck in his shirt. I couldn't move; I didn't know if I should. He pulled down my skirt and pulled me up from the desk, his body still behind me and briefly kissed me on the top of my head. He released his hands from around my waist and moved back toward his chair.

He turned his attention to his computer. "You need to add David Richards and Matt Barnes to that list, and then I think you've got everyone. Thanks, Leah, excellent meeting."

Feeling incredibly well-fucked, I replied confidently,

"It was my pleasure, Mr. Armitage." Daniel smiled at his computer screen as I left.

As I closed the door behind me Gail smiled sweetly, "Did you get everything you needed?"

I was caught a bit off balance. Had she heard anything? "Err, yes, I think I have everything. Thanks Gail."

I went straight to the bathroom and removed my panties; they were destroyed so I threw them in the bin and tidied myself up before heading back to the big meeting room. I was sure I smelled of him, of his sweat and his come between my thighs. The thought made my knees weak and before they buckled I scrambled to my chair.

"You OK, Leah?" David asked me, watching me intently.

"Yes, fine. Just a little overwhelmed. We have such a lot to do."

He smiled and nodded and I started sorting through some of the materials that we'd been given during the course of the day, trying to act as if my mind was on the job.

Back at the office I plowed through my emails and when I next looked at the clock it was 7 p.m. I grabbed my phone to see if Daniel had contacted me. I'd agreed that I would stay with him tonight, but we'd not agreed timings. There was a text from him.

**The car is outside. When you are ready, Phil will take you to Anna's to collect your things and then bring you home to me. Dx**

I scrambled to log out of my computer. I couldn't get out of there quickly enough.

When the car pulled up outside Daniel's house I felt a swell of nervousness in my stomach. Daniel's driver carried my bag up the steps and let himself in, putting my bag in the hall and wishing me a goodnight before he turned and left.

Where was Daniel? He didn't seem to be downstairs in the open plan area. Not wanting to shout out to him I went looking for him, eventually finding him in his study. He didn't see me. He was staring intently into the screen on his computer. I leant against the door frame, taking him in. It was so good to be able to unabashedly gaze at him.

"Hey, stranger," he said without turning around.

"Hey." I moved across to him and slid my arms around his waist.

He twisted toward me, took my face in his hands, and crashed his lips against mine. He ran his tongue along the inside of my top lip and darted in and out of my mouth, teasing my tongue. He kissed me like it was our first kiss and it seemed to last forever. It was such a contrast to our earlier, urgent fucking that it took me by surprise a little.

"Hmm, I needed that." Daniel sighed as he pulled away looking at me. "Let's have dinner. I've had my housekeeper prepare something but I have no idea what it is—we should investigate."

"Your housekeeper?"

"Yes, Mrs. Bayliss. She cooks for me if I ask her to."

"Oh," was all I could say. I'd never met anyone with a housekeeper before, but I guess if you lived in a house like this, a housekeeper was a natural accoutrement. Suddenly his revelation really bothered me. "I really don't know anything about you, do I?"

He looked confused. "I'm not hiding anything, Leah; we've just been busy with more pressing priorities than discussing my housekeeper." He chuckled and pulled me toward him burying his face in my neck and kissing me to distraction. I relented and pushed my hands through his hair, savoring the silkiness. God, he felt good. No wonder I didn't know about his housekeeper. I could no longer think about anything but his mouth on me.

His hands were roaming further and further down my body and I could see where this was headed. Not that I wanted it to be headed anywhere else but neither did I want our relationship to just be about sex. I pulled him away.

"Let's eat." I said to him. "We have plenty of time tonight." I could tell he wanted more, the evidence was right there in front of me, tempting me to touch him but I resisted. He took a deep breath and we set about dishing up the dinner left by Mrs. Bayliss.

We caught up on our day. Neither of us mentioned what had happened in his office. I told him about Brendan's pouting over me not telling him who my flowers were from. After dinner, we moved to the biggest of his sofas and he motioned for me to tuck in under his shoulder as we sat leaning into each other, our legs extended on the footstool that was nearly as long as the sofa itself.

I gave him a run down on my evening with Anna and how she was considering meeting with Fran. He didn't pass comment on whether he thought Anna should meet her or not. His attention was focused elsewhere.

"Have you heard from Charlie?" he asked as he pulled away.

"Not since the email he sent about the joint account and stuff." I looked back at him, trying to work out why he was asking. I was trying not to keep my worries inside so I thought it was easiest to just ask him. "Why?"

He snuggled back into me. "I just wondered. I just don't want him hurting you anymore. You'll tell me if he gets in touch or wants to meet you won't you?"

"Yes, if you want me to. But I don't think he can hurt me anymore. I don't think I care enough about anything he might say to be hurt by him."

He kissed me on the top of my head. "You'll let me know, though?" I nodded.

"What about you, though? Did your ex-wife hurt you? Have your girlfriends since hurt you?"

"Well, didn't I just open Pandora's box?" He chuckled and he kissed my head again. "The quick answer is yes and no. Yes to Georgina and no to the girlfriends."

I waited, willing him to expand on the quick answer, but he was steadfastly quiet.

"Georgina," I muttered to myself. I hadn't thought about what she might look like before now. We hadn't talked about her since Daniel had put her on speaker phone in his office. Georgina—just her name sounded sophisticated, I bet she was extraordinary and glamorous and clever—all the things I wanted to be. And above everything else she knew him better than I did and I felt a stab of jealousy. Then the thought of his subsequent girlfriends overrode my thoughts of Georgina and added to the jealousy that was now running through me.

"So, how many girlfriends have you had since Georgina?"

"Girlfriends? None."

"Are we about to have a semantic argument here?" I asked, picking up on his concentration on the word girlfriend. "I have to remind you I'm a lawyer."

Daniel smiled at me and took a deep breath. "I'm not trying to hide anything from you, Leah, I never am. It's just there's been no-one I cared about since George. There have been women but nothing serious."

"Lots of women?"

He laughed at my question. "I wasn't keeping count, but no, not lots. But I guess it's relative. How do you want them categorized? Women I had dinner with, women I kissed, women I saw naked?"

I was being silly. "I'm sorry, it's just I'm not used to this. This history thing. Charlie and I were together for a long time and before that I was with Matt since University. Their previous relationships didn't seem important."

"Mine aren't, either," Daniel spoke softly, patiently. "But I'll tell you whatever you want to know. I just want to make you happy."

I reached up for him and brought his lips to mine. "You do. I'm sorry."

"Don't be sorry, seriously. Whatever you need." He paused and then continued. "I had a few one-night things just after Georgina and I split up. I didn't see any of them more than once—I never even gave out my number. I was a bit of a mess and working through things, and I'm not proud of my behavior during that period. I'm used to getting what I want, and George leaving was a shock for me. It took me about six months to realize that trying to block out the pain with meaningless sex wasn't going to work, so I stopped sleeping around and got a therapist."

"Most men would have thought that was a bad trade—frequent, meaningless sex for a therapist?" I was trying to lighten the mood. He attempted a half-hearted chuckle but it wasn't very convincing.

"So during that period it was a couple of women a week for about six months."

That sounded like a lot to me, but like he said, it was all relative.

"Then since then, I've taken a couple of women to dinner in New York. Three women, to be exact, but I didn't sleep with any of them. In fact I only had a second date with one of them."

"How come?"

He shrugged. "I don't know. I just didn't connect with them. Something wasn't right. Maybe I wasn't ready."

"I noticed some very beautiful women in your office today. Were any of them the lucky women that you took to dinner?"

"I told you, Leah, all three were New Yorkers and I like to keep my work life and my personal life separate. Unlike your boss, David."

"What do you mean, unlike David?"

"Well, you know he had an affair with his secretary a couple of years ago?"

"I did, but how did you?"

"I got him checked out. I hate that you work with him so much."

I tutted at him. He could be so over the top at times. "Daniel, he's not interested in me and I'm certainly not interested in him."

"He is interested in you. I caught him staring at your chest in the meeting today, I nearly punched him."

"Is that why you summoned me to your office? To get me out of his clutches and to stake your claim?" I giggled at him and then flushed at the thought of our meeting. I don't think I'd ever been so turned on as I had been during out encounter this afternoon. I'd never done anything like that before; it had been clandestine, urgent, and very, very hot. The thought made me very aware of my body so close to Daniel's, and I shifted my weight away from him. He wouldn't let me go and pulled me closer.

"Something like that. I'm sorry about your underwear; I couldn't get to you quick enough."

"Yes I've been without panties all day, thanks to you."

"Jesus, Leah, are you serious? Thank god that you didn't tell me that earlier. I'd have done no work today whatsoever." And he cupped my bottom over my dress and there it was, that feeling of desire for him that was constantly simmering away suddenly started bubbling in me. He reached for the hem of my skirt pulling it up and reaching beneath it to my stocking tops trailing his fingers along the top where the lace met my skin. I could see his pants start to bulge and relief flooded me, he would be inside me soon. He seemed in no hurry though and just kept up the stroking of the outside of

# FAITHFUL

my thigh. Finally his fingers crept to the inside of my thigh but I kept my legs pressed together, not allowing him through, so he trailed up until he found my folds and forced his hands in and my thighs parted.

"Have you been wet for me like this all day?" Daniel whispered in my ear.

"I'm always wet for you. I just have to think of you." It was true and telling him seemed the natural response. I didn't feel embarrassed. I knew my words would excite him as they excited me.

I reached for the bulge in his trousers but he pulled my hand away and moved to stand up.

"Come with me." He held out his hand and wordlessly I stood up, took his hand and he led me to his bedroom.

As soon as we entered his bedroom he stopped and pulled me toward him. He removed my dress in one fluid movement over my head and ran his hands from my face down my throat, over my breasts, stopping just momentarily to rub his thumbs over my lace covered sharp nipples and then down to my waist. He lifted me from the waist onto the bed and pushed me to my back. I threw my head back in anticipation.

"Look at me. Always look at me, Leah."

I brought my eyes to meet his. He looked so serious, so dark. He stood over me, his eyes trailing down my body.

"Feel how wet you are, Leah. I want to see your

wetness on your fingers." He pulled off his t-shirt and his trousers and stood naked before me. He was so beautiful; I took in his muscular body and could feel my skin respond to the sight of him, tightening all over in anticipation of his touch.

"Leah," he reminded me of his request, and looking directly at him, I trailed one arm down my body, running my fingers across my breasts, hardening my nipples. My other hand reached between my legs and Daniel's eyes followed it as it flitted across my sex, delving between my lips, feeling how ready I was for him. Daniel groaned and I pulled my hand from my wetness and brought my fingers to my mouth and sucked off the glistening moisture.

"Your wetness is for me to taste." Daniel pushed himself over me and his tongue delved into my mouth in what felt like a bid to reclaim me from myself. His possessiveness was intoxicating and I reached between our bodies to try and position him inside me.

"Always so eager, baby." Daniel pulled out of my mouth and seemed amused at my need for him. I wrapped my legs around his waist, opening myself for him, desperate to feel him filling me.

"Please, Daniel, I want you inside me, please."

"You know I love it when you beg." And he thrust deep into me in one movement, giving me exactly what I wanted. I cried out.

He withdrew from me completely, pushing his length against my stomach and kissed me deeply. No, I wanted him buried in me. I reached for his hips desperately trying to position him, he was immovable. I squirmed beneath him and turned my head away from his kiss. If he wasn't going to give me what I wanted, I wasn't going to give him what he wanted.

Holding my head still between his hands, he looked at me. "Tell me what you want, Leah, I need to hear it."

"I want to feel you inside me. I want you filling me up. Please, Daniel, please fuck me, I need you inside me, please." I sounded desperate and I was.

He closed his eyes at my words and slid into me. I gripped his buttocks with my hands, desperate for him not to pull out and leave me empty like before but he pushed against them pulling out.

"No," I shouted and he slammed back into me and I was overcome with relief. He found his rhythm and after a few more thrusts his teasing stopped. I could stay like this forever, him inside me rocking backward and forward. I looked at him and he read my thoughts like they were typed out on my forehead.

"I want to stay inside you forever, fuck you forever, never leave your bed." I felt my body convulse at his words and I ground my hips and arched my back as my orgasm took me. Daniel didn't change his rhythm and kept sliding in and out of me, my flesh was so sensitive after my orgasm it was nearly painful and I squirmed. He held my upper arms to hold me still.

"Don't resist me, Leah. You'll make me come and I want to fuck you all night, relentlessly. You are going to come so much you won't remember your own name."

# Chapter Twelve

Daniel was true to his word: he fucked me for hours. I wasn't sure that I was going to be able to walk the following day. The sex was nothing I'd ever experienced before. I didn't realize it could be like this. I wondered if it was as good for him as it was for me. He certainly knew what he was doing. Maybe it was just normal for him. I finally drifted off to sleep.

The next day I woke to an empty bed again, but I had to get to the office and so jumped in the shower and quickly got myself ready for work. Daniel dropped me at the office. I could get used to not having to suffer the tube every day. There were certainly perks to having a super-rich boyfriend.

Brendan seemed to have forgiven me for keeping Daniel's identity secret as he asked me to finish looking at his dating profile over lunch. I was relieved. Although Brendan was a drama queen and his work output was completely dependent on his mood, I really liked him and I hated him being angry with me. We finalized his profile and finished our lunch at his desk as we both apologized to each other.

In the afternoon I got an email from Anna saying that she was going to meet Fran for a coffee after work and that she'd call me when she was done. I got a knot in my stomach. Charlie and Fran had disappeared from my life which made it easier to deal with what they had done. Was that denial? Anna meeting Fran brought to light that they were still very much around, just not in my life. I felt emptiness overwhelm me. Maybe I had just been pushing my feelings to one side and filled the gap with Daniel. Was I using him? Perhaps these feelings I had for him were as a result of me not wanted to deal with my feelings about Charlie and Fran. I hated doubting my relationship with Daniel. It felt so real and I wanted it to be.

I promised to stay at Daniel's every night until he left for New York. The thought of him being away for three days was almost unthinkable, but as much as I would miss him, my head thought it seemed to be a good moment for us to have a few days' break from each other. Perhaps it would give me space to deal with some Charlie and Fran stuff.

Daniel picked me up from work—but I couldn't leave until 9 p.m. I started interviews with Daniel's executives tomorrow and I needed to be prepared. When we got back to Daniel's, I was exhausted and distracted as I was very aware that Anna was probably talking to Fran at that precise moment. Daniel suggested a bath, which sounded like a great idea.

He came to find me fidgeting around the kitchen, not really sure what I was doing. Walking from the fridge to the cupboards to the TV and back.

"What am I going to do with you?" He enveloped me in his arms and started walking me backward toward his bedroom.

"I'm restless." Talk about stating the obvious.

He laughed. "I can tell."

In the bedroom he undressed me as I continued to pout. Then he led me to the huge bath and held my hand as I got in. The water felt delicious and my mind start to drift away from my distractions to the moment in hand. My refocus on the here and now was helped by the fact that Daniel re-entered the bathroom completely naked. His body was ridiculous. I thought men only got definition like his if they were athletes or models. Each inch of it was hard, precise, and exactly how it should be. I couldn't tear my eyes away from him.

"Should I stand here a bit more and let you objectify me, or can I get in?"

"Either way is good for me."

He laughed and climbed in behind me. He pulled me into his chest, kissed me on the head, and passed me a chilled glass of wine. Oh my god, he was so perfect. I ran my hand up and down his muscular thigh and felt myself relax.

"I'm sorry, I'm distracted. You know that tomorrow is a big day at work because I'm starting the due diligence interviews and Anna is meeting Fran tonight. I've just got a lot on my mind." I felt relieved to tell him.

He just lay behind me and I talked to him about my feelings about Fran explaining what she had done. How I was conflicted as I didn't want Anna to have anything to do with her but didn't want her to end her friendship with Fran because of me. He just patiently listened without offering comment or solution. Whenever I tried to talk to Charlie he would just try and solve whatever problem I had and that's not what I wanted—Daniel seemed to understand that. Talking about things lightened my mood and I was suddenly aware that I had a sexy naked man behind me. I brought his hands to my breasts and ran my hands up and down his inner thigh. He felt so strong behind me like he could protect me from the world. I'd never felt as safe.

When the water was practically room temperature we dragged ourselves out of the bath, dried ourselves, and slipped into bed. Daniel pulled me toward him his hard chest pressing into my back. "Sleep," he whispered into my ear, and as usual I did as he said.

I awoke in the same position. Daniel was running his hand up and down my thigh. "I love your beautiful skin ... so soft," he whispered into my ear and I reached around and found his bottom, pulling him toward me. His erection pushed at the cheeks of my bottom. I groaned as my desire overtook me. Pushing my nightdress to my waist he cupped my sex and pushed his fingers through to my core. "Always so ready for me, Leah." I tensed at the touch and gasped. He kissed my neck. "Just relax, concentrate on your breathing—don't focus on what I'm doing."

I did as he said and stopped providing any resistance to his fingers. He just kept pushing and stroking and circling, and I just lay there as the pleasure built and built. Every time my breaths shortened and I came close to climax he reminded me—"breathe deeply"—and I steadied myself, pulling myself away from the brink, my mind away from what his fingers were doing and back to my breathing, holding off my climax. We stayed like that for what seemed like hours on the edge, but finally the pleasure became too much and I came—shuddering and gasping silently. It was the most intense orgasm I had ever experienced.

Daniel pulled away from behind me and lay me flat on my back and looked at me as he pushed himself into me. I was still floating from my climax and could do nothing but stroke his beautiful shoulders, tensed above me as I gazed at him.

As I gained back control over my legs I wrapped them around his waist and pulled him into me deeper and harder. I saw in his eyes he was close. I loved that look he got, his eyes intense and never leaving mine, not for a second, not even to blink. And that was it, I was clenching around him as I felt another climax run through.

"Oh, Leah," he gasped as his own climax gripped him. I loved it when he called my name as he came. It sounded so desperate, like he needed me like I needed him.

"Let's call in sick and do this all day," he sighed as he pulled me over his chest.

"I think my boss might have a problem with that. He's less forgiving than your boss." Despite Daniel being his own boss I doubt he ever pulled a duvet day—he seemed far too driven for that. "But I'll make you a deal. I'm free all weekend so you can have me to yourself from tonight after work until you fly to New York on Sunday."

"Hmmm." Daniel was contemplating. "Can I do exactly what I want to do with you?" My head darted up to see the look on his face. Was now the moment I was going to find out what the catch with him was? Did he want to dress me in PVC and chain me to his bed? Mind you being chained to his bed probably would be very enjoyable. He read my expression perfectly and started to chuckle. "I'm not thinking kinky, Leah. I want you to meet my parents. They are having a dinner on Saturday night and I'd like you to come with me."

"They know all about you and are dying to meet you.

My mother has been so worried that I haven't found someone since George that if you had two heads and nine kids by nine fathers she'd be delighted with you. There's no pressure at all." Wow, they knew all about me and were dying to meet me? When did that happen?

I pulled away from him. I needed to get dressed and into work. It was going to be a busy day.

"Well, I'm not calling in sick, so I guess you've got a deal."

He pulled me back to the bed and kissed me as if he was never going to see me again. I pushed him away eventually and headed to the bathroom. I could hear Daniel singing in the next room as I stood under the shower. He was in a great mood. My mind was imagining what Daniel's parents were like. Would they judge me for starting something with Daniel so soon after being engaged to Charlie? Would they think I was using Daniel as a rebound? My internal judge and jury kept finding reasons to find me guilty of not being worthy of this gorgeous man.

I took a deep breath and tried to put those thoughts at the back of my mind. I had a busy day ahead and I had to focus. My day was going to be spent at Daniel's offices and I was excited to be so close to him for the entire day. Daniel wandered into the bathroom as I was at the vanity unity combing my hair with my towel wrapped around my body. He was completely naked.

"You just love being naked, don't you?" I teased him. He came up behind me and took my comb from me and continued to remove the tangles from my wet hair.

"I love being naked *with you*." He kissed me on my shoulder and stepped into the shower. My eyes followed him watching the water run down his hard, perfect body.

*Get a grip, Leah.*

─────

On the ride to work, Daniel explained that he would keep out of the way today so unless we bumped into each other in the corridors, we wouldn't see each other. I agreed that that sounded like the best approach. I was having a hard enough time keeping focused at work without Daniel being physically there to distract me. Plus we couldn't have sex in his office again, I'm sure Gail had heard something which was beyond mortifying, although as I remembered how hot the sex had been, my embarrassment was totally worth it.

When I got back to my desk, Brendan bounded over with a huge grin on his face. "Can I come to the interviews today and take notes? I hear from Deb that the CEO is hot."

Well, I couldn't deny he was right about that. Brendan was training as a Legal Executive and was always trying to find non-PA work that would be more interesting to him, so although I'm sure Deb would have told him Daniel was hot and wanted to see for himself, really he was trying to be keen without anyone realizing. It was part of why I put up with him. He was very bright and with a different background could be sitting where I was sitting rather than as my PA. But he was almost embarrassed to want more. I understood that feeling.

I grinned at him. "I can't take you today, but I'll make you a deal." Another deal, was this wise? "If you type up the disclosures Deb and I get today super-quick, you can come to one of the meetings on Monday if David agrees. I'll also explain how the whole process works and you can have a go at some drafting."

"Really?"

"Really." I felt good that I was able to give him something like this when he had worked up the courage to ask me. If I'd said no, he'd have been crushed.

"Thank you—I'm going to be the best PA you've ever had today." I laughed. He at least had enough self-awareness to know his increased enthusiasm for his role wouldn't last beyond today.

I realized I'd not heard from Anna and I sought out my phone from my bag and saw two missed calls from her, one from last night and one from this morning. I'd completely neglected her. She would have found the meeting with Fran almost as stressful as I did.

When I returned her call, she was in the middle of something, but we agreed to meet at lunchtime so she could debrief me. My meetings at the Gematria offices started at two, so I finished my prep and packed my bag so when I came back from meeting Anna I would be all ready to go. Deb and I had had a pre-meeting and I had done thousands of these interviews before, so I was feeling confident.

Anna had already grabbed me a sandwich and found me a table when I arrived at Eat. She looked exhausted, like she'd not slept.

"I'm so pleased you called. I thought you couldn't bring yourself to speak to me because I'd agreed to meet her," she blurted out as I sat down.

"Oh my god, of course not. I've just been selfish, wrapped up in work and Daniel. I didn't finish work until late and then I was so knackered I fell asleep early." Anna looked relieved. "So, tell me. What did she have to say?"

"You don't have to hear this. It was stressful and I want to tell you to get it off my chest, but if it's too much for you we can talk about something else."

God, she was really wound up about this. And I really wasn't, well at least as not as much as Anna seemed to be. "Seriously Anna, tell me everything. I want to know—I wasn't avoiding you last night, honestly."

She started explaining how awkward it had been trying to be polite when she first saw Fran. Particularly as the pregnancy was starting to show. Apparently Fran had started crying almost as soon as the conversation started and continued to do so on and off throughout their meeting.

"Apparently, she ran into Charlie at a bar about six months ago. He was drunk and leaching at a girl and she went over to give him a telling off and he ended up grabbing her and kissing her, against her will. She said she fought him off and ran out of the bar. A couple of days later he turned up at her flat, drunk, and she let him in and ... one thing led to another."

"One thing led to another?"

"Her words, not mine. She didn't go into details and I didn't want her to. But she said she hated herself and kept telling him it wasn't going to happen again but he would turn up and ..."

"One thing would lead to another?"

"Apparently, Charlie didn't know she was pregnant until you mentioned it to him. They hadn't seen each other since she found out that day shopping that you two were engaged. He had told her that you two ... were over ... were like brother and sister ... blah blah blah. You can imagine she was quite shocked that he was asking you to marry him while screwing her behind your back, so she had refused to see him until he found out she was pregnant. He was furious about the pregnancy, apparently. He was vile to her, accused of trying to trap him and ruin his life, demanded a paternity test. Of course, this is all according to Fran."

"It sounds believable enough. God, how could I have been with him as long as I was and fail to see what a complete idiot he was? Or ... is." I sighed. It was better and worse than I expected. Better because hearing it didn't hurt as much as I expected, but worse because it had been going on so long, longer than I let myself imagine. I felt like a fool—a naïve, trusting fool. "So, did she have the test? Are they together now?"

"Yes, she had the test. It's his. It sounds like they are somewhere between being together and not being together. It sounds like she's forgiven him for his initial reaction to the pregnancy, but I guess it's not the best start to a relationship."

"Wow." It was all I could manage.

I wandered back to the office in a bit of a daze. Lunch had been short because of my meetings that afternoon, but I had heard enough. I needed to get a hold of myself. I got back to my desk and was greeted with another huge bunch of white roses. I smiled as I opened the card.

I hope you managed to catch up with Anna and that you are OK. Call me if you need me.

Dx

Dear god he was perfect. I picked up my phone and wandered into the back staircase to call him.

He answered on the first ring.

"Hey, stranger."

"Hey, perfect guy. Thank you for my beautiful flowers."

"You're welcome. How are you doing?"

"I'm good. I did catch up with Anna, but I'm all good."

"Wanna talk about it?"

"Later, maybe, but seriously I'm fine, and better because I'm talking to you. Anyway, I'm just about to head over to your office and I don't want to be late so I'd better go. Will you pick me up at 7:30?"

---

The afternoon passed in a blur. We managed three meetings back to back, and my head hurt from trying to concentrate and remember all the information we had gathered. But it kept my mind off Charlie and Fran, and for that I was grateful.

I caught sight of Daniel a couple of times. I'm not sure if he saw me, but he didn't acknowledge me. The first time was while we were waiting for our first interview. He was in a meeting room and I saw him through the glass. There must have been half a dozen people in the meeting room and Daniel was at the head of the table flanked on one side by one of those women that make you feel frumpy just knowing they exist. She was ridiculously beautiful—selfishly so.

I looked at her and then back at Daniel. They looked like the perfect couple. She was hanging on his every word and seemed to have perfected her pout with her perfectly plump lips every time he directed his attention toward her. I hated her. I hated that she obviously knew him, worked with him, saw him regularly. I wanted to go in there and sit on his lap for the rest of the meeting, to make sure she knew he was mine. But how could I compete with that? I couldn't even keep Charlie happy. I forced myself away from staring at them and realized Deb was watching me, so I tried to distract her and myself by testing her on some facts about the Palmerston business.

The second time I saw Daniel I was on the way to the restroom . He was standing at the end of a corridor with his back to me, talking to a blond supermodel. Jesus, did he only employ the best-looking people in London? At one point she grabbed his lower arm and I couldn't watch any more, couldn't bear it, so I scurried back to the interview, no doubt giving myself kidney damage in the process.

Back in the office, with all our notes handed over to Brendan, I headed to the restroom to reapply my makeup. I had a lot to compete with. Daniel had a lot of other choices.

Daniel's car was sitting on the curb as I came out of our offices and I slid in beside him, desperate for his arms around me. He didn't disappoint. His intoxicating smell enveloped me as he wrapped himself around me and pulled me toward him. I buried my head in his neck wanting to get closer to him.

"I thought we'd go out to dinner. What do you think?"

I just wanted to get home and get him naked. I wanted to feel how much he wanted me.

"OK. I thought we could do something that involved less clothes, but OK."

Daniel laughed, pulling me closer. "I'm always up for that, but let's do dinner first. You said I could do with you what I wanted from tonight."

Well that couldn't be a good sign. He could do with me what he wanted but he didn't want to have sex? Maybe things were starting to fizzle out for him. Just as my anxiety was reaching new highs, Daniel grabbed my chin with his hand and pulled me in for a long, deep, soft kiss that seemed to last all the way to the restaurant. When we finally came up for air, he seemed to have extracted my thoughts through our kiss.

"I will never tire of seeing you naked, Leah, ever. I want you every minute of every day. But it's more than that between us, I hope. I want to talk, share our day, woo you, romance you. I want you to feel for me what I feel for you."

I couldn't help let a tear escape my eye. I turned away from Daniel so he wouldn't see. Of course, he didn't miss a thing.

"You've had a lot going on, and it's bound to be emotional for you. But don't hide from me."

I kissed him on the cheek. He was so incredibly good to me. I was never going to be able to keep him happy.

We went to Daniel's favorite local Italian restaurant and I was greeted like a long-lost daughter. It was sweet how much Daniel liked the place. With all the money he had, he could dine out at Michelin-starred restaurants every night of the week, but he chose simple and unfussy dining most of the time.

I told him all about my conversation with Anna about Charlie and Fran and he just listened patiently, grabbing my hand in his at various points as if he was trying to take away my pain by transferring it to him. I didn't know if it was because Daniel was in my life or because I had come to terms with things or a mixture of both but it seemed like a distant pain, something from a long time ago and it didn't sting as much I had expected it to. Then I brought up my sightings of him in his office. I tried to do it in a light, non-bunny boiler way but didn't manage to pull it off.

"So I saw you a couple of times today in the office." I exhaled as I said it. What was I expecting him to say?

"You did? I didn't see you at all. Thank goodness, because I probably wouldn't have been able to keep my hands off you."

"Yes, you seemed taken up by those supermodel women you work with ..." I was smiling, pretending that I was teasing, but I meant every word.

Daniel grabbed my hand again and looked at me intently. "Leah. If I had wanted to sleep with my coworkers, I could have started when my ex-wife left. There is no need for you to be jealous."

I felt really pathetic. I'd never been like this with Charlie or Matt—so needy. Although in many ways I seemed to be relatively OK or resigned to what had happened with Charlie, it occurred to me that it had affected me in ways I'd not expected. Was this it now? I'd turned into one of those girls or would things get better with time. Given time, I hoped I would return to normal, but I'd have probably driven Daniel away by then.

"I'm sorry," I said. "I don't know what's wrong with me. You are so patient, you must think I'm completely mental."

"Not mental, just a bit of a headcase." Daniel grinned at me.

# Chapter Thirteen

By the time we got back to Daniel's place it was getting late so we headed straight to the bedroom to get ready for bed. As I brushed my teeth staring into the mirror I realized that there was only tonight and tomorrow night and then I would be without him for days—what would I do with myself? Daniel came up behind me and snaked his arms around my waist, seeming to read my thoughts.

"You can stay here while I'm in New York if you'd like to. I'd like you here, knowing where you are, able to properly picture you and your surroundings. I hate leaving you." Daniel buried his head in my neck, sucking and licking.

"You'll be distracted with a bevy of New York supermodel beauties, I'm sure," I said avoiding his invitation as I rinsed my mouth and turned in his arms to face him.

"Why would I want anyone else when I have this gorgeous woman in front of me?"

He lifted up my nightdress, pushed it over my head so I was completely naked, and pulled me to him as he bent to suck my nipple. I buried my hands in his hair and my head fell back. How would I cope without him touching me for four days? It was an addiction, he was my addiction. He moved his lips to my other nipple, grazing the first with his nails which sent intense pangs to my stomach. He brought his hands to my waist and abruptly lifted me to the vanity unit. Standing between my legs he pushed closer and I felt his erection, through his boxer briefs, nudge at my entrance.

"This is the perfect height," he breathed in my ear. I felt his mood change. "The perfect height for my dick to rock right into your tight pussy." He was rubbing up and down my sex, teasing me. I reached down between our bodies but he grabbed my hand before I reached him. He pushed down his underwear with his other hand. With my free hand I reached for him again, wanting my fingers around his thickness. He pulled me back and pinned each of my hands behind me on the unit under his.

I squirmed, unable to move from where he had placed me. I could tell he was enjoying my helplessness. But he refused to enter me and just continued to rub up and down my sex. He just stared at me as I wriggled beneath him, becoming wetter and wetter in anticipation. My orgasm crept up on me, I was so focused on when he would finally push into me that I didn't notice the pleasure that was already building within me. Suddenly it was upon me and there was no going back and without my eyes leaving Daniel's I shuddered into my climax.

Daniel thrust into me, as if seeing me come finally broke his resolve and he slammed into me furiously, pushing right to the back of me. It was as if he didn't fuck me as hard and as fast as he could, the world would collapse. It made me feel powerful when it seemed he couldn't control himself around me. It was as if he couldn't get enough of me. I might not understand his need but I could see it, I could feel it. I felt my orgasm build again and I was vaguely aware I was calling his name over and over asking for it harder, deeper, faster. With his final thrust he let go of my arms and I slung them around my neck as my orgasm clenched the last drops of him.

He stayed buried within me, his face in my neck his arms wrapped tightly around my back until I pulled back slightly so I could see his beautiful blue eyes.

"You are incredible," I said. "You make me feel incredible."

He kissed me in response—a deep urgent kiss, as if he were trying to bury himself him in me.

Pulling away, he looked at me and said seriously, "You are everything I ever wanted, Leah."

I bent my head and pushed the top of my head onto his chest.

"Daniel," I said, pleading with him to stop embarrassing me.

"You don't get it, do you?" Pulling away from me he lifted me off the countertop and turned me around to face the mirror. Instantly my hands reached to cover my breasts, embarrassed at facing myself so naked. He moved my hands aside gently replacing them with his own. "You just don't see you how I see you." He started teasing my nipples until they were swelling and hard under his touch. He snaked one hand down to my mound and his fingers found the nub of my pleasure. I let my head fall back.

"Look in the mirror, Leah. See how you respond to my touch." I complied, meeting his eyes in the mirror. "Do you know what that does to me? Do you know how hard you make me? Do you understand what you do for me? You can't possibly know, or you wouldn't believe I would look twice at those women in my office. I don't notice them. Wherever I go, I see only you."

I could see he meant every word.

"But I have to leave you for four days. Four days when David could pounce on you, Charlie could beg for you back, any of the millions of guys in this city could try and pick you up."

"Daniel, I'm not interested—"

"I need to make sure that I'm all you're thinking of." And with that, he thrust into me. "Lean forward," he said sharply.

I put my hands against the mirror. He continued to

thrust, pushing my shoulders down to meet him. He was so deep inside me, he felt like part of me. There was no doubt he was all I could think of at that moment, this gorgeous man behind me, pounding into me.

"Look in the mirror, Leah. See what I see." I saw the desperate pleasure on my face, my hair in disarray around my face. I looked wanton, my body moving in response to what Daniel was doing to me, being forced further and further forward. Daniel hooked his arms under mine and pulled me back toward him.

The change in position suddenly brought Daniel even deeper into me and I cried out. Daniel grunted in response. I loved how he took pleasure in my pleasure, that my gratification gave him gratification. He was unrelenting, never breaking pace. Bringing my eyes back to the mirror, I met Daniel's gaze over my shoulder. He looked almost violent, like he was trying to contain himself.

"You're not to let anyone else touch you while I'm away, not ever. Do you hear me?"

I couldn't respond. I was overtaken my heightening pleasure as he kept hitting that spot so deep inside me.

"Leah, look at me," Daniel barked and my eyes found his again.

"Only you, Daniel," I said as I came watching him watch me. And I watched as my orgasm brought release to him. My knees weakened and as I slumped against him Daniel scooped me up and walked me over to the bed, lay me down and crawled in behind me.

"I meant it, you know. I can't have you touch anyone else while I'm away." He sounded wounded, like he expected me to fight his request.

"Daniel, of course not. I love you. I would never even look at another man." I couldn't believe this was how he felt.

"But men look at you all the time, flirt with you, come on to you. I've seen it. It's not that you would be looking for someone, more that they would come looking for you."

I turned around to face him and cupped his face in my hands. "Daniel, you make me sound like I'm beating them off with a stick which is just not true. And anyway, I don't want anyone but you. It's four days. I would like to say it will go quickly, but I'm not sure it will for me. But my heart won't wander. I love you."

"I love hearing you say that. I was beginning to think you regretted saying it the first time. I love you, too." He pulled me into his arms putting my head on his chest, and took a deep breath and we fell asleep.

Still in the haziness of sleep I felt myself begin to waken, that heavy feeling of being deeply relaxed and not quite ready to come around and face the day. My mind wandered to what Daniel had done to my body the previous evening and I reveled in the memory, feeling sensations between my legs that brought me up a level of consciousness. I couldn't want him again, so soon after last night, but I did. I really couldn't get enough of him, his touch, his closeness.

The sensation between my legs intensified and I reached over to Daniel, wanting him, but found an empty space. Then I gasped as I felt his tongue thrust inside me. Daniel was still in bed and between my legs.

Best. Wakeup call. Ever.

He replaced his tongue with a finger and continued to lap at my clitoris, circling it, teasing it. I threaded my fingers through his hair, watching him watching me as I writhed against him. He pulled out his finger and I whimpered in disappointment for a second before I was filled up again with a finger from each hand, each working its own direction around my opening, his tongue never faltering. Deep inside my stomach I felt my orgasm build and I thrust my hips upward, desperate for release. I couldn't believe my body could give me any further pleasure after so much being wrung out of me last night. But that's what Daniel did to me. He constantly kept me wanting, needing more.

He crawled up the bed to me. "Hey, stranger." Daniel looked pleased with himself and kissed me on my forehead.

"Hey stranger, yourself," I replied, sated but no longer sleepy. I ran my hands over his chest, loving the feeling of his physical difference from me. Reaching around to cup his buttocks, I pulled him toward me and I felt his hardness press into my thigh.

"I love that feeling," I said dreamily.

"What feeling, baby?"

"The feeling of your need for me, pressing against me. Knowing you desire me."

He pulled away from me, looked at me, and then pushed himself inside me. "All the time, baby. I want you all the time."

And he rocked in and out of me, so gently, so slowly and soundlessly that I thought I would burst. I saw him trying to hold back and I whispered, "Please don't stop yourself. I love that you want to come so quickly. I want you to come right now." And he shuddered against me and collapsed as my orgasm took me yet again.

We lay like that for what seemed like hours. Him covering me, pinning me to the bed with his weight.

Eventually we were going to have to get up. Lunch with the parents. I sighed. Why on earth had I agreed to that? Daniel seemed genuinely excited that they were going to meet me. The last time I'd met Charlie's parents it had been to tell them about the engagement and it was the beginning of a horrifying set of revelations. That neither he nor they thought I was marriage material, that he didn't think I was feminine, that he was fucking my friend and had gotten her pregnant ... the nightmare flooded back.

I had brought a number of outfits over from Anna's for the weekend but none of them felt right.

"What would you like me to wear?" I asked Daniel, feeling unsure about everything. I didn't know whether his parents were formal, relaxed. This was all too much.

"Wear what you want to wear," he replied.

"I have no idea what they will be expecting, Daniel. You need to help me out!" I was increasingly anxious.

Daniel turned away from what he was doing and captured me in a hug. I tried to push him away but he just pulled me toward him like I was a child having a tantrum.

"Leah, they are not interesting in what you are wearing. They are interested in *you*, not your clothes. Lunch is at their place, probably in the garden, and my brother and his wife might come. Everyone will be very casual, but if you want to wear a ball gown, it's all good."

"So jeans are fine?" I asked his chest, feeling more than idiotic.

"Jeans are fine. It's what I'm wearing."

I managed to suppress my anxiety enough to get in the car at least. I insisted we stop on the way to pick up some flowers and some wine. Daniel tried to argue with me, but relented when I started getting worked up. The drive into Hertfordshire would take us just over an hour—plenty of time to wind myself up again. Daniel did his best to distract me, and it worked. He seemed to regress to about 17, insisting that we play Red Hot Chili Peppers at full volume and yell-sing along. Daniel seemed to know every song word for word—I enjoyed watching him sing as if his life depended on it. He was so playful and cute you would never know he was responsible for a multi-million dollar empire.

As we arrived at his parents' house, I gathered myself and took a deep breath. As we drove up to the modest but very comfortable detached family home, the front door opened and out bobbed a chocolate Labrador, and then a golden Labrador, followed by a very handsome woman dressed in slim-fit cropped trousers and a t-shirt. She called to the dogs to encourage them out of the way so we didn't run them over.

"Oh, I love labs! What are their names?" I wanted to get out of the car to greet them with as much enthusiasm as they seemed to have for our arrival.

"Headley and Baxendale," Daniel replied.

"Are you serious?"

"Yeah, my Dad named them—it's some legal case isn't it? You know he's a lawyer right?"

I started laughing—how cute and how completely geeky! I loved it. Headley v. Baxendale was a case that you learned in your first term at university. It wasn't well known outside the legal profession, but it was one of the most important cases in the history of contract law. My nerves disappeared. This family seemed very unselfconscious.

Daniel's mother greeted me in a big bear hug like a long-lost daughter. His dad followed his mother out and Daniel and his dad had a quick, manly hug, which was adorable. Then we swapped parents and the hugging continued. Daniel seemed so pleased to be with them; he was beaming—flitting his gaze between them and me, his eyes excitedly dancing among us all. He parents were equally happy and after Headley and Baxendale had been given all the attention they needed we all headed inside.

Inside there was a glass of Prosecco waiting for us—always the sign of a friendly household!—together with Daniel's brother and his wife. Gosh, I was right in at the deep end. Edward and Polly were as delightful as Daniel's parents, however, and Edward started baiting Daniel from the moment we walked in. Daniel's mother, Gwen, ushered the four of us outside with the dogs so she could finish preparing lunch with Daniel's dad.

"So, I hope Daniel's treating you as he should—he is famous for his bad behavior," Edward teased me.

"Bad behavior?" Daniel interrupted incredulously. "I'm not the black sheep of the family, Edward. You are! Have you still not made partner yet?" Apparently Edward took after his father and was also a City lawyer.

Edward ignored him. "I hope he's not trying to take advantage of you. He's a bit of a cad."

Daniel pouted and grabbed my hand. "Leah, he's

# FAITHFUL

being sarcastic because I got married so young. Edward, stop winding her up."

"Daniel would never try and take advantage—neither of us believes in sex before marriage." I deadpanned.

If only Edward knew about his brother's voracious sexual appetite and the fact he had given me more orgasms in the short time we had been together than I had ever had in my life. Daniel pulled me in and kissed me, the sort of kiss that was a prelude to hot, sweaty sex. I pushed him away—I was not into PDA, especially in front of newly introduced family! Daniel, Edward, and Polly just laughed and we all took our seats at the enormous outdoor dining table.

Polly offered to take me on a tour of the garden, I quickly agreed, wanting to see where Daniel had played as a child. As we walked and admired the garden, Polly asked about me and Daniel. I kinda guessed that was the main purpose of our walk from her perspective—girl talk. I was hoping to glean some insight myself. I explained how we had reconnected on LinkedIn and how I was at the end of my relationship but was still a bit bruised. I didn't mention the engagement—if you could really call it that—or the fact that Charlie was sleeping with a friend. It genuinely didn't seem important.

A lot of things came out that I hadn't really pieced together before, not even in my own head. I explained that in many ways I was trying to take it slowly with

Daniel but I felt I was pulling against an overwhelming force. It didn't make sense, and any outsider looking in would say it was way too soon since Charlie, but it felt right. Polly seemed genuinely delighted at Daniel being with someone. She said she hadn't known Georgina when she and Daniel had been married.

"They seem to be genuinely very amicable with each other. I guess it doesn't hurt that Daniel was very generous in the divorce settlement, from what Edward told me. But that's Daniel. I think he felt responsible for the split."

"I thought she had initiated it." I shouldn't be prying, but of course I wanted to know what happened. I wanted to know everything about Daniel.

"Oh, she did. But they married before Daniel had built his business, and that's where his head was during their marriage—in his business. Georgina was convinced he was cheating at various points because he worked such long hours and spent so much time traveling. He just wasn't focused on her or their relationship—it was all about the business for him, from what Edward says." He never mentioned that Georgina thought he was cheating. Is that the sort of thing you mention to your new girlfriend? I guess not.

"He's more balanced now, I think. He's established himself and maybe he learned his lesson with the divorce. He was devastated, apparently." I nodded again. "Which is why it is so lovely to see him so happy with you." I smiled.

I felt a sudden pang of guilt for talking about Daniel behind his back. I didn't ask for the information, but I certainly hadn't tried to change the subject. What was most comforting was how much of it I already knew. Daniel himself had told me most of what Polly said.

We wandered back to the gazebo where Daniel and Edward were watching us. Everyone had moved on from Prosecco to beer. As we reached the patio, a worried look overtook Daniel's face. I bent down to kiss him, hoping to reassure him that there was nothing to worry about—nothing Polly said had freaked me out. I could see him relax and I pulled my chair closer to him before I sat down.

Gwen let me help clear the empty plates from the table. It also gave us a little time for some one-on-one time. While we were loading the dishwasher and putting the leftovers in the fridge, she quizzed me a bit about my job and my family, even whether or not I saw myself with children. I found myself being completely open with her. She probed in such a gentle, non-threatening way that I hardly noticed. By the end of our conversation she probably knew more about me than many people I'd known for years! Eventually Daniel came in to see what kept us and dragged us both back out to the garden.

Edward and Daniel continued to tease and bait

each other, both reverting to the teenagers they would have been when they lived in this house. Gwen lovingly admonished them for their bickering and back and forth, and their father just ignored it. They were such a genuinely happy family that it made me nostalgic for something I'd never had. My parents were not unhappy people, but neither were they as full of life as Daniel's were. As an only child, and a girl, there was just a lot less noise in our house. Daniel's life was charmed and in the nicest possible way. I envied him.

"So, I've not mentioned grandchildren for the entire afternoon. I think I've been very contained, but Edward, are you ever going to get on with it?" Gwen suddenly blurted out and everyone laughed. But then her eyes shot to Daniel. "And don't think I'm not going to come after you, too, Daniel."

Daniel groaned. "Mum, I spend a lot of time trying not to freak Leah out, and you go and say something like that? You are really not helping!"

I squeezed Daniel's hand. "It's OK. I'm not freaking out."

Daniel looked at me intently, trying to see if I was faking it. I laughed at him and looked away.

"Convince her to move in with me first, Mum." Clearly Daniel saw an opportunity to push his luck. I excused myself to the restroom. I needed to contain the anxiety that just hit me. Did he just suggest living with each other?

When I came out of the restroom, Daniel was waiting outside.

"Sorry, baby." He looked at me sheepishly and pulled me into him.

"You don't need to be sorry."

"I don't?"

"You don't."

"What? So ... what? Does that mean you'll move in with me?" I laughed and pulled him closer to me.

"No, I'm not moving in with you, Daniel. We've been seeing each other five minutes. But I'm not freaking out, either. So maybe one day."

Daniel kissed the top of my head. "One day, *soon*." I laughed and we went back outside.

Daniel's parents did their best to try and convince us to stay over until the following morning, but I wanted Daniel to myself on our last evening together for three days and four long nights, and Daniel seemed to feel the same way. He promised his parents that we would stay on our next visit.

Daniel's buoyant, playful mood continued all evening. We opened some wine when we got back and he put on Luther Vandross and made me dance with him. When we finally sunk into bed, we were both too hazy with wine and tired from a wonderful day to do anything but sleep.

Daniel made up for an evening without sex the next

morning. Managing to awake before him, I quickly brushed my teeth and wiped off the mascara under my eyes. When I slipped back into bed, he kissed me from my forehead right down my body, not missing an inch of me. He turned me over and back, lifted one arm and then other, as if I were a science experiment.

When he was done I escaped from under him and pushed him back on the bed. I meant business and had no intention of wasting any one of the moments I had with him. I knelt between his legs and took him in my mouth, giving him the second blowjob of my life. When he'd come deep inside me, I turned him over to his side toward me and let him sleep. After about half an hour of watching his shallow breath raise and lower his defined abs, I woke him, selfishly wanting him inside me before he left.

Despite my protestations, Daniel left me with a key to his house. My plan was to pack up my things and head back to Anna's once he left, but he insisted he give me a key anyway. He said it wasn't just for while he was away—he wanted me to start feeling at home in his home. He showed me where he cleared out some space for my things in his wardrobes. It may have all been too much for me a couple of days ago, but the fact that he was leaving, even if only for a short time, somehow made it OK. I needed some kind of reassurance of his commitment to me.

Daniel's driver was dropping him at the airport, so after a thousand kisses and a million reassurances that we would speak each day, I peeled myself off him and pushed him out the door, standing on the step while I watched the car pull out.

I felt horrible as soon as I closed the door. A big lump of darkness at the pit of my stomach I went back upstairs and started to pack up my things. I hung up a dress from my case in the wardrobe and fished out a pair of flip-flops to leave beneath it. It was a start.

So I was ready to go. I could call myself a cab. It was the last thing I wanted to do so I climbed back into bed, and pulled Daniel's pillow to me and breathed him in.

# CHAPTER FOURTEEN

I awoke to my phone ringing. I can't have been asleep very long. It was Daniel to say that he was all checked in and in the lounge. He asked me again if I would change my mind and come with him, and I assured him I wouldn't and that I would see him on Thursday, which was really no time at all.

"Where are you, at Anna's?"

I was embarrassed to admit I still hadn't left, even though Daniel had really wanted me to stay.

"Err, no I took a little nap and have just woken up."

Daniel laughed and told me again how he'd like me to stay at his.

"When you unpack at Anna's, make sure you check the inside pocket of your overnight bag."

That sounded ominous. "Why?"

"You'll find out when you look!"

Of *course* I couldn't wait. As soon as we said our goodbyes, I scrambled off the bed to investigate. My stomach turned over as my hand found a velvet box where Daniel had left it. All I could think was it was too big to be a ring box.

Opening the box I found the most beautiful bangle made up of three rows of diamonds. It was stunning. Immediately I tried it on. *Wow*. There was a note tucked in the top of the box. I took a deep breath. How was I going to accept this?

My beautiful Leah,

Please wear this everyday so I can feel as if a part of me is with you always.

I love you.

Daniel

Well, I couldn't refuse a request like that, could I? I was easily convinced. I slipped the beautiful bangle over my hand and reached for my phone. He would have turned his phone off by now, but I wanted to ensure he received my thank-you as soon as he landed. As I was typing my text Anna called. I promised to be there as soon as I could. We had a nice few days planned, starting with a night out.

Being with Anna kept me busy and my mind off the fact I was going to be without Daniel for four days. I needed to stop doing a constant countdown, otherwise I was going to become one of those awful, needy girls who couldn't be without their boyfriend for longer than five minutes. In reality, it might actually be too late to avoid that particular metamorphosis, but I needed to at least pretend otherwise in front of Anna.

Anna bought an array of pampering products for

us to indulge in, so we sat around for the rest of the afternoon with face packs on, catching up with what we had missed in each other's lives in the last few weeks.

"So, it seems really serious between you and Daniel." Anna finally broached the subject she was clearly itching to address since we started talking. It wasn't like her to beat around the bush.

"It feels serious." I started fiddling with my bracelet and then caught myself and stopped. "But I know what you're going to say—it's very soon after Charlie and it's all happened so quickly—and I'm really conscious of all that, but I can't seem to stop, to slow things down."

"Actually I wasn't going to say that, I think you probably started getting over Charlie before you split up, and anyway, where's the manual that tells you how long you are supposed to wait between relationships? But do you want to slow things down?"

"Honestly, I don't know if I want to or whether I feel I should. I feel OK, I feel like I'm over what I went through with Charlie, but I keep waiting for something to happen to prove me wrong."

"I get that, and I have a cure." Anna stood up and started giggling. "Wine and a night out!"

I joined Anna in her giggles and nodded as she held up the bottle, half-waiting for me to tell her we shouldn't start drinking this early.

We were having such a nice time catching up in the

comfort of our dressing gowns that we almost didn't make it out of the flat. But about nine we did finally pile into a cab and head out for more drinks. Anna gave the cab directions to the club where one of her work colleagues was having their birthday drinks and my phone rang. It was Daniel.

"Hey, have you landed?"

"Yes, just in the car on the way to the hotel. Where are you?"

"Just heading to a party with Anna."

"Well, you are clearly taking advantage of me being out of the country." He sounded pissed off. I didn't know what to say. "Where are you going?"

"Somewhere in Shoreditch. I'm not quite sure where." Now I was pissed off at having to explain myself.

"OK, Leah, I have to go. Speak later." And he hung up. Just like that. I was stunned. A feeling of nausea washed over me and the buzz from the wine completely disappeared. Bloody hell, he had no right to be pissed off at me going out when he wasn't even in the country. What was his problem? Anna was busy chatting to the cab driver so hadn't witnessed the exchange. I plastered a smile on my face determined to enjoy myself.

The party was absolutely packed when we arrived. It really wasn't my scene—too studenty for me—and it didn't help that I felt stone-cold sober after the call with Daniel. After being introduced to 110 people, none of whose names I remembered, I found a place to sit and collapsed. My heels were killing me. I wondered how long I'd have to stick it out before I could tell Anna I was leaving. I watched her talking to a guy across the room. Anna didn't really have a type, but I wouldn't have expected her to give a second look to the guy she was talking to. He looked a bit older than a lot of the other partygoers and seemed almost like a biker. He certainly had tattoos on his arms and biker boots. He was stocky and a bit scary, but he was laughing at whatever Anna was saying, and she had her hand on his upper arm as she leaned in to him.

I felt myself rock toward the center of the couch as someone sat beside me. I almost tipped my drink on myself.

"Sorry, did you spill anything?" the twenty-something who was sitting a little bit too close for comfort asked as he steadied my arm.

"No, I'm good, thanks." I forced a smile at him and prayed he didn't want to talk to me.

"I'm Andrew. What are you drinking? I can get you a top-up." Oh god, he *was* going to try and talk to me.

"Honestly, I'm fine, thank you though." I tried to shift away from him without appearing rude. His leg was right up against mine and as he spoke to me he rubbed his leg up and down mine. I wasn't sure if he was being deliberate.

## FAITHFUL

"So who do you know here?" he asked.

At that moment someone tapped me on the shoulder. "Miss Thompson, I have a call for you." A very out-of-place burly guy handed me a phone.

"What the fuck are you doing, Leah? I told you that no one was allowed to touch you." As the voice bellowed into my ear, the realization rained down on me. It was Daniel on the phone.

I didn't answer but got up from the sofa, with the intention of finding a quiet corner of the party to tell Daniel I thought he was a complete lunatic. How the hell did he find me here? Who gave me the phone? What was going on? Was he having me followed? The room went dizzy as my anger overtook me. Eventually I found myself outside.

"Leah! Answer me?" Daniel was shouting down the phone.

"I do not owe you an explanation. You do not own me. You are crazy. Leave me alone." I hung up. The burly man who handed me the phone was beside me. Had he followed me in to the party?

"Can I drive you home Miss Thompson?"

"Who are you?" I spat.

"I'm part of Mr. Armitage's security team. He was just concerned about you, that's all. He asked me to keep an eye on you."

"He asked you to spy on me, you mean."

"It's not like that. He's just protective." I did want to leave the party and turning down a lift was cutting my nose off to spite my face.

"I need to tell Anna I'm leaving and see if she wants to come. I'll be back down in a minute." I didn't want to spend another moment at the party. Not leaving just because Daniel's driver was offering me a lift home seemed ridiculous.

"I'll be here, Miss."

Anna and Biker Man were pressed up against each other when I got to them and whispering in each other's ear. There was definitely heat there. After making Anna promise not to get a minicab home, I went back outside to pick up my ride.

---

The movement of the car combined with far too much wine made me very sleepy and I lay my head back and felt myself drift off. Not fully asleep I heard the driver on the phone. He was clearly telling Daniel he was taking me home.

When I got in I got ready for bed straight away. I wondered whether I should try and speak to Daniel before going to bed. I shouldn't have hung up on him. But he shouldn't have me followed! Probably best to wait for the wine to wear off. He knew I was safe.

The next morning I woke just after 8. I'd forgotten

# FAITHFUL

to set my alarm. What a brilliant start to the week. That's what happens when you go out on a Sunday night I guess. It served me right. I grabbed my phone to see if Daniel had texted or called last night. Nothing. New York was five hours behind so he would be fast asleep for a while yet.

Anna wasn't home when I went to check to see if she was up. There was no way of telling whether she had been home and gone to work or never been home. I sent her a quick text

**Are you OK? Please let me know. L**

I got ready in a record 35 minutes, which meant I shouldn't be more than ten minutes late for work. Donning dark glasses, I made it out into the bright sunlight to find Daniel's regular driver waiting for me.

"Hi, Phil."

"Good morning, Miss Thompson. Are we going to your office?" There was no fighting this.

"I guess we are. Thanks."

As I settled myself in the back of Daniel's car I grabbed my phone to text Daniel. A reply from Anna was waiting for me to say she had been back to the flat last night and was at work. I started my text to New York.

**I'm sorry I hung up on you. We need to talk. Lx**

My phone rang precisely three seconds after I pressed send on the text.

"Hey, stranger," I answered.

"Hey stranger, yourself." It was lovely to hear his familiar voice. "I know I was completely over the top." He sounded awful.

"I'm not going anywhere. But we should talk about this. Not now, I need to get to work and it's silly o'clock where you are. You should go back to sleep."

"I don't sleep much when I'm here. I'm fine. Should I come back? I need to know we are OK."

"No, Daniel, please. We are fine, but we are working each other out and there are bound to be bumps in the road. Let's just take a breath and talk tonight."

"I'll call you before my evening engagement. Are you in tonight?"

"Yes, you can call your security team off. I'm having a quiet night in. Sounds like you have something more interesting planned."

"I just have a reception—a charity thing. I wish you were here to come with me."

"I wish you were here. But I'll see you Thursday. It's only a few days."

Last night's drama put things in perspective. I might miss Daniel, but his going away was a good thing. It was allowing me to get some perspective. We really had a long way to go in our relationship. The fact that a short separation was causing so much anxiety on both sides brought me up sharp, and made me realize that what we shared was so intense that we needed some normality if things were going to last and not burn out. And I wanted this to last; I didn't want this to be a rebound thing.

I came back from getting some lunch to find a huge bouquet of white roses on my desk. They were beautiful but unnecessary. The card simply read:

I'm sorry. Daniel x

When we spoke that evening things were a bit tense. I'd spent all day at his office and it felt like the place was stuffed to the gills with beautiful women. I found myself feeling intensely jealous and wondering whether or not Daniel flirted with them and whether they fantasized about being with him. They must do, they weren't barren of all senses.

Of course I was completely hypocritical criticizing Daniel for his overbearing behavior last night when if I had the resources I would happily pay to have someone ensure he wasn't flirting with anyone while I wasn't around. My mind knew it was a crazy way to think but I couldn't bear the thought of another woman even looking at him. By the time I spoke to him that evening, I was angry at him for what he might do. The poor guy didn't have a chance.

Daniel opened our discussion by repeating his apology of earlier in the day. I cut him off mid-sentence.

"You don't need to apologize anymore. I get it." I gave him a watered-down version of my jealous imaginings of the day. I heard him chuckle into the phone at various points.

"You know there's no one I'm flirting with, don't you, Leah?"

"A part of me does and another part of me thinks, 'well, I thought that of Charlie.' I'm not saying it's rational. It's just how I feel."

"Well, I certainly can't claim my behavior is rational when it comes to you." No, having me followed wasn't rational, that was for sure.

"I'm not a cheater, Daniel. You can't have me followed 24 hours a day to ensure I don't speak to any other men. It will make me feel like a prisoner."

"I don't think you would cheat. It's the men I don't trust. And I suppose if I'm honest I don't want you to have room to experience anyone else or to doubt us."

I exhaled. He was right—it wasn't rational, but I got it. We were both hanging on so tight as if any moment the bubble could burst and these intense feelings that had appeared so quickly could float away into the ether. So what was the solution? Would more time with each other make things better or worse?

"I'll be back on Thursday, and we can get back to normal. But will you please use the driver when you want to go out?"

Things settled down; Tuesday and Wednesday were relatively uneventful. Daniel and I spoke at least three times a day. It was nice to know that we had so much to talk about when there was no possibility of any sex. It really comforted me to know that, while he couldn't physically touch me, he still wanted to speak to me, to know me. And I felt exactly the same. As much as I knew it was more than sex, a part of me was always looking for the darkest possible reason for Daniel's interest in me and my feelings for Daniel.

Daniel seemed pretty stressed about the things going on in the New York office. Apparently his Managing Director there was taking meetings with private equity houses to try and launch a management buyout. Daniel was going to have to fire him and dampen down reports that the business was in difficulty and would potentially be up for sale. It put my week in the office in perspective.

Daniel decided to promote the Operations Manager to the role of MD. She was a woman and Daniel told me in advance of me seeing any press coverage so I wouldn't overreact and think he was sleeping with her. I felt a bit stupid when he told me that. He wouldn't be the success he was if he was fucking half his staff!

I spent the rest of the afternoon googling his name. I hadn't done any internet stalking since we were first back in touch. I suppose I'd been looking for different things then.

There were numerous photos of him and his wife. *Ex-wife*. She was beautiful and very natural-looking. In my head I had pictured some kind of plastic, Beverly Hills wife who had too much plastic surgery and did nothing but shop and lunch. She looked about as far away from that as was possible. Glossy brown hair and kind, smiling eyes. She was a teacher, apparently.

Then there were pictures of the hotels and news coverage about the possible management buyout and how Daniel had found out and fired the MD. There were pictures of what looked like him arriving in New York a few days ago. I didn't realize he dealt with this level of press attention. He was dealing with so much and I was just been adding to his stress.

When I spoke to him on Wednesday afternoon between meetings, he asked me to stay at his house that evening so he could see me before I went to work. He was landing at 6:30 a.m. I was desperate to see him.

I arrived at his house after going back to Anna's and packed a weekend bag. I brought enough things for a couple of days. Letting myself in to the house felt strange, I felt like I shouldn't be there without Daniel. There was a note on the kitchen counter from Mrs. Bayliss telling me she had left me some dinner in the fridge. Daniel must have told her I was coming.

I carried my bag upstairs and unpacked. Normally I would just keep everything in my suitcase and dig things out as I needed them, but I wanted to feel more comfortable here and I knew it would make Daniel happy. I had even brought a few bits I could leave when I went back to Anna's if I felt like it. I was just finishing emptying my washbag when my phone rang.

"Where are you?" Daniel seemed anxious.

"In your bathroom, unpacking my toothbrush. Why?"

"That's the best news I've had all day. What are you wearing?"

"Daniel!" I admonished.

"Tell me, I need distraction." There was no arguing with him and my answer wasn't going to be titillating.

"I'm just about to change. I'm still in my work clothes."

"Put me on loudspeaker and describe what you are taking off as you do it."

I suddenly felt self-conscious. And turned on.

"Every detail, Leah."

"I'm unbuttoning my blouse."

"Which button did you start with? The top button?" He wanted serious detail.

"Yes, the top button. I'm taking my blouse off."

"What bra do you have on today, describe it to me?"

"It's black, lace, half-cup."

"How does it feel? Can you feel your nipples through it?" I froze. Could I do this? I brought my hands to my breasts, feeling my already beaded nipples straining at the lace.

"Yes. I can feel them," I said weakly

Daniel groaned at my reply. "I want to be there covering them with my tongue."

"Now I'm unzipping my skirt. My panties match my bra, and that's all that's left."

"Lie on the bed." His voice was more urgent. I could feel my sex pulse. I didn't know if it was the control he had over me when he was in this mood or my anticipation that was making me come to life. I lay back awaiting further instruction, my hands wandering over my breasts and stomach.

"Are you wet, Leah?" I was; he was miles away and my body was begging for him.

"Yes," I whispered.

"Feel it. Dip your fingers in under your panties. Feel your wetness, Leah."

I slid my hand down and trailed the slit of wetness that ran under my panties. I felt myself gush as my fingers explored.

"Leah, tell me how you feel."

I couldn't speak—not from embarrassment, but because I wasn't sure what would come out of my mouth. My fingers moved with now urgent need and let out a small whimper.

Daniel groaned down the phone. "Baby, I wish I were

there filling you up. Do you want that, too?"

"Oh god, yes, I want you inside me." The rhythm of my fingers increased as I imagined the feel of Daniel's cock buried deep inside me.

"Oh, yes. I bet you are so slippery wet, so ready for me. I want you to lick your fingers. Leah, taste yourself." I'd never tasted myself before Daniel, but right now I would do anything he wanted. Why couldn't he be a cab ride away rather than a continent? I sucked my juice from my fingers, and buried them back between my legs. My breathing was increasingly ragged and I could feel my climax start to build.

"I love to hear you excited, Leah. I love what I do to you."

"I love what you do to me," I gasped. I thrust my fingers deep inside me, pushing my clitoris with my thumb. I wondered whether he was hard. Was he touching himself as well? I didn't have the courage to ask him, but just the thought together with having been denied the real thing for what seemed like an eternity I clenched around my fingers into climax.

"You sound so sexy when you come, baby."

I giggled into the phone. "Your power over my body can be used remotely, apparently."

"I'm very glad to hear it. But no more orgasms for you until I am there in the flesh. Do you hear me?"

"Whatever you say," I said softly. I meant it. I wanted

to please him. "When are you back?" I asked, wondering how long I would have to wait.

Reading my mind, Daniel laughed. "You won't have to wait long, baby. I promise. I'll be there when you wake up." I felt myself relax at the thought of having him back. I'd missed him.

# Chapter Fifteen

The first thing I was conscious of the next morning was that intoxicating smell. I smiled, remembering his promise that he would be in London when I woke and I opened my eyes. His beautiful eyes were staring back at me.

"Hey, stranger," I croaked, my voice still full of sleep.

"Hey, beautiful." He was stroking my hair away from my face.

"How long have you been watching me sleep?"

"Only a few minutes. You looked so peaceful."

"You should have woken me. Let me quickly brush my teeth so I can say hello properly." I scampered into the bathroom and quickly freshened myself up. I was so excited to see him. I wished I had booked the day off from work.

Daniel was lying on the bed fully dressed except for his shoes and his overnight stubble. God, even after an overnight flight he looked delicious. He did look tired, though.

*I should let him sleep,* I thought halfheartedly. I had

to leave for work in just over an hour—that didn't leave us long together. I snuggled up beside him.

"Hey, what about my proper hello?" he demanded.

I turned my head to see his face and he pulled me on top of him and crashed his lips against mine. Oh, that perfect pressure of his mouth on mine. His tongue stroked the top of my mouth and then pushing urgently against mine. I pushed my hands into his beautiful hair, he was here. We kissed for what seemed like hours. Like teenagers.

I loved kissing.

I loved kissing Daniel.

I became aware of Daniel's erection pushing against my thigh and I moaned at the anticipation of feeling him. I couldn't wait any longer and I snaked my hand down to see how much he had missed me. Before my fingers found their destination Daniel flipped me over to my back and pinned me to the bed. My arms restrained by his hands and my thighs by his knees. He started kissing my neck, over and over, tracing my collar bone from one side to the other and then up my neck to my lips again. His tongue trailed across the outside of my lips and dipping into my mouth to find my tongue. He released my hands to run his hands between my breasts to my waist. My arms found his hard back; the feel of him was so reassuring and so sexy. I needed him now.

Abruptly he pulled away from me and pulled me with

him so we were suddenly standing. "Come on, you. You need to get to work and I'm not going to be able to stop if I don't stop now." I was confused. I didn't want to stop.

"Don't look at me like that. I've been without you for days. Once I start properly, we won't be done for hours."

"I'm not going to be able to concentrate today, the state you've worked me into."

"It's all part of my evil plan." He grinned at me and pecked me on the lips. "I'm going to make a few calls. The car will take you to the office. I'm going to work here this morning. Can you leave the office early tonight?" He was all business. How very disappointing.

"Well, I can probably leave on time," I said heading to the bathroom.

"Good. I'll be here. The car will bring you back to me. We'll have no interruptions tonight." He pulled the bedroom door shut behind him. I was going to have to wait nine hours.

The day passed so slowly, I kept checking my mobile to see if he had called or texted. I was desperate to feel close to him and he felt miles away from me. In the end I gave in and texted just before lunch.

**I miss you. I'm looking forward to tonight. L**

That just made things worse. I found myself checking my phone even more to see if he replied. He didn't.

To distract myself I arranged lunch with Anna. I wanted to hear about her shenanigans last night. The date with biker boy. Apparently on Sunday night she gave him her number but she hadn't let him get anywhere past flirting. He called on Monday and she agreed to go out with him last night. When she walked into Eat with a massive grin on her face. It could tell it was an "I just got laid" grin.

"Someone looks happy!" I grinned back at her—it was infectious.

"He is so, so sexy," she said, knowing what I really wanted to know. "We had such a nice time. He was such a gentleman. I'm totally into him." We were laughing. Anna might be blunt but she could laugh at herself so much more easily than I could.

Anna had said this a million times before, and as much as I hoped that he would be the one she was going to grow old with, it was likely that we would be having a conversation in a couple of months about how boring/unreliable/sex-crazed/unfunny/too-funny/stupid/rich/not-rich-enough he was. But it was nice to see her happy for now. We spent lunch trying to decide when the perfect time was to have sex with him for the first time, which of course took the entire hour despite us both knowing it would probably happen on the date Anna drank a bit too much.

In the end I left the office just after 6 p.m. When I arrived at his house I rang the doorbell. I didn't want to use the keys he'd given to me. Daniel answered the door. He chin was covered in stubble and he stood there barefoot in faded blue jeans and a t-shirt that looked well-worn and well washed. He looked amazing. I loved Casual Daniel. I couldn't help but grin from ear to ear when I saw him. He didn't take his eyes off me when he told whoever he was speaking to on the phone that he had to go. I flung my arms around his neck and he lifted me off the ground and into the house.

"Why didn't you use your keys?"

"I don't know. Shall we have some wine?" I was trying to divert his attention. I didn't want him to think I wasn't making progress with feeling positive about our future together. I'd unpacked my case and hung stuff up in his wardrobe. That was enough progress for now. I kicked off my shoes and followed him into the kitchen. The wine wasn't even poured before he pressed me against the fridge, exploring my mouth with his tongue. I relaxed. It felt so familiar. I was so pleased to have him back.

Daniel finally poured us both a glass of Rioja. "You have far too many clothes on." Daniel growled at me as we clinked our glasses together. He took me by my free hand and led me up to the bedroom. Finally, I had been waiting far too long for this. My knees trembled in anticipation as we climbed the stairs, my breathing became shallow, and I tightened my hand in his.

Daniel let go of my hand and slumped in the silver

gray armchair in the corner of his bedroom and took a sip of his wine. I was expecting him to ravage me not sit down for a rest. But he didn't take his eyes off me as I tried to work out what was going on.

"Far too many clothes. Take them off. Please." His voice was low and serious. He had every intention of giving me everything I'd been wanting all day, but he was going to try to kill me with the anticipation first.

I felt the wetness pool between my thighs. I placed my glass of wine down on one of the various chests that littered the huge room and I stood in front of him. I fingered the top button of my shirt and tentatively undid it, watching Daniel watching me.

Skimming my skin as I went, I released one button after another and then pulled it off my shoulders and it pooled at my feet. Bringing my hands back up, I traced the edge of the cup of my bra then slid my hands down my body to my waist. Daniel's eyes followed my hands, every now and then glancing back up to my face with a dark serious look.

I unzipped my skirt and it fell to the floor with my shirt. Daniel took a deep breath but said nothing, his arousal very evident by the tenting in his trousers. There I stood in my bra, panties and hold-ups. Daniel's examination of my body from his chair was so intense it was as if he were caressing and stroking me all over with just his brooding stare. My urge for his body increased with every moment. His desire for me was emanating from his intense staring at my body, like he couldn't tear himself away even if he wanted to, even if the house was on fire. It made me feel so powerful, so desirable, so ready for him. Every moment he didn't touch me I wanted him more.

I reached around my back and unclasped my bra and pulled it away from my body, freeing my breasts. My nipples were painfully erect and desperate for his tongue. He knew it, he could see. I unintentionally groaned, unable to hide my arousal at his enjoyment of my body from a distance. Without thinking I reached for my breasts and kneaded them together desperate for release, letting my head fall back relishing the sensation of my smooth, tight skin.

"Panties, Leah." His sharp tone reminded me that however powerful I felt, he was in charge. I let my breasts drop and hooked my thumbs into my panties. Leaning forward with my eyes on Daniel, I stepped out of them. I was left with just my black hold-ups on. As I straightened my back, Daniel stood up. I expected him to reach for me but instead he just very slowly circled me, taking in every inch of my body without a single touch. The anticipation was unbearable. I could feel the wetness against my thighs. How long could he hold out? My god, was he ever going to touch me?

He was so close behind me that I could feel his breath.

"Daniel, please!" I stammered, dizzy with craving.

"Have some self-control, Leah," he teased.

My knees weakened as he appeared in front of me again. I tentatively lifted up a hand to touch him.

"Hands by your sides." I let my hand swing to my side and barely able to focus I dropped my head defeated.

Then finally he reached a single finger under my chin and brought my face up to meet his eyes. I felt my skin light on fire at his touch. I tried to push myself against him but he kept a single finger on me.

"Look at me, Leah."

He then brought that finger tantalizingly slowly down my neck. My breathing increased and I felt waves of pleasure build deep inside me as he followed a path down between my collar bone and between my breasts. As if barely able to contain himself, he paused and exhaled and then his finger continued down my stomach. It was unbearable, I was desperate, my breathing ragged I then I couldn't stop it my climax washed over me—I came screaming his name, begging for him to touch me. In the midst of my climax I stumbled and Daniel grabbed me and pulled me toward him. The feeling of his fully clothed body against my naked one seemed to extend my orgasm and I just continued to gasp for air unable to believe the shudders continuing to pass through my body.

"Baby, you've got it bad. If that's what I can do with one finger on nowhere in particular, you are going to have the night of your life." I couldn't speak, but he was right. I wanted him so badly that he could make me come just by looking at me.

He pushed me back onto the bed and I lay temporarily sated watching him undress. He was as hard as I'd ever seen him when he freed himself from his boxer briefs. I pushed myself up to sit so I could get a better view.

"See something you like?"

"Oh, yes." I grabbed his bottom and pulled him between my legs and on top of me as I lay back. The feeling of his weight on me, his skin touching mine, his smell surrounding me wakened my senses and I moved my hips against him. I wanted him inside me.

"Leah, stop. You're going to make me come."

"That's the idea. I want to feel you. Please, Daniel."

I didn't have to wait another second. He plunged into me, driving right up to the hilt, catching me by surprise. My nails dug into his shoulders so hard I must have drawn blood but I couldn't think about that. All I could think about was the feeling of fullness I was experiencing, as if it were for the first time.

"I'm not going to last long, Leah," Daniel said between his slow thrusts.

"I want to see what I do to you." I meant it. I wanted to concentrate on him. I clenched around him and he threw his head back and moaned and I watched him fall apart.

Daniel rolled off me and pulled my head to his chest. I could feel his heart hammering away in his chest as I gently stroked his chest. I could stay like this forever I thought. We both lay there wordlessly until Daniel's heart rate returned to normal. I pushed myself up on my elbow and pushed my lips against his chest.

"Stay there," I said as I went to move off the bed.

"Don't leave me."

He sounded so sad that I brought our still joined hands to my lips and kissed his fingers. "I'm just going to run us a bath. Is that OK?" He nodded but his voice bled into his expression and he looked worried.

I pushed on my pink robe and slipped into the bathroom, turning on the taps to fill his huge around bath. I added some oils and switched the dimmer switch on the lights and arranged my iPad to put on some soothing music that reminded me of our first date together.

When I came out of the bathroom Daniel was scrolling through his emails on his Blackberry and when he looked up and saw me watching him he looked guilty and dropped the phone onto the bed.

"I'm sorry," he said, weary.

"Sorry for what? The emails?"

He nodded. "Don't be. I get it. Do you need to work? I can have the bath on my own."

He stood up and grabbed me before I had a chance to finish my thoughts. I wanted to reassure him I wasn't angry with him, why would I be? I understood how work could take over at times and he was in charge—that must be super demanding compared what I did all day. But he was raking his fingers through my hair and kissing me as if it were our last few minutes alive on earth and I forgot what I was going to say.

"I can't think of anything I'd rather do than have a bath with you."

He led me into the bathroom room, peeled off my robe, and held my hand as I stepped into a bath the size of a hot tub. The water was a perfect temperature.

We lay in the perfectly temperate water, me between Daniel's legs, my back against Daniel's perfect chest. We talked about Anna's new biker friend, Brendan's sudden upturn in productivity and how things were going in the office generally. Daniel didn't offer anything about work. In fact, he seemed very quiet. Was it jetlag?

"How was the flight? Did you manage to sleep? You seem tired."

"I slept a little." He scraped his fingers over my breasts grazing my nipple. I tried to ignore the sensation that small movement brought to life in me.

"What's going on at work?" I asked.

"Later," was all he said as his other hand delved between my thighs. I was lost; my ability to form sentences left me completely.

I could feel his erection building behind me and I slid around so I was astride him. I clasped his face in my hands and moved forward to kiss him which moved my sex along his hardness and I felt him twitch beneath me.

Breaking our kiss, I reached between us and positioned him at my entrance. Daniel reached around my waist and forced me onto him, impaling me on him, hard and fast. I gasped and he pushed me away slowly and then again, with force pushed me down. I held my hands against his chest trying to keep my balance. The water rushing against my clitoris felt glorious. Daniel continued to push and pull my body, creating the perfect rhythm. I was vaguely aware of water spilling out of the bath but I couldn't care. I just wanted him to never stop.

Daniel pulled me toward him to grasp one of my nipples in his mouth and the slight change in position together with the pressure to my nipple intensified the thrill across my body. I threw my head back and Daniel's hand dived toward my clitoris. I tried to push my body away from his. It was too intense. I screamed that it was too much, but he ignored my cries as the pleasure crashed over me and I felt him shudder beneath me.

The bathwater was cold when we finally emerged. Daniel dried my body with one of his impossibly fluffy towels and combed through my wet hair. I loved how he looked after me physically like he did. I felt cherished. When Daniel was dry we headed downstairs, me in my pink robe and Daniel in his pajama bottoms and an old t-shirt. We investigated what Mrs. Bayliss had left us for dinner. Fish pie. Between us Daniel and I set the table, replenished our wine glasses and dished out dinner. He still seemed distant, distracted, but more relaxed.

"So tell me what's going on at work." We sprawled out on the largest of the sofas as Daniel channel surfed. He ignored me, seemingly engrossed on whatever rubbish filled the screen. I rubbed his arm that was wrapped around me. "You have to talk to me, Daniel. I can't be the one that does all the opening up."

I had his attention now and he looked at me with that same forlorn expression.

"I just don't want to bother you with anything. It's not about you and me, it's all work." He forced a smile and pulled me closer to him.

"I get that. But I want to hear about it. Don't shut me out. When something's bothering you, I want to hear about it. It doesn't matter that it's not about us."

Daniel sighed. "You see things differently." I didn't say anything, hoping the silence would force him to elaborate. "I'm not used to talking about work outside of work."

"You mean I see things differently from Georgina?"

"I'm sorry. I'm not comparing you, it's just different, and I'm not used to it."

"You have nothing to apologize for. I'm adjusting to having so many orgasms."

"Want another?" Daniel whispered and buried his

face into my neck, kissing and sucking me. I pushed him off.

"Stop trying to distract me. Talk to me," I said seriously. "Did Georgina not like you talking about work?"

"No. By the end, I couldn't glance at my Blackberry without it turning into a full-blown row. But she was right, work was my priority. I thought I was doing it for the both of us. I *genuinely* felt that, but she just wanted my time and attention." He fingered the beautiful diamond bracelet he bought me.

"It must have been difficult."

"It was. And I don't want to repeat my mistakes with you."

I nodded. "We need to share stuff in your head as well as mine. I like you to talk about your work. I'm not going to get mad about you looking at your Blackberry or having to work. I'd be a hypocrite if I did. I like to work and I get that you do, too. But share it with me, please?" Daniel hugged me so hard it winded me and then he started to talk.

The New York MD that Daniel fired had left a trail of destruction behind him of which they were uncovering more each day. He had falsified financial figures reported to London, he had told suppliers that he was going to buy Daniel out of the business and some of them had stopped working with Daniel as a result. There were also suspicions that a couple of the suppliers were dummy corporations that the MD had been using to siphon off money from Daniel's business. If they came across more evidence then they might have to involve the police which would have serious PR implications.

"I dropped the ball. I should have seen all this stuff for myself, I should have known." I suddenly felt guilty. Had he been less attentive because his attention was directed on me?

"You can't blame yourself for someone else's dishonesty and bad behavior."

Daniel stayed silent for a moment.

"Try taking some of that advice for yourself sometime," he replied finally. He was right. I did still blame myself for what happened with Charlie. But I was beginning to realize that it wasn't a rational reaction, even if I couldn't stop doing it yet.

"It's so much easier to dish out than it is to take yourself," I laughed. "But seriously, am I a distraction to you? Should we calm it down a bit, just until the New York situation sorts itself out?"

"No," he said simply.

We lay back down on the sofa me on top of him, Daniel stroking my back. I must have fallen asleep like that as the next thing I knew I felt Daniel placing me in bed. Sleep fell so heavily over me I couldn't open my eyes and I let him pull the covers over me and place a kiss on my forehead. "I love you," I mumbled. I heard him sigh.

I awoke hot, aware that it wasn't morning. Looking at the clock beside me I saw it was 3 a.m., but the bed beside me was empty. After stripping off the layers of covers over me I went to find Daniel. I could hear him in his study. He was on the phone. Well, it must be to New York at this time of the night. Even there it must be late. The talking stopped and I pushed open the door. He looked so tired.

"Hey stranger." He looked up when he heard the door.

"Hey stranger, yourself. Are you OK?"

"Yes, sorry. Did I wake you? Let me take you back to bed."

"No, you didn't wake me. Will you come with me? You need to sleep, Daniel."

"I have so much to get through, Leah. I'm so sorry."

"Bring your laptop and work in bed. At least then you don't have to go far when you're done." He grinned and followed me with some papers and his laptop and I quickly drifted back to sleep the sound of him typing lulling me back to my slumber.

# Chapter Sixteen

I was excited that it was Friday and I was going to get to spend two full days with Daniel without *my* work, at least, interrupting. When I woke Daniel was upright, resting against the headboard but asleep, his laptop on still on his lap. God knows how little sleep he had last night.

My shower must have woken him. When I emerged from the bathroom, he was typing away as if he'd been there all night. We agreed that I would collect some more clothes from Anna's this evening and stay until Monday. I made him promise that he wasn't to put work on hold for me and that he could work from home. As long as he was near me, I was happy. He seemed to have relaxed a little from yesterday, although he still had exhausted eyes. I would have to think of how I could make it better for him.

The atmosphere at work was great. It was always a bit more relaxed on a Friday, but people seemed really upbeat. Maybe it was just me.

Brendan was doing a great job on his interviews and we pulled together a first draft disclosure letter, which was looking pretty good. I had a meeting with Jim on Monday to go through the first draft agreements, but we were on schedule and things were going really well. Brendan and Deb worked really well together. I was concerned that Deb would feel like Brendan was taking good quality work from her—quality work was the goal of all trainees—but she was generous and wanted to help him. Even better was they were totally and completely loyal to me. Some trainees were always finding ways to report to the partner on issues that came up before I got a chance, which led to me looking like I didn't have a grip on things. But Deb wasn't like that—she just wanted to do a good job. And I was keen to create a good impression—after all, ultimately Daniel was the client.

Just before lunch my personal phone rang. It was a number I didn't recognize.

"Hi, Leah, is that you? It's Polly, Edward's wife."

"Oh hey, how nice to hear from you. Are you OK?" I was surprised that she had called, we hadn't swapped numbers.

"Yes, I'm fine, I hope you don't mind me calling. I'm in the neighborhood and wondered if you fancied a coffee?"

I glanced at the clock on my computer. It was nearly noon. "Yes, that would be lovely. Do you know Simmons? Shall we go there? I'll be about 15 minutes, if that's OK."

I quickly hurried off an email before I left and

stopped by the bathroom to check my makeup. Did she have a specific reason to meet with me?

Apparently it was just a catch-up. It was nice to see her. She told me all about how she and Edward met and how they got married after just a year. She just knew he was the one. I'd heard stories about couples like that but never actually met one. All my girlfriends seemed to have terrible luck in the dating department. I seemed to be the one that was most fortunate, well until the Charlie stuff of course.

I opened up a bit more about that to her. I didn't mention the pregnancy but I did admit that Charlie had cheated on me with a close friend. She was horrified, so goodness knows how she would react if I told her Fran was pregnant. I tried to reassure her that Daniel wasn't some rebound guy. I'm not sure why I felt the need to do that. Did I want to ensure his family liked me or was I trying to convince myself?

Although in many ways it felt like Charlie and I had ended ages ago, every now and then I was reminded otherwise. I still had to tell some friends I'd not spoken to for a while that we were no longer together. It's not like I could send out some big announcement. I checked and there didn't seem to be any `My fiancée cheated on me and is having a baby with another woman` announcement cards available. It might have been easier, to have the plaster ripped off like that. The alternative was to regularly explain what happened and then endure people's sympathetic but awkward response. I couldn't even distract them by announcing that I had moved on and was seeing someone. The only person that I had told about Daniel was Anna. Of course Edward and Polly knew about us as did his parents but that had been Daniel's decision. I remained distracted by thoughts of who should know and who I should tell as I retook my place at my desk.

Brendan appeared out of nowhere. "Where have you been?"

"Having coffee with my boyfriend's sister-in-law," I said. Maybe I should start being more open. I was sure of my feelings for Daniel, wasn't I?

"Are you messing with me?" It wasn't the response I expected. I didn't know what to say. "Are you serious? You call him your boyfriend and you are meeting distant family members and you won't tell me anything about him?"

"Yes, he's my boyfriend, but we have been taking things slow and seeing how things go. It's no big deal."

"Leah, you are meeting his sister-in-law for coffee. That sounds serious to me." I guess it was. "So who is he, what does he do, what does he look like, is he rich, is he good in b—"

"Brendan!" I cut him off. "Stop. No more details until you do some work!" He slunk off, pretending to be in a mood but I could tell that he was delighted that he had been able to get some information out of me.

At exactly 5 p.m. I shut down my computer and grabbed my bag. I wasn't alone. There was a small group already huddled waiting for the elevator all desperate to begin their weekends as soon as possible. I told him it would be best for his driver to pick me up from Anna's rather than from work as getting out of the City was bound to be impossible on a Friday afternoon. So I hopped on a bus but soon gave up and decided to walk. The traffic was at an absolute standstill.

When I arrived at Anna's, she was already home and more than a little bit flustered. Oh yes, it was date number three (if you counted the flirting at the party, which we both agreed, for 'how long to wait before sex' purposes, was entirely acceptable.). While I was packing my case she ran in and out of my room in various outfits asking for my opinion. It was like some kind of movie montage. This needed alcohol. I poured us a glass each from the bottle in the fridge and forced a glass into Anna's hand.

"Please take a sip, I can't have you hyperventilate on me—I'll spend all night in A&E and I'd planned to spend the night having sex with my boyfriend."

Anna looked at me shocked. "Jesus, Leah, have you had a personality transplant?" I shrugged. "Don't try and pass it off as no big deal. You just called Daniel your boyfriend—I've never heard that before—and you just offered, without me asking may I add, that you planned to spend this evening shagging! I'm so proud. It must be living with me!" We both started laughing.

I finished packing and after hauling my case to the front door I collapsed on Anna's bed to try and help her come up with the most perfect date three outfit of all time. It must be sexy but not slutty. It must say, 'I might be up for a slice, but I'm not a sure thing.' It must be super flattering, but not require control underwear, just in case. It was an almost impossible task.

My phone rang. It was Daniel. Gosh, I'd been distracted.

"Sorry, I got caught up with Anna. I'm just going to leave now."

"OK, baby, just making sure you were OK." I could tell that look was back on his face. A dull ache rested in my stomach.

"I'll be there in a few minutes." After hanging up I turned to Anna. "I'm sorry, I have to go. Things are tough for Daniel at work and I want to cheer him up. But call me tomorrow because I want to hear all about tonight!"

I raced downstairs as far as I was able with my suitcase. I'd overpacked. I had no intention of spending much time in any of my clothes this weekend.

When I arrived, I hesitated but fished out Daniel's keys from my purse and knocked on the door using the shiny brass knocker and then tentatively let myself in. He was walking toward the door as I stepped in and a big smile crossed his lips. He pulled me toward him in a tight embrace.

"You used your keys."

"I did."

He pulled his head from my neck and kissed me on the lips, long and hard. Daniel picked up my suitcase in one hand and took my hand with his other and led me upstairs.

I didn't get a chance to even unzip my suitcase before Daniel came up behind me and snaked his hands around my waist burying his face in my neck again. I laced my fingers through his as he walked me over to face the bed. He unclasped me and began to methodically undress me from behind me, kissing various exposed areas of flesh every chance he got. When he kneeled down behind me to take off my shoes and hold ups he took a sharp intake of breath. My body had betrayed me again.

"Leah, I can see how ready for me you are. You are so sexy."

I shuddered as he reached between my legs and caught the drips of my desire on his fingertips, leaving me craving a more thorough exploration. Standing up he massaged my wetness on my nipples, so they were straining almost ready to burst. I reached up and behind me for his head and he pushed his face into my neck, nipping at the delicate flesh. I tried to turn around but he stopped me.

"Bend over the bed, Leah." I did as he asked and bent over onto my elbows. I could feel my wetness increase in anticipation. I heard him quickly remove his clothes. I felt his hands grip my hips and then his tongue on my inner thigh. That was an unexpected sensation. I expected him just to slam into me, knowing how ready I was for him. His tongue gradually moved up to the lips of my sex and teased me running up and down the slit, clearly feeling no rush to bring things to the next stage.

"Daniel, please," I begged.

"Tell me what you want, Leah."

"I want you. I want more of you, Daniel. I want all of you."

Daniel plunged his tongue forward and reached my clitoris circling and stroking. My breathing grew shallow and the pleasure built from deep inside me. Without warning Daniel replaced his tongue with his thumb on my clitoris and thrust his tongue deep inside me. My head spun as I came, thrusting my hips, pushing him deeper and harder against my body.

Before my orgasm was over and he changed position I felt his hands on my shoulders and him pushing into me from behind.

"Feeling and hearing you come gets me so hard. I couldn't wait another second to be inside you, Leah," he gasped as he pounded into me pulling me back against him, taking me so deep I could feel him right at the end of me. I wanted it to never stop.

He ran the fingers of one hand down my spine, the sensation increasing my desire to almost unbearable levels and I bucked against his touch, arching my back and throwing my head back. I heard him groan and he circled his hips and it was over for me as another orgasm crashed through me and I clenched him as tight as I could. Through the sound of the blood pumping through my ears I heard him climax behind me.

He circled his hands around my waist and pulled me up onto the bed bringing my head to his chest in a now familiar post coital position. Both breathless and without words, we lay there waiting for our bodies to regain their energy.

---

The next morning I called Anna, eager to hear how about her date.

"So?"

"So what?"

"Anna Jane Kirby, you have never been coy in your life. Now is not the time to start." Anna laughed.

"I'm trying to turn over a new leaf," she giggled.

"Well you can stop that right now and tell me what happened."

She sighed and breathlessly declared, "It was wonderful."

Oh my god. Where was Anna and who was this imposter?

It sounded like the biker, whose name was Ben—which was perfect as I was very fond of alliteration—was a hopeless romantic. There had been no sex but a more than perfect kiss followed by another perfect kiss and a promise that he would cook her dinner the next evening. I think Anna would have been less coy had they had mind-blowing sex all night. It was the intimacy that she was embarrassed about.

"So if we are having an at-home date, we're having sex, right?" Anna rarely asked me about the rules of dating. She was a self-proclaimed master.

"I guess." Having dated exactly three men, I wasn't the best person to answer.

"If the sex is as good as the kissing, I might have to marry him." I'd never heard Anna mention marriage before, not even as a joke! It was like she was allergic to the concept or something.

We had another detailed outfit discussion. The at home date always has the added complication of having to look super natural but still sexy. We decided on the mixture of freshly mani-pedi'ed nails, not too much make up, skinny jeans and a low back, long sleeved gray Jigsaw t-shirt. Precautionary measures included her taking condoms and texting me his address in case I never saw her again and he turned out to be a serial killer.

Anna never gave me grief about spending too much time with Daniel. I guess she was pleased to have the flat to herself. But she seemed to get how Daniel and I were together. We were together from the very beginning. I wished her luck and told her I wanted a full report tomorrow.

I spent the rest of the day pottering about. I did some yoga. I read at least three articles from the economist and texted Anna to tell her I was so proud and then resorted back to Grazia. I also caught up with a couple of my favorite TV shows—anything to do with the law, it was always so much more exciting on TV than it was in real life.

In between I kept Daniel supplied with tea, water and a shoulder rub that almost turned into something more before I turned very stern and told him that he was to stop trying to distract himself and to work hard today so maybe he could have some time for me on Sunday. I just liked being there in the house with him. Just to know he was in the room upstairs was comforting. It made me feel like we were really part of a couple and we weren't just caught up in some wild affair. It made me feel even better that I had started telling people that I was seeing someone. I guess my parents would be next.

I wondered how they would react. I think they were relieved that Charlie and I weren't together, although of course they never said anything. "We just want you to be happy darling," was my mother's eternal cry.

After sharing takeout from Daniel's favorite Italian place in his office, I cleared up and took a long hot bath. I took my book and a glass of wine to bed and waited for Daniel. I didn't hear him come to bed, but he was there when I woke up the next morning. Even sleeping he looked tired. Pulling on my robe, I went downstairs to make some fresh coffee and to see what was in the fridge. I would go shopping today so I could cook this evening. Perhaps I could make some breakfast as well?

The day followed much of the same pattern of the previous day although I didn't even pretend to look at *The Economist* again, but I did go for a run, which I thought if we were measuring virtue, would balance out.

"Leah?" Daniel was calling for me from his study. I was messing about in the kitchen, preparing some virgin mojitos for cocktail hour.

"I'm in the kitchen. Give me a second and I'll come up to you." Despite my offer, I heard Daniel plod down the stairs to come and find me.

I was very pleased with my cocktail creations and grinned as I offered one to him. He took it from me but placed it straight on the counter behind me without taking a sip. He looked serious. Worried.

"What is it?"

"I have to talk to you. Come sit with me."

We sat on the sofa. He was really worrying me now. There could only be bad news coming. What could have happened? He just remained silent as we sat there.

"Please, Daniel, I'm going to have a heart attack. Just tell me what's going on."

Daniel's head was in his hands, his elbows on his knees. He wasn't looking at me. This was bad. I wanted him to spit it out. Was he trying to end things with me?

"I have to go to New York." My chest dropped. Was that all?

"OK, well that's not so unusual, is it?"

"I have to go for a while. Until the next set of financial results are released." How long was that?

"Our share price has taken a battering over all this MD stuff and I need to go and shore things up, oversee what will be a criminal investigation, and reassure investors. But I want you to come, Leah. I don't want to leave you. I can't."

"How long until your results are released?"

"About two and a half months. But you'll come with me, Leah, won't you?"

*Two and a half months? Wow. I couldn't go to New York for two and a half months. I had a job. A life.*

"Let's just calm down. Virgin cocktails are just not going to cut it. Can we have some wine, please?" Daniel headed back to the kitchen. It gave me a chance to collect my thoughts. This was a shock. I knew Daniel wouldn't want to leave me so it must be serious.

We didn't speak while Daniel was organizing the wine. When he came back to the sofa I took a large swig and set my glass down. I took Daniel's hands in mine. He scanned my face, trying to read my reaction before I started speaking.

"Look, this is no big deal." I hoped I sounded more convincing than I felt. "It's two and a half months out of our lives. You'll be working a lot, anyway so even if I was there all the time, you would just feel guilty for working so much. You can work constantly if I'm not there. I'll fly out to see you as much as I can, and before you know it, you'll be back." That seemed logical, right?

"You won't come with me." It wasn't a question. Daniel looked defeated. I climbed on to his lap and pulled his face toward mine.

"Daniel, I can't just drop my job. You know that. And I don't want to put that much pressure on this relationship so early on. And even if I did come with you, I wouldn't see you because you have to concentrate on work. Please don't make this a test of my commitment to you."

"You're right. I've been fighting this all weekend, trying to find another way, a way that would keep me in London, but tonight I realized what everyone is telling me is right. I have to be there. I'm sorry."

"The only thing you need to be sorry for is for keeping this from me for as long as you have. You need to share these things. Otherwise I just worry because I can tell you're keeping things from me." Daniel nodded and pressed his lips against mine.

"When do you have to leave?"

"Tomorrow, or maybe Tuesday."

"Well, we'd better make the most of it." I turned around and straddled him, stepping my legs over his, pushing my hands through his hair and delving into his mouth. I was going to miss this.

"I want you in my bed." Daniel slid me off his lap and stood up, holding out his hand to me. I took it and he led me upstairs.

We quickly and silently undressed. I was anxious. Wanting him but wondering where we were left after such a bombshell. There was no time to process any of it; I just concentrated on reassuring Daniel.

I slid my fingers up his arms, from his hands to his shoulders, and then around his neck. The feel of him was so reassuring. He reached under my bum and lifted me to the bed. There was no thinking about anything now as Daniel dropped his head to my nipple and licked and sucked.

"You taste delicious." I arched my back. The sensation was incredible but I wanted something more. I wanted him deep inside me.

In a very calm voice I told him, "Daniel, I need to be close to you." It wasn't a desperate cry to increase my pleasure, but a serious request. And he knew exactly what I meant. He entered me so deeply I placed my hands against the headboard to provide resistance.

"I need to be deeper, Leah." I could feel him as deep as he could be, I thought, but I was wrong. Daniel shifted and moved my legs over his shoulders so my pelvis tilted up. I cried out as he touched that spot deep inside. He rolled his hips and pushed and pushed until my arms gave out and he grabbed my shoulders to stop my head crashing into the headboard. His movement again forced him into me at a slightly different angle and the combination of sensations so quickly sent quivers down my body. I was so close to my release, Daniel could tell.

"Breathe, Leah. I'm not ready for you to come yet." Daniel seemed so determined in his request that it staved off my orgasm. I pulled my legs down and clasped them around his waist pulling him in with my legs. I reached around his back and ran my fingers down the valley of his tight muscles and along his spine. I felt him buck beneath my touch. He got into his rhythm and was just pushing in and out of me over and over.

I pulled his face from my neck. I wanted to look at him. When our eyes met I saw sadness. I didn't know if he was desperately trying to hold off his release or he was sad about him leaving me.

"I love you," I whispered, my eyes not leaving his. He pushed his head back into my shoulder and sucked.

He never lost his rhythm, and every unrelenting movement created another layer of pleasure building up around me. I clenched and he moaned.

"Leah, I'm close, baby." That was all I needed to light the touch paper of my climax.

"I'm there Daniel. Come with me." And we both dissolved.

# Chapter Seventeen

Daniel left the next afternoon.

It was all happening so quickly. I tried to pretend to myself that I would see him in just a few hours.

We agreed that I was going to fly out to see him a week on Friday which meant it would be ten days before we saw each other again. I had thought four days without him had been a struggle. What was ten days going to be like?

I didn't go to see him off at the airport. He was flying with colleagues and anyway it would have felt too dramatic. I kept reassuring him that this was going to be no big deal. I kept telling myself the same thing. My feelings were still in a box which I had no intention of opening at the moment.

The rule about no contact during working hours got well and truly trampled. Every morning when I woke up there was an email waiting for me from Daniel and I made sure I sent one to him for when New York's sun rose. I'm not sure how much sleep Daniel was getting. Quite often when I emailed him in what should have been the dead of night in New York he replied or called me. We spoke at least twice a day and if I tried really hard I could imagine he was just around the corner. The closer my visit to him, the more relaxed he seemed.

The sun was out, which improved my mood. After all it was a Monday. I took the opportunity to take a walk to find my lunch a little further away from the office that my usual haunt. Work was frantic and I needed 20 minutes to myself with no phones ringing, no people throwing questions at me from every which way. When Brendan offered to get my lunch I refused. I wouldn't get out until late tonight so there was no chance of seeing daylight again if I didn't take the opportunity then.

I wandered to a deli that I particularly like and collected a salad and my favorite smoothie. As I headed back into the sun I caught sight of a couple on the opposite side of the street laughing. The sun helped everyone's mood. The guy was stroking the woman's pregnant belly, his eyes not leaving hers as they laughed. It seemed such an intimate moment and I replaced my sunglasses to begin my walk back to the office.

And then I froze.

It was Charlie and Fran.

I couldn't pull my eyes away from them. I stood there just staring as the rest of the City became a haze.

I was vaguely aware of being knocked into by various people inconvenienced by my petrified state but I really couldn't focus. I couldn't move. I realized they were standing outside Anna and Fran's firm. Why did I come this way? I didn't think about running into them.

Despite our lives having been so entwined just a few weeks ago, until now it was as if they had fallen off the face of the planet. They had fallen off the face of *my* planet but here they were, getting on with their lives as if they were just any other happy couple. As I continued to stare they eventually kissed briefly and Fran headed back inside, then Charlie strode away.

That's when the nausea kicked in.

It was overwhelming. The metallic taste in my mouth was a sure sign I was was actually going to throw up. Oh no, I couldn't let it happen here. The panic forced me back into reality and I focused on the road just a few steps away from me and stuck my hand out for a cab. I mumbled Anna's address to the cabbie, still trying desperately to convince my body that I wasn't going to be sick.

I made it to Anna's without vomiting. As soon as I was through the door I ran to my bathroom and emptied the contents of my stomach. Even when my stomach was empty the heaving wouldn't stop and I clung to the bowl, afraid that if I let go I would fall all the way to the floor. Tears ran down my cheeks and I wasn't sure if I was crying or if it was just the strain of the vomiting. And then it was clear I was crying. I didn't even know why but I couldn't stop it.

My body stopped heaving and I pulled myself off my knees and tried to go about cleaning up the bathroom and myself. Black mascara marks had settled on my cheeks and as I tried to wipe it away new mascara replaced it. I tried to take a deep breath. I needed to get back to the office. I had so much to do. I started to panic. Why did I come home? I should have thrown up in the office. And then the heaving started again and I rushed back to the toilet bowl. There was nothing left to come out but I just stayed there alternating between sobbing and heaving as pain started coursing through my stomach muscles.

At some point I forgot about work and gave in to the tears. I couldn't just clean off the smudged mascara and dance back into work as if nothing happened, my whole face was swollen and red, and I was still heaving, although there was now more sobbing than heaving.

When the sobbing seemed to have won out, I tried again to pull myself up. I didn't even bother looking in the mirror. I just rinsed my mouth and found something to tie my hair back with. My clothes were disheveled and I pulled them off myself and found my way to the shower. The crying then found a new lease of life and I just stood under the warm water and didn't try to stop it.

Eventually the water ran cold, and when I started

shivering I climbed out of the shower and wrapped in a towel crawled into bed. The sobbing seemed to have subsided, for a time anyway, and I heard my phone ringing somewhere outside my bedroom. It must be work wondering where I was. I rarely took lunch and now I'd been gone for hours. I started crying again, these tears were bitter, bitter that Charlie still had this power over me and then sorrow consumed me again.

I staggered out of my bedroom to find my phone. I couldn't speak to anyone but I should let the office know I was OK. There were nine missed calls. Most of them were from Brendan and then there were two from Anna. I texted Brendan saying I had come down with something really suddenly and was at home. Just as I pressed send, my phone started buzzing in my hands. It was Anna. The tears intensified. What was I going to say to her? I took a deep breath and answered.

"Leah, is that you? Are you OK?"

"Yes, fine."

"You are clearly not fine. What's going on? Brendan called to ask if you were with me because you didn't come back from lunch. Where are you?"

"I'm home. I'm fine. I'll see you when you get home." And I hung up, a wave of grief passed over me and new tears were falling. It had taken every ounce of energy I had to put that sentence together in something resembling a normal voice.

## FAITHFUL

I slunk back into bed and pulled the covers up. I couldn't get warm. At some point I must have cried myself to sleep. The next thing I knew I felt the bed sink behind me and I felt a body climb in beside me. But something wasn't right. It wasn't the right smell next to me. It wasn't *Daniel*. My eyes flew open—no, not Charlie? I sat bolt upright and was confronted by Anna beside me.

"Oh, thank god. I thought it was Charlie." I lay back down but on my side my body facing Anna.

"Why would Charlie be in your bed, Leah?"

"I don't know." I was disoriented and so thirsty. Why was I so thirsty?

"Leah, what's going on? You are really freaking me out. It's 4 p.m. on a Tuesday and you are in bed. Do you need to go to the hospital?"

"What? No. I need some water. Please will you get me some water?"

Anna returned a few minutes later with two glasses of water with lemon. She was so thoughtful to think of putting lemon in the water. I would never think of that. I started to cry again. Perhaps if I was thoughtful like that Charlie wouldn't have cheated on me with my friend.

"Oh my god, Leah. Are you OK? Why are you crying? Is it because you miss Daniel?"

I ignored her but took the glass from her hand, and greedily drank down the water as I cried. I must have sounded like I was choking.

"Leah?"

I took her glass from her and drank that straight down, as well. And then it was back, that metallic taste. I leapt out of bed and rushed to the bathroom just in time to have all the water I just drank pour into the toilet. I sunk to my knees.

Exhausted, I stopped crying and was just staring into the toilet bowl, grasping the seat with both hands as if the ground underneath me wasn't steady enough to keep me upright. Anna followed me in to the bathroom and rubbed my back. I'd dragged her out of work, all because of him.

"I saw them." I said quietly, still looking into the toilet bowl. "Charlie and Fran. Outside her building. I had almost forgotten it all and then *I saw them*. I saw her with what was meant to be my life. Pregnant with Charlie's baby, kissing Charlie." I wretched into the toilet again.

Anna didn't say a word. She didn't say, "I thought you were over this. I thought you'd moved on. You've got Daniel now. You're better off without him. They deserve each other." She didn't offer any of those useless platitudes that made rational sense but just didn't matter. She understood. She pulled me to my feet, wiped my face with a warm cloth, and then made me wash my hands and rinse out my mouth. She led me back into bed and brought the covers up right to my chin. She left the room but came back two minutes later with more water.

"Just sip. Tiny sips." I took the glass and took a few little sips and handed it back to her.

She climbed back into bed with me. I managed to fall asleep again, but kept waking, replaying the scene of Charlie and Fran together outside her office. My imagination extended it, seeing them in my old home, with Charlie's parents. I was replaying their whole existence around and around in my head.

I had been awake for the last two hours when the clock went to 6:30 a.m. In my head that was the earliest possible time I could get up without Anna thinking I was still freaking out. And if I was in the office for 8 a.m., I could be there before everyone else and catch up on some of the stuff I missed yesterday.

Anna caught me as I tried to sneak out of bed.

"Don't argue with me. You are not going into work today and I'm working from home." As she said it I realized I wanted someone to tell me not to go to work. At that moment, I never wanted to go to work again.

"You need to give yourself a break; one day isn't going to kill anyone. My clients don't know I'm not in the office, and if I am in the office, I might be tempted to rip Fran's head off. And I'm pretty sure that wouldn't go down well with any jury, so I'd very likely go to prison, and then my clients really would be inconvenienced. On balance, I think it's probably best to work from home until the feeling passes. Just to be sure." I half-smiled, went to the bathroom, and then climbed back into bed.

"I hate him."

"Good."

"Good? I want to do him physical harm. That's not good."

"Leah, when you met Daniel, all your feelings about Charlie disappeared and you magically got over a six-year relationship in days. You are just catching up on what you've been putting off. And anger is good, anger is normal."

"You're been all wise again and it's freaking me out."

"Sorry."

"No, I'm sorry for being a bitch. You think that being with Daniel is just a rebound thing?"

"That's not what I'm saying, and I have no idea, Leah. All I know is that you've been able to escape from Charlie to Daniel. I'm not saying that's a good or a bad thing. It just is."

She was right. I had forgotten about Charlie until yesterday when I was confronted by the reality. Daniel allowed me to do that.

By early afternoon I summoned the strength to make it to the sofa to watch trashy TV, and although I'd not eaten anything for 24 hours, the only thing I wanted was ice cream, obviously.

Anna and I didn't talk much, but neither did I concentrate on what was on the TV. My mind wouldn't let me. I just kept thinking about Charlie and Daniel and about Charlie and me and Daniel and me. Was what I was feeling for Daniel real or was it my way of just making sure I couldn't feel what I felt about Charlie and me? I couldn't help but think that Daniel's trip to New York was a sign. It was an opportunity for me to find out the answers to all these questions. I was going to have a lot to talk to Daniel about when I went to see him later that week and I wasn't sure he was going to be happy with what I was going to say. It was clear to me now what I needed to do.

---

I had pleaded with Daniel not to come to the airport to collect me. I tried to convince him that it would be wasted time for him which he could use to work so he would have more time off when I had arrived. He had grudgingly agreed but only if I agreed to being collected by his driver. That was an easy give from my perspective.

After I landed and waited for four weeks for my bag to be spat out on the conveyor belt I secretly hoped that Daniel had broken his promise and come to collect me. I was more than a little gutted when I saw a piece of card with my name on it waiting with excited friends and family of my fellow passengers. I wanted Daniel to make it all better.

"Good evening, ma'am."

"Hi." I sighed, not hiding my disappointment.

Somehow the driver managed to park directly outside the entrance to the airport and as he put my bag in the trunk I took my hand luggage and opened the door, desperate for the air conditioning. It was a scorcher.

The smell was what hit me first. That delicious Daniel smell and then I was greeted by his megawatt smile in all its glory. It hit me out of nowhere how beautiful he was. There wasn't a part of him that I didn't want.

"I couldn't have you in New York and not be here. But I stayed in the car and worked so you can't be mad."

All I could do was grin at him as I climbed into the car in a very unladylike way, far too concerned with getting to touch him rather than elegantly entering the car. On my knees on the backseat I pulled his face toward me and kissed him.

"How could I ever be mad at you?"

He grabbed my waist and pulled me onto his lap and pushed his lips onto mine. My hands travelled around his head and through his silky hair. It had grown noticeably since I last touched it and I momentarily felt a pang of regret. I didn't want to miss a minute with him. He ran his tongue across my lips, prolonging the moment when he would crash into me. I couldn't wait and opened my mouth, urging him in. When his tongue met mine, I couldn't help but moan and collapse against him, feeling his hardness growing against me. I didn't think I could wait for the 45 minutes it was going to take us to drive into town. We had to talk before anything. I had promised him that I would tell him what was on my mind and he deserved that. I slipped off his lap and grabbed his hand in both of mine, trying to dial it down a notch.

Conscious of being overheard by the driver we made small talk on the journey into town but I couldn't stop smiling and staring at him and touching him, unable to believe how totally perfect he was and how he was right here beside me. He was like a drug that transported me to a happy place and blocked out anything bad in my life. But blocking out the bad stuff was only a temporary solution. I didn't want Daniel in my life because he fixed me, I wanted Daniel in my life because I loved him and he loved me.

"Are you taking me back to your flat or do you have to go back to work?" Daniel's apartment was just off Central Park on the Upper East Side. It made sense because he was in New York so often. He didn't ever really talk about it, but I presumed that's where we would be staying.

"No, I'm done in the office for the weekend. I thought we could go back and relax, I guessed you'd want to change after your flight and I wanted to stay in tonight and catch up."

I released Daniel's hand as it travelled up my thigh. I felt the familiar heat with his touch and my nipples beaded beneath my white lace bra. Oh god, just the slightest bit of attention sent my body crazy for him. I grabbed his hand and placed it in mine again. I was going to have to be quick if I were going to keep my resolve and tell him how I was feeling.

"Sounds great. I thought it would be good to talk as well. You know ..."

His idea of catching up didn't have anything to do with chat but we needed to talk or at least I needed to talk. I looked out of the window, trying to avoid looking at him so I didn't worry him but I felt something shift between us and he kissed me on the top of my head and squeezed my hand.

Daniel seemed to have dialed down his touching me as we made our way into his flat. I was so totally distracted by the apartment I nearly forgot about what I was about to do. The place was enormous with huge windows facing the park in every room other than the kitchen. The decoration was very similar to his London house, just a little bit more modern but still opulent and comfortable in a palate grays and silvers and creams with huge lamps and overfilled cushions finishing the place off. I felt at home despite never having even been anywhere so glamorous.

I shook myself out of the Kelly Hoppen trance and turned to find Daniel behind me. I wrapped my arms around his waist and buried my head in his chest. I didn't know if I could do what I was about to do.

I took a deep breath. "You know you mean more to me now than ever man ever has ever meant to me don't you? You have to know that Daniel?"

"Leah," he said cautiously, "what's going on?"

"You know, earlier in the week, when we didn't speak for a day or so?"

I made it back to work on the Wednesday and I seemed to be fully functional so I managed to call him then. We hadn't spoken since Monday lunchtime when I'd seen Charlie and Fran. I'd texted and emailed him and just said I was stuck on conference calls. And then when I was subdued on Wednesday, I just passed if off as tiredness and tried to be as excited as possible about my flight on Friday and my weekend with him.

"Yes, you were busy at work. What's going on?"

"Well, I saw Charlie and Fran together. They didn't see me but I saw them together, across the road, as a couple and her bump is quite big now and they kissed and ... well ... the whole thing kind of freaked me out."

"Why didn't you say? Of course it must have been upsetting. Are you OK?"

"Well, it just brought a few things up for me." I didn't need him to know what a complete wreck I had been, how I'd been unable to function for 24 hours, how I'd thrown up until I thought I might pass out.

"So it occurred to me that Charlie and I haven't even spoken since I found out he was cheating. I mean, come on, you have to admit that is a little crazy. What's even crazier is that I haven't even wanted to talk to him. I haven't even really thought about him or us or what happened between us. I've just moved on as if he never existed."

"What are you saying? That you want to speak to him? That you want to try and resolve things, get back with him?"

"Oh my god no. I don't want him. At all. And I don't want you any less than I have done from the moment we met. It's just I doubt myself, I doubt my judgment because of what happened between Charlie and me and it's that I need to resolve, not my relationship with Charlie. Don't for one moment think that this is about him."

Daniel didn't say a word he just stared out onto the city.

"It's just that since we met my mind has been full of you and that has been wonderful but there has been no room for anything else. No room for me to finish up my old life in order to start a new one. No room for lessons to be learned. It must be at least part of the reason why I have all these insecurities and why I'm a 'headcase' as you put it."

I moved in front of him, putting my arms around his neck but he still didn't look at me.

"I want to be able to see me the way you see me and

# FAITHFUL

I want to love you the way you deserve to be loved but I don't think I will be able to any of that until I sort some stuff out. And this time while you're in New York seems to be the perfect time to do that."

"Leah, what are you trying to say?" He pulled me away from him and held me out in front of him by my shoulders, finally trying to look me in the eye.

This time I couldn't look at him, so I just stared at his chest as his eyes bore holes into me. "I'm just saying I think we need to take this time, when I go back to London and you are here in New York, we kinda just need to take a time-out for me to get myself together."

"But ... I don't understand, what do you mean time-out?"

I paused, this was it. I had to say it but I just didn't know how.

"Like, a little pause, a break."

Daniels arms dropped from mine and he sat on the sofa behind us and ran his fingers through his hair and slumped forwards, his elbows on his knees.

"You'll be back in London before you know it and I will have had time by then."

"I'll come back to London. I'll fly back with you on Monday. I'll manage things from there somehow." He didn't raise his head, he wasn't looking at me.

"No, Daniel, I don't want that responsibility. You said yourself you need to be here and anyway, I don't need this time because you are in New York, even if you were in London, I would still need to get my head together."

"But if I hadn't left ..."

"Daniel, this was going to have to resolve itself one way or another and this way, hopefully we have more of a chance."

"You seem happy when we are together. I just don't get it, Leah."

"I am happy. You make me so happy. You transport away from anything remotely bad in the world and that is fabulous but it doesn't mean the bad stuff isn't there. It just means it seeps back into my head when I'm not expecting it."

"So, what you don't visit while I'm here but we still talk, we're still friends?"

I paused. No, that wasn't how I needed it to be. How could I tell him? I walked over to him on put my arms around him.

"We're not just friends though, Daniel, we never were. My feelings for you are far too strong to be just your friend. Let's just take a break until you come back to London after the results are published."

"Fucking hell, Leah, that's exactly the point isn't it? We are so much more than friends. I don't want a break from you. I want you all the time."

I couldn't argue with him, I felt the same. Maybe I

was just forcing something I didn't need to? Maybe just the physical distance would be enough. I sighed knowing I was trying to convince myself. I knew that if we were in contact, I would still have a head full of him, full of worrying who he was with, who was flirting with him. I would still have that feeling of him saving me and it was time I saved myself.

"I guess you want a chance to be single. To play the field, after Charlie. I should have expected it and I can't judge you for it after what I did when I split with George."

"No! That is not what I'm saying! At all! I don't want anyone else, really. Anyone. This isn't about me finding someone else. This is about me finding myself. And I know that sounds cheesy but truly, that's what this is." God I was explaining myself so badly. "But I can't ask anything of you, I can't ask you to be beholden to me while we are apart. You shouldn't wait for me if you don't want to." I took a deep breath. I'd thought about this, it was only fair, but it was going to kill me to say it. "You can consider yourself single while I've asked you for this time. You don't owe me anything, including your fidelity."

"Fucking hell, Leah. I don't want anyone else." Daniel grasped his hair tightly in his hands and stared at the floor.

"And I don't want you to want anyone else, but I can't have myself being consumed with jealousy, not knowing who you are with because *I'm* not with you. I need to be able to tell myself that you are free to be with whoever you want to be while we are apart."

Daniel stayed silent. God, it would kill me if he found someone else while we were apart. Maybe I was crazy for saying what I did. Crazy for asking for a time-out. What was I doing?

"Please, Daniel. I need this. We need this. I don't want to be a paranoid headcase waiting for us to fail, making us fail. I don't want to doubt you, doubt myself. It's exhausting."

"Whatever you want, Leah. Always." Daniel slumped back on the sofa, his head tipped back, defeated.

# Chapter Eighteen

I shrugged off my blazer and shifted my weight so I was straddling him. He hands went to my hips and his head snapped forward.

"What are you doing?"

"I just want to enjoy our time together this weekend." I started to undo his tie.

"So you are going to use me for sex and then dump me?" The corners of his mouth turned up just a fraction and I grinned at him.

"I'm not dumping you, but the sex thing sounds like an *excellent* suggestion."

"As I said, anything you want." And he pulled me forward, brought my lips to his.

---

The weekend together was incredible. Difficult but incredible. We took in some sights, ate at amazing restaurants, wandered around the park hand in hand, and spent a lot of time in bed. I was sure that he was trying to convince me to change my mind, but he never said anything and I was grateful. Even so he succeeded in convincing me a hundred times. I doubted myself for the entire trip. I was genuinely happy with him. He made everything so much better.

Every now and then I would get a reminder of why I needed our time-out. Women took him in everywhere we went, blatantly looking him up and down at times and at other times openly flirting with him right in front of me when I was clearly with him. It left me feeling unworthy of him and I found myself imagining the possibilities he would have when I returned to London. That paranoia and insecurity was something I'd never experienced with any man. It can't have just been because Daniel was so handsome, so perfect. Charlie and Fran crept into my mind at various points, too. That box of emotions was well and truly open and although there were no more tears, there was a deep dark pit at the bottom of my stomach that never left me.

On Monday, after breakfast, I insisted Daniel went into the office. I was being picked up at 10 a.m. for my flight and I couldn't bear the thought of an emotional airport goodbye.

"So this is it." He clung to me as if were the last time he was ever going to see me.

"It's just two months Daniel."

"And at the end of two months, if you need more time or your feelings for me have changed or you've fallen for someone else? There are so many uncertainties, Leah."

"None of that will happen. It's much more likely you will run off with a Victoria Secrets model." The thought sucker punched me in the gut. That was the risk I was taking. The risk that if I gave him up for two months, so I could be sure of me, sure of my feelings for him, that I would lose him forever.

I pulled him closer. He didn't respond. He knew the possibilities; he knew before he flew out two weeks ago. That's why he'd been so upset. He placed a firm kiss on my forehead and without looking at me again headed out of the door.

Oh god. What had I done?

---

I got back to London with a plan. It was raining. Of course it was. I came in drenched and pissed off at the world and Anna was on the sofa channel surfing. It was just after midnight, so I knew she was only waiting up for me. I poured myself a glass of wine and collapsed on the sofa next to her.

"You OK?" she asked.

"Yes, I think I'm going to be."

She smiled and patted me on the leg. "Wanna talk about it?"

"Actually no. I'm good. Or at least I will be. Let's talk tomorrow, I need to unpack and get to bed but thanks for being so fantastic."

"Well, in the words of Scarlett O'Hara, tomorrow is another day."

Indeed it was and that's when my plan would kick in.

The next morning I felt OK, in control. I took a deep breath and pressed send on the familiar number. He answered after just one ring.

"Hello?" the voice sounded uncertain.

"Charlie, it's Leah. I was wondering if you had some time after work this week to meet with me?"

He was clearly shocked but he quickly agreed to meet me on Thursday evening. Good. Step one was in place.

The next thing I did was book some therapy. I wanted to do this properly. I would go every a week. Working it around David and my clients was going to be difficult but I was determined to make it work.

I wasn't sure what to do about Fran, whether I wanted or needed to confront her. I knew I had to see Charlie but with Fran I wasn't sure. I put that on hold.

Despite me thinking I was just going to be able to press pause on Daniel and have him drift out of my mind, it wasn't that easy. I thought about him every day. For the first few days I thought about little else. I wondered if he would be able to stop himself contacting me. I convinced myself that he wouldn't find it difficult. Men were so much better at compartmentalizing things. Then I wondered if I would be able to stop contacting him. That was the real question. I nearly picked up the phone, texted him, emailed him a million times. It was like those early stages of dating when you really like someone and you want to tell them everything but you know you have to hold yourself back. Having made a big fuss about a time-out I couldn't exactly change my mind after a few days.

Gradually it got easier, not just because I managed to contain my thoughts about him to a few times a day rather than all day but because I focused on seeing him in just a few weeks. It made it easier somehow knowing that if I kept my resolve now, it would be all the sweeter when out time was up.

One of the times I allowed myself to think of Daniel was reading the daily alert I had set up for the Gematria group. I justified the google alert that I set up as because of the Palmerston deal but on the basis I only set it up after I came back from New York, I'm not sure who I was trying to kid. I wanted to know if any more bad news came out about the New York office. I'm not sure what I would do, whether I would reach out to him, but I wanted to know.

The following weeks were tough. One by one all my boxes were opened and all the feelings about so much stuff that I'd not thought about in months, years in some cases, came out and raged through me as if brought to life by the sunlight I revealed them to. There were plenty of ups and downs, lots of tears and anger and swearing and wine drinking. I tried to balance out the wine drinking with running and that helped with the emotional weight that I felt, it made me feel lighter and stopped me thinking about all the sex with Daniel I was missing out on. It felt like I was in training for a marathon, physically and mentally. Daniel's return was D day and I wanted to be as ready, as fit as I possibly could be.

Meeting Charlie was difficult. I don't know if I expected seeing him to magically make me feel better but I don't think I expected how odd it would be. In so many ways it was like it always had been between us. I knew him so well and I'd forgotten that somewhere. He ordered my wine for me before I arrived and we traded information about parents and jobs as if we were chatting at home while making dinner together. I don't think I'd expected that familiarity to still be there. Since I'd let myself think about him, I'd turned him into a monster in my head but here he was, same as ever, his monstrous parts well hidden.

Eventually we navigated the elephant in the room. I didn't scream or shout or swear or punch him, which I thought was remarkably restrained of me. He apologized. He said that he had probably been trying to make me hate him by sleeping with a friend of mine but it hadn't been conscious. I said he'd succeeded. He said he wanted out of the relationship and should have never proposed I agreed but admitted I should have never accepted. I knew things weren't right between us when I accepted. I'd just been on a road, wanting to get to the end of it rather than asking myself if I was going in the right direction. I had to take some responsibility for that. We talked about when it went wrong, but I don't think either of us knew. Maybe it had just never been right. There were lots of apologies and regrets on both sides. In the end he thanked me, and I believed it was a genuine thank you, for picking up the phone. It felt like it had been the right thing to do.

When I relayed it all to Anna, almost word for word, she agreed our meeting had probably been for the best but said she still would hate every bone in his body until the day he died. She really was the perfect friend.

Three weeks into the eight week separation I got called into David's office. I was worried I was going to get a bollocking for taking up so much of Brendan's time. He was really proving himself working with Deb on the disclosures and he was so enthusiastic I couldn't do anything but reward him by giving him more and more to do, which he loved. Although he said he could balance my work with the PA stuff David required, I had my doubts. David was almost certainly feeling neglected.

"Leah, I need you to send an email out to the team on the Palmerston deal. The whole thing is on hold."

I was shocked. Daniel and I had never talked about

the deal when we were together but I couldn't help but think that if we weren't on our time-out, I would have known about this before David.

"Oh, OK, that's fine. Should I tell people why or whether it's likely to come back on?"

They were all valid questions but I was fishing for information for my own personal reasons, unconnected with the content of any email I was going to draft.

"I don't have much info. Just that it's unlikely to come back on. What is weird is that my wife mentioned that apparently there's a re-launch of a New York hotel that's happening this week, she knows they are a client and I think she was hoping we would get to go." He laughed. "It just seems a little strange that they were refurbing a place that was going to be part of the sale. Who knows what's going on?"

Leaving David's office my paranoia ran free. Had the deal been pulled because of our time-out? Was he punishing me? Perhaps Daniel had found someone else and wanted to cut any links with me. He had never mentioned a re-launch of any of his New York hotels but I guess he didn't really mention any specifics about work, other than what he'd told me about the New York MD. Were the two connected?

Oh god, I just wanted to speak to him. I wanted him to reassure me that he still loved me and that there wasn't anyone else and that I was just being paranoid. I grabbed my phone and wallet from my bag and ran out the door. I'd go and get coffee which would be an excuse to get out of the building. In the elevator, I scrolled down my phone and hovered over Daniel's number. He would want me to call him wouldn't he? If he knew how I was feeling? If it was over between us I wanted to know now, I didn't want to have to wait another five weeks just to have my heart crushed. Better the devastation starts as soon as possible and then it would be over sooner. But I couldn't make the call. I was the one who initiated this time-out and I had to stick to it. My paranoia would just have to eat me alive.

Anna and I went out for drinks that evening. We drank and chatted around a table with the buzz of the bar surrounding us rather than on our sofa with the television in the background but it was good to get out. We saw a couple of people we knew which was nice. Catching up on other people's news really distracted me from my drama. I realized I'd not really seen anyone other than Anna and Daniel for what seemed like months. It probably was months. I was deliberately staying under the radar since Charlie and I split. I didn't want people feeling sorry for me and I didn't want to have to put up with people's sympathy faces. And because Daniel was always there, either physically or in my head, I couldn't face people because I felt guilty that I didn't feel worse about what had happened with Charlie. Daniel made me feel better about everything.

About a week later, I was just beginning to convince myself that I was being paranoid and that if Daniel wanted to cut all ties with me he wouldn't be so cruel as to wait until our time-out was over. Then I opened that day's Google alert. David's wife had been right: One of the Palmerston New York hotels was being relaunched. There were a few press articles covering the unveiling. They all seemed to mention the misconduct of the New York MD and what was now a criminal investigation, although there weren't many details of what the criminal allegations were and they also showed pictures of the refurbished hotel. Any publicity was good publicity I suppose.

Trailing through the articles, there were photos on the red carpet of various celebrities attending the event. My heart actually stopped when my eyes found a picture of Daniel with his arm around a woman's waist smiling into the camera. When I looked closer I could see it was his ex-wife Georgina. What was going on? Was this an old picture? I was scrambling between all the pictures in the different articles and it was clearly a picture from just last night. So that was that. He was with his ex-wife. I was wrong; he had taken me at my word and not contacted me for any reason, not even to tell me he was back with his ex-wife.

I called Anna and in barely understandable English told her what I was looking at. I wanted her to tell me

I was overreacting, that it didn't mean what I knew it meant. Of course she couldn't do that because what she saw was what I saw.

What had I done? I'd pushed away the person who I wanted to be closest to. It was all my fault. I'd taken a huge risk and it had backfired.

The phone ringing jolted me out of my haze of confusion, sorrow, and regret. I answered it without thinking but I could barely say my own name.

"Hi, Leah, it's Polly. How are you?" She must be ringing to check how I was.

I tried to pull myself together and sound normal. "Hi, Polly, it's so nice to hear from you. I'm good, how are you?" Well that sounded vaguely normal, didn't it?

"I'll be near your offices again later today and I wondered if you have time for lunch?"

Before I knew it I accepted. In the back of my mind I felt that having lunch with her would somehow bring me closer to Daniel and I grabbed the opportunity. It was only after we made the arrangements and I tried to turn my attention back to my emails that the anxiety crept in. Was she calling to check that I was OK after Daniel's reunion with his ex-wife? Was she going to give me Daniel's side of the story? To stop myself from talking myself into crazyland I went to check on Brendan. He was still smarting over the Palmerston deal aborting and was back doing full time PA work and he wasn't happy about it.

I arrived slightly early at the restaurant. I wanted to have time to check my makeup and decide what I would order before she arrived, that way I could spend all my energy trying to pretend I was fine.

"Leah!" she exclaimed when she saw me. She was smiling brightly as she kissed me on both cheeks. She collapsed opposite me and deposited a couple of shopping bags either side of her chair. "It's so good to see you. You look amazing. I love this place you picked," she said as she looked. Juno was one of my favorite places in the City; it was small but very glamorous, with crystal chandeliers hanging all over the ceiling and baroque furnishings.

"I'm so glad you like it, and you look amazing, too. Have you been shopping?" Polly then proceeded to pull various things out of bags for my reaction.

"I shouldn't have been near any shops as I had a meeting by Liverpool Street, but I so rarely come into London, I couldn't help myself!" She was positively gleeful. Was she trying to pretend like nothing had happened? Perhaps she was trying to cheer me up. I didn't say anything, taking my cues from her.

It was easier than I would have thought to chat about nothing in particular and to act happy and upbeat. She was so lovely and bubbly that I imagined no one could be unhappy around her.

After our plates were cleared she put her hand on my

arm and leaned in to speak to me so no one else could hear. I tensed. This was it. This was when she was going to say something that would crush me.

"How are you getting on with Daniel being in New York? Are you finding it difficult?" I was stunned. I didn't know what to say. Perhaps she didn't know about his reconciliation with his ex-wife. "I'm sorry, am I being insensitive?"

I didn't speak because I didn't know what to say.

"Yes, it's very difficult to be apart from him, and I miss him dreadfully. I'm trying to use our time apart to sort out some stuff with my ex."

She looked at me sympathetically. "You poor thing. Only another month to go. Are you going to go out to New York again before he comes back next month?"

She can't have known about his ex-wife. In fact, she didn't even seem to know about our time-out. I could do nothing but roll with it. "No, I don't think I'll make it out again. I've got so much to do." It was the truth and that's all I had.

"Well, what are a few weeks in the scheme of a life together?" she squealed. "I shouldn't say stuff like that, should I? I just can't help myself. He just seems so happy with you, and I think you are just perfect for each other!"

I smiled and I felt tears well in my eyes, so I took a sip from my glass of water and tried to make sure I didn't get emotional. Well, *more* emotional, anyway.

Back at the office, because the Palmerston deal had aborted, my workload was more manageable and I left the office just after 6 p.m. I headed home, picking up a bottle of wine on the way. It was a sorry state of affairs. Here I was, thirty, pretty much single, and headed home on a Friday night to drink alone. I was halfway through the bottle when Anna got home. She looked thoroughly pissed off.

"You OK?" I asked. I tore my eyes away from my laptop, where I was pretending to be on Twitter but really I was back to cyberstalking Daniel.

"Actually, no, I'm in a foul mood. I've got far too much to do at the office and I've just abandoned it—if I worked non-stop for a week without any sleep I don't think I'd get through it, so really, what's the point? I might as well come home and drink wine. And, I called Ben today and I didn't get a response and he didn't call me back, which is just bloody rude. I really needed a shag tonight. And what's worse, I don't think it's just the shag. I think I might like him, which is really annoying."

"Have some wine."

"Are we self-medicating, do you think, drinking like we do?" Anna asked.

"Of course we are self-medicating." We both laughed.

"So, you like this guy?" I asked.

"All right, you don't need to go on about it," she snapped.

I laughed. "You are a crazy cow. Do you want to talk about it?"

"No, I do not."

I didn't say anything.

"But I just do like him. And I just don't know what to do with myself about it," she said softly.

"Well don't ask me, I'm a complete headcase. My fiancé ran off with a friend and Daniel was the love of my life and I pushed him away trying to do the right thing."

"Leah …" It was Anna's warning tone. Without saying it she was trying to remind me what my therapist said. My therapist reasoned that if Daniel had gone back to his ex-wife while we were on a short break, which was by no means a certainty, then our relationship was never going to last in the long run and better to know now before I was in deeper. As Anna helpfully told me—I could have just watched Indecent Proposal for the same life lesson and it would have been about 500 quid cheaper—but still, it didn't make it any the less right. At the same time I couldn't help but wonder what if?

"Do you know what we need?" I perked up.

"What?" Anna was less enthusiastic.

"A night out. That's what we need. A proper, dressed up to the nines, girls night out. None of this you taking me out for a quiet drink, trying to cheer me up or sitting here on this sofa moaning to each other. Tomorrow night we are going to go out and have fun. Let's invite Bridget and Alice and we'll go out and dance and laugh. We need a blow-out." I was decided. This is what we needed to break the cycle of misery in this flat.

"OK. If you say so."

"I do, and even if we have to fake it, we're going to have fun. And I know I shouldn't comment because I have no expertise in this area whatsoever, but give Ben a chance. It's not like he's not called you for weeks, it's just been a few hours."

# Chapter Nineteen

Bridget and Alice were two of our friends from law school. The four of us were all friends but Anna and I were always closer and Bridget and Alice were closer to each other than to either of us. We were like two couples who liked to double date. We saw each other fairly regularly but I'd not seen anyone recently so we were well overdue for a night out. It wasn't unusual for Fran to join our double dates but clearly things had changed. There was no way anyone was inviting Fran. Anna had filled in Alice and Bridget about what had happened with Charlie and me and both of them had tried to call but I just hadn't been up to talking to them about it. We had all known each other long enough to accept these things about each other without holding a grudge. They knew that I wasn't one for oversharing.

Anna was always the one that, although she didn't crave being center of attention, neither did she mind it. Alice and I would run in the other direction when Anna and Bridget would insist on being the first on the dance floor, the first one with their hands up in lectures, the first one to be PDAing with a stranger at the law school ball, not caring what anyone else thought. Bridget was a more extreme version of Anna but less funny. A night out with Bridget was guaranteed to involve some sort of drama—one of us would be arrested or proposed to or come home in a different outfit from the one we left in. And drama that didn't involve my love life was exactly what I needed.

After a run in the morning, after which I felt fantastic, I set about clearing out my wardrobe. It always made feel productive and renewed when I finished a clothes clear out. I set about pooling clothes into three distinct piles one for throwing away, one for taking to charity and the final one that needed dry cleaning or mending in some way. I was feeling very virtuous when Anna crashed in.

"Bridget has managed to get us into that private member's club in Mayfair that you like." My stomach dropped. I didn't want to go to the Coltrane Club—that was Daniel's and my place. Oh no, how did I tell her without sounding pathetic.

"So I thought we could get a cab to Berkeley Square because it's so difficult to get to. We can find us some rich hedge fund guys who'll buy us champagne. In the words of ... whoever ... the best way to get over a guy is to get under another!" Anna was really excited. It seems Ben was just a distant memory and she clearly thought that I should move on as well.

I was relieved. She meant Lawtons, not the place Daniel and I had gone on our first date. I loved it there; it was a great way to start what was going to be a great evening.

"Fantastic," I said and I meant it. "What are you wearing?" My clothes were strewn about my floor

"Something short, something slutty," Anna said. She was on a mission.

I wore skinny jeans with my favorite platforms that were a Dune version of Jimmy Choo patent leather wedges that I couldn't justify spending £400 on and a backless bright blue blouse that looked quite prim from the front. I always felt great in that top. I didn't have time to finish my wardrobe clear out. I could distract myself from my hangover tomorrow by throwing the rest out.

---

When Anna and I walked into Lawton's, I could tell it was going to be a night to remember. All eyes were on Anna and her fantastic legs. It was just the reaction she was looking for. When we finally found Bridget and Alice, Bridget had already managed to convince the guys sitting next to them to buy a bottle of champagne. What a great way to start an evening.

I briefly wondered whether any of the people here knew Daniel. I felt sure someone here would know him. I told myself to snap out of it. As I said to Anna, even if we had to fake it, we were going to have a good time tonight.

The three guys next to us bought us a second bottle of champagne and then Bridget thought it would be rude if we didn't ask them to join us. So, of course they did. There's no such thing as a free lunch, or a free bottle of champagne.

Bridget got very friendly, very quickly with one of them. They all looked like they were mid-thirties and were well dressed. The one Bridget had her eye on (luckily, the same one who had his hand on her thigh) was very pleased with himself. He was one of those guys that has plenty of everything—confidence, looks, money, women—everything a guy would want. You could tell he was a player. He was a better looking version of Charlie and watching him made my skin crawl. He was enjoying Bridget's attention but his eyes flitted around the room every couple of minutes, just to make sure he wasn't missing out on something better, someone hotter.

The guy next to me was less good looking and to be fair to him, he was really trying to be nice, asking me about my job, where I lived and all that stuff you're meant to ask about when really he just wanted to know whether I was easy and he was going to get lucky. I did a pretty good job at faking it I thought. As much as he seemed like a nice guy, I wasn't ready to start anything with anyone. Whatever happened with Daniel and me, I needed our break to recover properly, and that's what I was going to do. I couldn't even flirt with the guy next to me. Just because Daniel saw our time-out as an end and was moving on like lightening didn't mean I was going to do the same thing.

Eventually our group moved downstairs where there was a small nightclub. The guy that initially took an interest in me moved on to Alice, who was much more receptive and they were rubbing up against each other on the dance floor. It was as if I was watching everything from outside myself. I didn't really feel part of the evening. I wondered what Daniel was doing, wondered whether his ex-wife was living with him in New York now, wondered whether they would be remarried. Anna looked over me and I re-plastered my fake smile on my far too made up face. She had caught me and came over and dragged me to the bathroom.

"So I heard from Ben. I had a missed call and then he texted asking me where I was and apologized for not being in touch."

I could tell Anna was delighted but she was trying not to be too obvious about it.

"Right, that's good. Did he offer any kind of explanation?"

"No, but I guess he can't say much on text. I'll text him back tomorrow and see where things go." There was nothing I could say, but it sounded like a bit of a booty call, calling at this time of night on a Saturday night when he'd dropped off the face of the planet.

"So what's with the guy you've been dry humping on the dance floor? Is he going to get lucky tonight?"

"Urgh, no way. I'm faking it!" We started laughing. If we were both faking things to this extent, maybe it was a sign we shouldn't be here.

We left Bridget and Alice at Lawton's and headed home. Our hearts really weren't in it and I'd had enough faking it for one night. It was just after midnight and I hadn't really drunk after we had gone downstairs to the club so maybe tomorrow wouldn't be a complete right off. I would have no excuse not to go for a run.

As we headed upstairs to Anna's flat, there were big muddy footprints going up the stair carpet

"Gross, these carpets have just been cleaned. Some people are ASSHOLES," Anna screamed hoping to catch the attention of the upstairs neighbors who were three guys in their twenties and Anna was constantly battling with them over noise levels and the like. What weren't so familiar were acts of deliberate vandalism. As we reached the front door, it was open and the door frame splintered – the door was broken down. I felt my heart speed up and the pleasant alcoholic fuzz was replaced by pure adrenaline.

"Those fuckers! I knew they would try and get their revenge for me breaking up that party last week." Anna went to storm into the flat but I grabbed her arm to stop her.

"We need to get out of here. We don't know if it's the guys upstairs and we don't know if there's anyone in here." I could tell Anna was going to start arguing with me until she saw on my face how serious I was. "Come on. We need to phone the police."

Anna silently just followed me and we went to the end of the road, out of sight of the flat and I phoned the police. She was shaking and couldn't speak so I spoke to the operator and gave them details of what had happened and where we were. Anna started to cry as the police cars turned up and I put my arms around her to try and comfort her. She wasn't as tough as she made out. So much for our night of having fun.

The police established that the burglars were no longer in the flat and they asked us to go in so we could tell them what had been disturbed and what had been taken. We went in together clutching each other's hands. It was horrible, knowing an uninvited stranger had been in amongst your things. My mind started racing to my most precious possessions and I reached for my bracelet. My bracelet from Daniel that I never took off. That was the most important thing; he was the most important thing.

My eyes started to well up, I just wanted him to be here to blanket me in his arms and tell me everything was going to be OK. I missed him so much. I would never again feel that comfort from him and I needed to be strong and get used to it. I had made my bed and I was lying in it, all alone.

As we made our way into the living room, nothing looked different. I'd never been burgled before so my only reference point was movies and detective shows. I expected everything to be everywhere but the kitchen and living room looked as we left earlier in the evening.

"They seemed to have gone directly to the bedrooms, and specifically this bedroom." The female police officer was pointing at my room. So Anna and I headed there. My clothes were all over my bedroom floor as they were before we'd gone out, which I imagine why the police thought my room had been the target but the room was how I'd left it. My wallet was even lying on my nightstand from when I transferred my cash and cards into my evening bag. I went over to the bed to check my wallet and all the remaining store cards and credit cards were all still there—nothing was missing. I moved to my jeweler that I kept in a drawer in my wardrobe. The only proper jeweler I owned had been given to me by my parents or inherited from my grandmother and as I dived into the drawer as I came across each important piece my breaths got easier. None of it was missing.

"I don't know what they took?" I spun around to look at Anna. "All my jewelry and my cards are still here.

Let's go to your room." We hurried out and went back through the living room and into Anna's bedroom but everything seemed to be there.

"Were they looking for something in the wardrobe?" The policewoman asked looking at my clothes on the floor.

"No, I was clearing out my wardrobe. This is how I left it."

"Would they have been looking for something in particular?" Anna asked no one in particular.

"Usually these are crimes of opportunity and anything that would be easily sold would be taken but all your electrical goods are still here and your wallet. It is strange," the policewoman responded.

"Do you think they were interrupted before they got a chance to take anything?" I was trying to come up with an explanation, it seemed so odd. Someone had made a real effort to break the door down but hadn't taken anything? It didn't make sense. Before I could ruminate anymore Anna screamed at the top of her lungs and the police woman and I ran into Anna's bathroom after her.

On the mirror over the sink someone had scrawled in lipstick "Two days." My legs went weak and I grabbed Anna as we both collapsed. The relief that I had felt at nothing having been touch was replaced by fear. This didn't feel like a crime of opportunity, it felt like we were being targeted. Two days? What did that mean? We were quickly ushered out of the flat and into the back of a police car.

"What's going to happen in two days?" Anna was shuddering and could barely get her words out.

"I don't know Anna, I just don't know." My mind was blank.

The police questioned us for hours, separately. It was awful, they were clear that the message was aimed specifically at one of us and that one or both of us knew what it was all about. I got questioned on my job, about ex-boyfriends, whether I or Anna took drugs or owed anyone money. It was all ridiculous—neither of us were that interesting. But the police convinced me that they were right, that if I could just think hard enough then I would have the answer.

I went through the possibilities in my head. Could it have been Charlie? Was he trying to scare me? Frankly, he just wouldn't have the bollocks to break into someone's house and why would he? We had found some sort of peace with each other. What about Fran? I'd made no peace with her at all. I'm sure if she found out about Charlie and me meeting she would be pretty pissed off and her brother was a convicted criminal. But what would that message mean? And I'm sure she wouldn't want to upset Anna. Fran didn't make sense but nothing did. There was nothing at work that would make me think it was connected to anything I was working on. It wasn't as if I had Russian oligarchs or Sicilian mafia for clients. Most of my clients were in the FTSE 100!

It was about 4 a.m. when we got out of the station. There was no way I going back to the flat despite the police saying we could. Anna was still in no fit state to make any decisions—she was barely talking—so I got the police to drive us to a nearby hotel.

"Who do you think it was?" Anna was turned toward me in the bed nearest the window. I was just climbing under the covers in my robe after a hot shower.

"I have no idea. Really, no idea. Maybe they just got the wrong flat?"

"Do you think it was connected to Daniel?"

God, it hadn't even occurred to me.

"No, no not at all. Why do you?"

"Well no, not really, but won't he be back in London in a couple of days? It seems like a weird coincidence."

"What and he thought it would be a nice way to remind me by breaking into your flat and writing on your bathroom mirror?"

"Well, no I guess not." Anna was silent for a couple of beats and then said, "I don't think it was him, but maybe someone is trying to get to him and is threatening you."

"Look, I told the police about Daniel when they asked about ex-boyfriends, so if that is the reason, I guess they'll find out."

There was no way I was going to have Anna or me back in the flat before the "two day" deadline had expired but we couldn't stay in this hotel. We got a great deal last night because we checked in a 4 a.m. but this room would be around £400 a night so we had to move hotels today. We could stay with friends but I'd prefer to have my own space rather than sleep on someone's sofa. It's not like many of my friends have spare bedrooms.

I hadn't slept a wink last night but Anna had drifted off eventually. I decided to go and settle our account while Anna was still asleep, it would take my mind off things. The only thing I had to wear was my clothes from last night so without any of the fun, I endured the walk of shame down to the hotel's reception. Luckily this early on a Sunday morning the only people around were hotel staff.

"Hi, can I settle up for last night? We're going to check out this morning."

The receptionist was the one that checked us in last night, and I'd explained to her that we'd been burgled but she still looked at me strangely before she started tapping her keyboard.

"I can check you out but you're paid up for a week, and we were going to upgrade you today. Are you sure you want to check out?"

My brain wasn't fully functioning. "No, we arrived

last night, or early this morning really, I gave you my credit card details but I didn't pay anything last night." My credit card wouldn't have space on it for a week in this hotel.

"Yes, I remember, but your account was paid for a week just an hour or so ago."

"How?" My heart started to thud again. Maybe whoever had broken in last night followed us to the hotel and wanted us to stay here like sitting ducks?

"By telephone. Someone called Armitage."

Of course. A mixture of warmth, relief, and love washed through me all at once. I felt safer than I had done since before we had arrived back at the flat last night or even perhaps since I left Daniel. I had never experienced a man who looked after me before. Daniel was the first man that just made it all better.

Even when we weren't together.

Even when I asked him to stay away from me.

Even when he was back with his ex-wife.

"Oh right, OK. Thanks."

"You just tell us when you are ready and we will move you to your new room."

I smiled and nodded. I was afraid that if I spoke my voice would crack. I didn't want to lose it in front of the receptionist.

After I dried my tears I opened the door to our room. Anna wasn't in bed.

"Anna?" I called out.

"I'm in the bathroom. Where have you been?"

"Just sorting out the bill. We are booked in for the week but we have to change rooms."

"What? I can't afford that and neither can you. We'll have to go back to the flat."

"Daniel has paid the bill. We don't have to pay."

"What? What the hell is going on?" Anna stormed out of the bathroom and stood looking at me accusingly.

"All I know is that I went down to reception to pay the bill for last night and they told me that we were paid up for a week. When I pressed them they told me Daniel had paid, but we have to move rooms. That's all I know. There's no point getting snippy with me."

Anna slumped on the bed next to me. "I'm sorry. I'm just completely freaked out. How did Daniel know we were here?"

"I have no idea. But Daniel has a way of getting any information he wants."

"Do you think he's the reason we got broken in to?" Anna was calmer. I could understand her being freaked out.

"I really don't know, but my gut instinct says no. But maybe that's just because I'm in love with him."

"Still?"

"Always."

"You need to call him."

"And say what? 'Sorry for being a selfish idiot and needing time away from you'?"

"Or you could just say 'thank you for picking up the tab for the room'!"

We both started laughing. It was the first time either of us had cracked a smile since the club.

"You're right, I should call him. It's polite." I took a deep breath. I needed to do this. He was days away from being back in London and sooner or later I was going to get the closure I'd been dreading. "I can't do it until this afternoon though, he won't be awake."

Anna jumped up and looked at me. "Let's go and get some stuff from the flat and then come back here and have some lunch."

"OK, sounds like a plan. But let's check into the new room first."

We didn't have much with us to pack up so we quickly made our way to the lobby and reception. The receptionist came up with us to the new room which I thought was a bit odd. I guess it was a Sunday morning and she wasn't busy. We were on the executive floor so we needed to use our key in the elevator. The executive floor was decorated in a slightly different way to the rest of the hotel. It was more modern and less traditionally English. It reminded me of Daniel's house. I didn't have to look for reminders, he was just everywhere I went, everywhere I looked, he was in my heart.

Anna went first into our room. "Oh my fucking god." I hesitantly smiled at the receptionist, embarrassed not only that we were dressed in last night's clothes but now because Anna was swearing like a navvy. I hope she didn't think we were prostitutes.

"Thanks for showing us up. We're just going to pop back to our flat and pick up some things if the police let us." I was desperate to remind her why we were here dressed like we were.

"If you have a few moments, I'd like to show you a few things in the suite." She gestured for me to follow Anna into the room. The suite? I guess that answered the question as to what Anna was shouting about. Of course Daniel would get us a suite.

And of course it was beautiful. Anna and I had a bedroom each and it made Anna's flat look like a shoebox. It had amazing views of the City. Once we were finished with our tour of the suite and directions on how to use the steam room, the sauna, and the hot tub on the balcony, I showed out the receptionist. Anna managed to get a grip of her excitement, but I knew it couldn't last and I wanted us to be on our own before she exclaimed that the bathroom was bigger than the Blue Banana. I could just tell it was coming.

"Oh my god. Can you fucking believe it?" Anna whispered to me when I found her on the balcony

"Come on, let's go."

The suite was beautiful, but if felt bittersweet. Part of me wondered if Daniel was trying to make up in advance for the fact he was going to have to tell me he was back with his ex-wife.

We were just headed across the lobby when the doorman approached us.

"Good morning, Miss Thompson. I can have your car brought around for you if you are going out." He must have mistaken me for someone else. Someone rich so that was some consolation.

"That's OK, we're going to walk."

"I'm sorry. I have strict instructions to ensure you don't leave the hotel unless you are with Mr. Armitage's driver."

I'm not sure I'd ever been dumbstruck before, but I couldn't form any words. I knew I should respond but I didn't know what to say.

Anna got there before I did. "Yes, please, could you get the car?" She turned to me. "He's obviously worried, so let's just take the car. It's not worth a discussion, especially when we're wearing these shoes."

It wasn't Daniel's usual driver and the driver wasn't on his own. There was a burly guy in the passenger seat who leapt out as soon as the car pulled in front of the revolving doors of the hotel.

"Miss Thompson, Miss Kirby. Good morning. I'll be providing you with security." Well, I was officially mute so I just nodded and got in the car. Without telling them the address, we pulled up at Anna's flat a few minutes later and were instructed to stay in the car until Burly Guy checked it over. We did as we were told and we were quickly in and out. Not long after we were back at the hotel and unpacked, showered, and sitting down to lunch.

"When are you going to call him?" Anna asked.

It was all I could think about and it was clearly etched across my forehead.

"Not yet. It's still early in New York and it's Sunday."

"Daniel doesn't strike me as someone who sleeps in."

"I'll call him later."

I would call him but I just didn't know what I was going to say. I wanted to make it easy for him. He didn't need to feel bad about reconciling with Georgina, but I knew he would. I told him I knew I was risking losing him, so it was my doing. He had nothing to be sorry about.

# Chapter Twenty

I couldn't put it off any longer. While Anna was in the main bathroom making the most of the steam room and sauna I took my phone into the bedroom Anna had allocated to me. I closed the door and slid down the inside until I reached the floor. It would be 10 a.m. in New York and Daniel would have been up for hours. I didn't know what I was going to say to him, I just knew I had to call him, to kick start the beginning of the end.

It answered on the first ring.

"Leah, how are you? *Where* are you?"

I missed his deep soothing voice. I had forgotten what it did to me. I could see him clearly in my head now. He was starting to go fuzzy in my memory but hearing him brought him in to focus. The beautiful body of his, those piercing eyes that saw right into me. His inky black hair, almost too long. And that smell, that intoxicating scent of his. I needed to snap out of this. He was seducing me in my head.

"I'm fine, I'm in the hotel. Thank you for all this. You didn't have to go to all this expense."

"Leah, it's nothing. I just want you safe."

"I am, thank you. I take it the police called you? I'm sorry you've got dragged into it all." I was trying to be matter of fact and business like.

"There is nothing to apologize for at all."

There was an awkward silence on the line. He clearly didn't want to tell me that he was back with Georgina over the phone and I just didn't know what to say. Before I could think of anything he interrupted me: "It's so good to hear your voice." My throat tightened. I couldn't cry.

"Yours, too." I managed to squeak out.

"I've missed you."

"Me, too."

He would never understand how much. I would miss him forever, there would be no one else for me after Daniel, I was sure of that. I played with the bracelet he had given me, which I never took off. It was my constant reminder of him.

"The results come out tomorrow and I think the market will respond well. I should be back on Tuesday evening."

So it had started. The two months were up and I had lost my bet. Now it was time to pay the casino.

"That's great, congratulations. You must be relieved." I sounded so cold.

"Did you do what you needed to do?" Why couldn't he be an asshole about it all so I could hate him?

"I did. I feel stronger. I feel better."

"That's good, I'm pleased for you. Do you feel ready to ... see me? ... on Tuesday? ... or maybe later in the week?"

Daniel sounded tentative, but it was clear that he wanted this over as quickly as possible. He was right to. We needed to rip the bandage off. It had been too long as it was.

"Tuesday sounds good."

"I'll pick you up from the office. If you need anything, please call me."

I just sat there for what seemed like hours after I hung up. The thought of it all being officially over on Tuesday was just too much. Just the thought of never speaking to him again was all it took to start my sobbing. I missed him. I missed the life I could have with him. Still crying I made my way into my bathroom, and turned on the shower. I needed to shock myself out of my mood. I made a choice and I was living with the consequences.

I wandered back into the living room to find Anna. I steeled myself. I felt stronger.

"I called Daniel to thank him. He's coming back on Tuesday and we're going to meet after work. I guess he'll officially tell me then."

Anna was on the sofa and reached out her hand to pull me down next to her.

"What did he say?"

"Nothing, we didn't talk long. He said he missed me and he asked me how I was, but that's it."

"Did you tell him that you missed him? He's worth fighting for, Leah. He should know how you feel."

"I did tell him I missed him, but I don't want to fight for him. I want him to be mine because he can't possibly be anything else. I want him to need me like I need him. I can't force or fight for that. I love him and if he's happy with his ex-wife then I'm happy for him. I'm sad for me, but happy that he's happy. That's what I want for him."

I was lucky to have had him in my life, even if it were for just the shortest time. Imagine if I had gone through my life thinking what I had with Charlie was as good as it got. With Daniel, I learned what love was. Real, earth-shattering, heart-stopping, world-changing love. How many people could really say that? I was lucky, and I would treasure forever the moments I shared with him. But now nothing else would do, and however many times Anna forced me out to meet new guys, however many times she told me that the easiest way to get over a man is to get under another, it didn't matter. No one else was Daniel. I felt sure I could get to a place where I was content with my life. But it would be different from how I had envisaged as a girl. There would be no wedding, no family. I would be on my own, without Daniel.

"Well, all that therapy seems to have worked, but I hope it doesn't mean we can't indulge in a little wine o'clock just because you're no longer self-medicating. Especially since we have a fully stocked wine fridge!"

"Only if you promise to help me look fucking *amazing* on Tuesday. He might be dumping me, but it doesn't mean he can't fancy me while he's doing it."

"As Oscar Wilde said, 'Crying is for plain women. Pretty women go shopping.' Tomorrow night, you and me in Selfridges. We are going to knock him dead.

"Oscar Wilde, hey? You're stepping it up!"

---

I stood in front of the mirror in the Roland Mouret dress, thinking up ways to justify the ridiculously expensive purchase. The dress did everything a dress should do for a woman. I loved it.

"I don't know if you are talking yourself into it or out of it, but it doesn't matter. You just *have* to buy this dress." Anna was slumped in a chair in the corner of the changing room.

"It's a lot of money."

"So, sell a kidney. We're not leaving here without that dress." Anna was quickly losing patience. We'd been having this back and forth for twenty minutes.

"You're right." I headed back to the dressing room to peel myself out of the thing and whip out my credit card before I changed my mind.

I felt physically sick as I typed in my PIN. I'd never

spent even half of what this dress cost on a piece of clothing, but if this was the last time I was going to see Daniel, I wanted to feel fabulous. And if he got a reminder of what he would be missing, well that was all right, too.

---

I didn't wear the dress to work. Knowing me, I would have spilled something on myself by 10 a.m., so I brought it with me. I left my desk dead on 5:30 to change. I wanted to be ready—mentally and physically. I thought that outside of the flattering light of the changing rooms and into the bright fluorescents of the ladies restroom the dress would lose its wow factor, but it absolutely did not. Although I couldn't say it aloud, Anna was right; the dress was made for boobs and a bottom like mine. The cleavage was just hinting at outrageous but the mid shin length with killer heels seemed to balance it all out to sexy. I was thrilled. I had treated myself to a blow dry at lunchtime so I just needed to touch up my makeup and I was done. I was back at my desk just before six. I checked my phone to make sure I'd not missed a call and there was a text from Daniel.

**No rush but I'm ready whenever you are. I'm downstairs. D**

He'd been waiting half an hour already. My heart started thudding like it was about to come through my

## FAITHFUL

chest. This was it. I was far more nervous than that evening all those months ago when we he had first picked me up from the office. I suppose I didn't know then what I'd be missing. I logged off and headed to the elevators forcing myself to take deep breaths.

I saw him as I came out of the elevator. He leaned against the car with his head was buried in a newspaper.

I stood there for a few minutes just drinking in the sight of him. His beautiful navy suit, my favorite. It skimmed every beautiful inch of him. His hair was just how I saw it in my head whenever I thought of him: almost too long, but the perfect length to slide my fingers through. My skin tightened all over.

As if he heard me inhale, Daniel looked up sharply from his paper and his eyes met mine. There was no going back. I started to walk toward him, but I couldn't pull my eyes away from his. I had forgotten the power he had over me.

He met me at the door

"Hey stranger." His velvety voice washed through me.

"Hey stranger, yourself." Despite my nervousness and anguish, I couldn't help but grin at him. It was as if he pushed a happy button inside me. I couldn't feel anything bad when I was around him.

He didn't kiss me, he didn't touch me. He wanted it to be clear how we stood from the start—he was trying to be fair with me and I appreciated him for that. It made me love him more.

He opened the car door for me; as I climbed in, his hand brushed my lower back. It was if I were on fire. Couldn't he feel that? I shivered as goosebumps covered my whole body and I felt myself moisten for him. He had barely touched me and I was ready for him, desperate for him. I scurried over as far into the corner of the car as I could. I would dissolve if he touched me again, and despite myself I would be begging for him to come back to me.

As the car started, I kept my eyes fixed forward.

"So, I saw that your results were really well received. You must be so pleased."

"Yes, relieved. The ex-MD has been charged. We're cooperating with the police and I've installed a new MD. Things can get back to how they should be now, I hope."

But he should be with *me*, that's how things should be.

We pulled up and I realized we were outside Daniel's favorite Italian restaurant. Oh god, why here? I suppose he wanted to break the news to me in public so I couldn't yell and scream at him. I loved this place. I wouldn't ever be able to come here again, not after tonight. I'm sure we would say we'd stay in touch, but I couldn't do that. I truly wished him happiness, but I couldn't be friends with him and watch him be happy without me.

## FAITHFUL

Daniel was made a real fuss of, as usual, as we were escorted to the same table we had on our first real date. I had managed to avoid looking directly at him since I got into the car, but there was no avoiding it forever. I lifted my eyes and found him looking right into me.

"There you are." He smiled cautiously and I couldn't do anything but smile right back at him.

As soon as our wine was poured, I glugged down half a glass. I wanted that numbness back. I didn't want all these feelings. I felt the warmth of the alcohol as it trickled down to my fingers and toes.

"Leah, you don't need liquid courage. It's OK."

But it wasn't OK. I couldn't bear it any longer—I wanted it done.

"Daniel, I just want you to be happy and I'm pleased you are. You're right, it's OK. I'm not going to make a big scene. You two have known each other since you were kids. I get it. It's fine."

We were interrupted as our starters arrived. The sight of the food made my stomach churn. I was sure it would be delicious, but the thought of eating anything was abhorrent.

I fixed my eyes on the tablecloth again.

"Leah, look at me." His tone was gentle, coaxing. I could do nothing but what Daniel asked of me; I met his eyes as requested. "I'm not following you. Who have I knownc since I was a kid?"

"Georgina."

"Oh right. Yes, you knew that though." He was right, I had known all along and I couldn't compete with that history. I nodded. I could feel the tears start to well in my eyes so I took another generous gulp of wine.

"So, tell me how you've been. What have you been doing? How are you feeling about ... well, everything?"

"Good, everything has been good. I feel like I've worked through a lot of things and I feel much better about everything. Well, most things."

"Good, I'm pleased. And have you been seeing anyone?"

What did he mean? A therapist?

"I'm sorry, I shouldn't have asked. It's none of my business." Daniel was the one to stare at the tablecloth this time. He meant romantically.

"You mean, like a man? Of course not." I didn't want to have to fight for him but surely he knew how I felt. "There's no one. There'll never be anyone, now. It will always be you for me." My voice cracked but I forced myself to carry on. I couldn't leave without him knowing. "Just because I'm not with you doesn't mean you won't always be with me, in my heart." As I spoke I felt calmer. "I've learned a lot about myself these past two months. I'm going to be fine. I don't want you to feel bad. I don't want you to feel guilty. I'm happy loving you, whether or not you love me back. I just want you to be happy, and if

I can't give you that happiness then all I can wish for you is that you've found it with Georgina."

"You love me, still?"

"Still and always." As I looked back at him I knew it would forever be true.

"I can't do this here." Daniel rummaged in his jacket pocket and threw some cash—far too much —on the table and stood up. "Let's get some air."

Daniel was through the door before I said goodbye to Luigi. As I stepped outside, Daniel pulled me to him. His looked at me so intensely, so intimately; I felt a fuzziness in my legs and thought I might collapse. And then he kissed me, delicately, softly. I reached under his jacket and traced his beautifully broad back. His tongue trailed between my lips; I was lost to him. I hadn't allowed myself to remember how it felt when he touched me, but I couldn't stifle the moan that betrayed me.

"Daniel." I pulled away from him.

"I'm sorry. I couldn't go another moment without kissing you."

"It's not fair on Georgina."

"What does kissing you have to do with George? If I didn't know better, I'd be jealous. You seem to have an unhealthy interest in her."

"You can't be kissing me when you are with Georgina, it's just not—"

"—With Georgina? What are you talking about? I'm not with Georgina!"

*What?* "But the pictures, at the launch?"

"She came to the launch, but not with me. I couldn't be with her again. I couldn't be with anyone who isn't you."

"You're not back with her?"

"Of course not. That launch was weeks ago. Have you thought all this time I was back with her? Why didn't you call me?"

My tears flowed uncontrollably. It was relief and happiness all mixed up. My heart tried to explode in my chest as he pulled me toward him. Daniel wiped my tears from my face. "Don't cry, baby. Don't be sad."

"I'm not sad." I sobbed. "I'm ... I don't know what I am."

"Mine?" Daniel suggested.

"Yours."

# EPILOGUE

"This is the smallest of the bedrooms, but a perfect size for a small study or maybe a nursery." The agent looked under her lashes at us, clearly trying to gauge our reaction.

Panic rumbled at the base of my spine, and then I heard Daniel's throaty laugh next to me as he pulled me toward him and kissed my temple.

"Breathe, baby. We don't have children." Daniel explained to the agent through his laughter. "Yet." He added raising his eyebrows at me. I play-slapped his stomach, but really rather than chastisement it was just an excuse to touch him.

We followed the agent out of this, the smallest of the five bedrooms in the apartment we were looking at. Since Daniel returned from New York we hadn't spend a night apart. Our separation made it clear to me that although I could do without him I would never want to and so I agreed to move in with him when he asked me exactly three weeks after our reconciliation. I moved the rest of my stuff out of Anna's. As soon as I was unpacked Daniel announced he wanted us to have our own place rather than share the place he lived in with Georgina so we were house hunting.

The apartment was incredible. Since the break in Daniel insisted we only look at apartments with 24 hour security. The police hadn't discovered who had broken in but I never went back there overnight and Daniel installed a security system before Anna went back.

As we left the building Daniel grabbed my hand as we started down the street. "So, what do you think?" He was grinning at me.

"It's amazing, Daniel. Big but homey. But we don't need all that space. It's huge."

"Would you be happy here?" He pulled me in. "I want you to be happy."

"I'm happy anywhere if I'm with you."

"Then marry me."

It wasn't the first time he'd mentioned marriage. He'd brought it up a couple of times. There'd been no formal proposal, so I'd never said no, but I hadn't said yes, either. I knew it was going to happen. I wanted it to happen, but I was in no rush. I looked up to him. He looked worried. I reached for his face.

"Hey. Don't look so worried."

"I want us to be together forever. That's all." I pulled his forehead to mine.

"We are going to be together forever."

"Then tell me you'll marry me."

"I'll marry you, Daniel."

# Acknowledgements

The process of writing this book has been so more fulfilling that I can have possibly imagined. Most people who have supported and inspired me along the way have no idea of the part they played but I thank them still.

Thank you to all my friends and family who have encouraged me (and not quite believed me when I told them I was writing a book).

Thank you Ashley Rutter – If I'd not found your blog, I'm not sure this would have ever happened.

Thank you Twirly for your help and excitement.

Read on for the first chapter of my novel Hopeful.

# Contact

If you enjoyed Faithful, please leave a review.
Good reviews really help indie authors!
Get in contact – I'd love to hear from you!

Tweet me
twitter.com/louisesbay

Friend me
www.facebook.com/louisesbay

Like me
www.facebook.com/authorlouisebay

Pin me
www.pinterest.com/louisebay

Friend me
www.goodreads.com/author/show/8056592.Louise_Bay

Add me to your circles
https://plus.google.com/u/0/+LouiseBayauthor

Follow my photos on Instagram
Louisesbay

Find me at home
www.louisebay.com

# Other Books by Louise Bay

## Hopeful

Guys like Joel Wentworth weren't supposed to fall in love with girls like me. He could have had his pick of the girls on campus, but somehow the laws of nature were defied and we fell crazy in love.

After graduation, Joel left for New York. And, despite him wanting me to go with him, I'd refused, unwilling to disappoint my parents and risk the judgment of my friends. I hadn't seen him again. Never even spoke to him.

I've spent the last eight years working hard to put my career front and center in my life, dodging any personal complications. I have a strict no-dating policy. I've managed to piece together a reality that works for me.

Until now.

Now, Joel's coming back to London.

And I need to get over him before he gets over here.

*Hopeful* is a stand-alone novel. Read on for the first chapter.

Praise for *Hopeful*

"This book contains **hot sex**, angst and you are so desperate to know what happens next." *Kindle Friends Forever*

"Louise skillfully combines humour and heartbreak with copious amounts anticipation to make this book **one of the great finds of 2014**. I loved every word, every feeling and every tear. " *Agents of Romance*

"It gave me the good ache! This is a true love story and **I couldn't put it down**! I highly recommend!" *Gwen the Book Diva*

"I really **loved this story** and this couple." *Slick Reads – Guilty Pleasures Book Reviews*

"If done right, all you need are amazing characters... check...enthralling storyline to keep you wanting more... check...and sizzling hot chemistry...double check! This book **hooked me right from beginning to end** and I sunk right into the turbulent depths of their journey." *Page Turning Book-Junkies*

"Deserves **more than five stars**!"

"**It was amazing**." *Summer's Book Blog*

"The chemistry and intensity going on in this book felt so strong and you could really feel it and **it was definitely hot!!!**" *Hooked on Books*

"Hopeful was **simply amazing** and soul consuming." *Just One More Page*

"This is a story that pulls at your heart all the way

through. I was so taken by this book **I couldn't put it down**." *Eye Candy Bookstore*

"Louise Bay did an amazing job making us laugh, cry and fall in love with JOEL WENTWORTH!" *Rude Girl Book Blog*

"Louise Bay creates such an engaging world that you can't help but **find yourself mesmerized**." *Cocktails and Books*

"This intriguing book is written and played out beautifully! **I've had tears and I've had tingles** - I've laughed too. A romance can't give us much more than that." *Cariad - Sizzling Pages*

# The Empire State Series

**Part One:** *A Week in New York*

**Part Two:** *Autumn in London*

**Part Three:** *New Year in Manhattan*

Anna Kirby is sick of dating. She's tired of heartbreak. Despite being smart, sexy, and funny, she's a magnet for men who don't deserve her.

A week's vacation in New York is the ultimate distraction from her most recent break-up, as well as a great place to meet a stranger and have some summer fun. But to protect her still-bruised heart, fun comes with rules. There will be no sharing stories, no swapping numbers, and no real names. Just one night of uncomplicated fun.

Super-successful serial seducer Ethan Scott has some rules of his own. He doesn't date, he doesn't stay the night, and he doesn't make any promises.

It should be a match made in heaven. But rules are made to be broken.

Praise for *The Empire State Series*

"An **unforgettable** first book in the series. It will leave you wanting more, but not frustrated. It was sexy and erotic, but felt authentic. I can't wait for the next two coming. I **highly recommend** it!!" *Books and Beyond Fifty Shades*

"The **writing is excellent** and you'll be hooked from the very beginning. I am definitely looking forward to the next instalment of the series. I was a fan of Ms. Bay's after reading her novel Hopeful earlier in the year and A Week in New York has only helped to make me a bigger fan." *Love Between the Sheets*

"Louise has done it again and created **a fantastic read**. This deserves every one of the **five stars** rewarded and more. Louise certainly can tell a story." *Kindle Friends Forever*

**"5 "I don't Bullshit" Stars**! If you haven't started this series, you need to now!! It's an easy, quick, and smooth read that you are sure to enjoy." *Book Bitches Blog*

"I've become a **total Louise Bay junkie**. Love everything I've read by her." *Bare Naked Words*

"I would **give it 6,7,8,or 9 stars if I could**." *Obsessed with Books*

"The Empire State Trilogy is one of the **not only good ones, but GREAT ones**. I am so in love with Ethan and Anna. *Book Briefs*

"It is **INCREDIBLE**!!! I give this book 5 stars with 5 hands down the pants. I CANNOT wait for the next book, hurry up Ms. Bay!!" *Beautifully RED*

# Hopeful
## Chapter One

*Present*

"I thought we were going to the pub, you boring bastards."

Adam was on one of his increasingly regular rants. Everyone reacted to the Big Three-O differently. Apparently, Adam was going to party as hard as possible and reject any evidence that he wasn't a kid anymore.

"We're going when this is over, so shut the fuck up." The six of us—even Matt and Daniel—were engrossed in sequin-covered, ballroom-dancing celebrities, but Adam was restless. He paced up and down behind us all. He'd been in a bad mood all day.

"Ava, I'm surprised at you, liking this glitter and sequins and dancing shit. You're such a girl."

"IQ points are wasted on you, aren't they? Get lost so we can watch this in peace." I hated to humor him when he acted like this, but reacting was wasted energy.

"Thank god I'm getting my wingman back for good. I'm going to nail a different girl every day this summer."

"Yeah, I'm sure," Daniel said as he headed to the bar.

"... won't mind you picking up his leftovers."

*What did he say?*

"No one says 'nail' anymore, Adam." Leah said. "This isn't 1996."

Jules turned to raise her glass to get a top-up from Daniel, the perfect man he was, who had brought the half-empty wine bottle over from the bar. "Has someone not snapped that delicious man up yet?"

*Who? What delicious man?*

"Nope. And I don't need his leftovers, so fuck off, Daniel. We're going to tag team it all across Londontown this summer."

"Not if I snap him up first!" Jules jiggled on the sofa.

Adam's mood was not improving. "And you can fuck off, Jules. Don't go near him when he gets back."

*Joel.*

*They were talking about Joel. Joel was coming back.*

*Fuck.*

---

It was so hot in the pub that I couldn't breathe. The sweaters I had on weren't helping. Nor was the open fire. Nor was the mention of Joel. The conversation had moved on to other things, but I was desperate to know more. When was he coming back? Why was he coming back?

# HOPEFUL

I hadn't seen him for so long—years. Not since July 10, 2006, if we wanted to be exact.

"You ok, Ava?" Jules asked.

My grin was too wide. "Of course. Just hot." I was going to have to work on my poker face. And my hearing: I couldn't hear anything. We were in a little local pub in the middle of nowhere, but it was so loud. Everyone's voices came out as incomprehensible vowel sounds. Maybe I was coming down with something. I just wanted to get back to the house and crawl into bed, but I was designated driver. Thank god we were all going home soon. I needed some space, some time to think.

Tomorrow was the end of our annual weekend away. Since University, we all got together every Easter. It had started as just a Sunday lunch and, over the years, had morphed into a weekend in the country. Daniel had become the richest man in England—technically, I think he was the third richest man under 40 in England, but whatever he was, he was far richer than the rest of us. He found us increasingly glamorous places to stay, which he insisted on paying for. At first we resisted, but it had been futile and we had all long since given in. He was just ridiculously rich. This year we were in a beautiful old castle in Scotland that had turrets and sweeping driveways and staff. It felt like a hotel, but with only us as guests. I'm not sure why we'd even come to the pub—we had a cook back at our castle.

It was a comforting ritual. Various girlfriends and boyfriends came and went, but the six of us were together every year. This year Daniel brought Leah; I wondered if by this time next year they would be married. They hadn't been together long but they were perfect together.

Neither Jules nor Adam had significant others this year. Jules had disposed of her latest victim last month, and Adam, for all his talk, was still licking his wounds over his girlfriend of five years rejecting his proposal this time last year. I'm not sure if he really was out "nailing" half of London, but I doubted it. He had never been good at casual sex. He was far too needy—one of several reasons there would never be anything romantic between us. We were teased about it from time to time. Matt and Hanna were convinced Adam and I would end up together, but Matt and Hanna wanted everyone paired off as soon as possible. They had been together since the first term at University and married just after graduation. They wanted everyone to be as settled as them, in the nicest possible way. They were so happy and wished that for everyone in their orbit. They had been the constant in our group—like the patient parents of four unruly children.

I'd never brought anyone along to our annual weekend in the country, but I'd never liked anyone enough to let him into this private world. Not since Joel.

Joel. God, I had to get out of there. My head was full

of him. Over the past eight years, I'd pushed him to the very corners of my memory. Within weeks of his leaving, I had started my training for one of the best law firms in the country, first at law school and then on the job. I had loved the long hours, the lack of sleep, the mostly unspoken competition between the junior lawyers, the whole brutality of the culture. It was my punishment. In those first few years I didn't see much of our little group; I deliberately kept my distance. I'd joined in on the odd night out, and of course we did our annual Easter thing, but generally it was all too painful. It reminded me too much of our shared history and of what was missing, who was missing. Work was the perfect excuse, and nobody questioned my absence, really. After a couple of years I had bought my first flat in Clapham, which was where Hanna and Matt lived, and slowly I began seeing more of them and then more of Adam and then everyone. I restarted my life outside work.

Of course, I didn't date. Not even a little. There were times that my lack of sex life was questioned. Jules regularly asked me if I was shagging my boss and Adam occasionally enquired whether I was a closeted lesbian. But eventually my singledom stopped being a topic of conversation. Hanna and Matt were married; Daniel had been in New York, married to his now *ex*-wife, George; Jules was a serial monogamist; Adam was a pretend serial shagger either side of a long-term girlfriend. And I was single. That's just how we were. That's how we saw each other and ourselves.

Joel's return threatened to put a proverbial cat among the Clapham pigeons.

*Past*

Joel was Adam's friend, initially. They were classmates—both economists—while the rest of us were thrown together in the same block of bedrooms in the dorm. Joel lived on his own off campus, so I'd only see fleeting glimpses of him when he came to visit Adam. On nights out, he would sometimes be there, but he seemed always slightly at arm's length from the rest of us. He and Adam were kind of a package deal. Whereas the rest of us were all firsthand friends, Joel was a secondhand friend—we knew him only through Adam. This thought only struck me when I saw him for the first time without Adam.

It was midmorning in the library at the beginning of our final year, it was packed, and I was desperately trying to find a desk. I had two or three secret spots on the first floor that were so tucked away that I could always guarantee one of them would be empty, but not that day. I'd been forced off the first floor that held the law library to the third floor when I spotted him. That was when I realized I didn't really know Joel. He was just familiar. I stood, half-concealed by a bookshelf, and watched him, his head bowed and his forehead creased, flicking between two books as if they were saying completely opposing things and he was trying to make sense of it. There was a space open opposite him; I wanted to grab it before anyone else did, but I felt awkward, shy almost. Looking—no staring—at him from this distance, I took him in. I usually avoided looking at him, desperate to ensure I didn't become one of the quivering women that seemed to be constantly buzzing around him. He had developed a bit of a half-beard, which made him look even more masculine than usual. He still had his summer tan, and his shirt clung to his broad chest. His sleeves were pushed up, emphasizing his strong arms and his very capable-looking hands. Had he always been this handsome? Totally out of my league.

As if he could feel someone watching him he raised his head, and I knew I should look away and busy myself with the bookshelf in front of me, but I couldn't. His eyes found mine and he broke into a grin. I forced a goofy smile back, did a stupid half-wave, and walked toward him. Jesus, I was pathetic.

And that's how it started; Joel became my firsthand friend.

"Hey, Ava. You studying or picking up books?"

"I'm trying to find a spare desk to start my thesis but the world's conspiring against me. This library's packed!" My voice was a least half an octave higher than any sane person. *Calm the hell down, Ava.*

"What bad luck. And that free desk in front of you right now is completely useless? Anyone who sits there will be infected by a curse which will cause them to fail their finals?"

"You heard that, too? Well, coming from an economist, I suppose I have to believe it—I thought it was just a rumor. See you around." I pulled my eyes away from his and turned to leave.

"Sit, Ava."

I said nothing, avoiding his eyes, and I set out my books and papers and opened my laptop.

I'd always recognized Joel as being attractive. That was just an indisputable fact; acknowledged by men and women alike. He was well over six feet tall, had a swimmer's body and that slightly longer, messy hair that just begged to be tousled. The boys would tease him about being pretty and the girls would flirt with him as a matter of course. It was his confidence that sealed the deal. I'm not sure if he was confident because he was so gorgeous or gorgeous because he was so confident. He wasn't cocky or arrogant, and he didn't enjoy other people's misery or disaster. He was just very comfortable with who he was—or so it seemed.

The world Joel inhabited wasn't like most people's: It was a privileged existence. He was served at the bar before others, strangers smiled at him in the street, and shop assistants were at his beck and call. From the outside, the sun just seemed to shine a bit brighter in his world. I had never resented his smoother path in life, never thought it was unfair. I just knew it to be different from the world I lived in, and I understood that our worlds wouldn't collide. But sitting opposite him did bring our worlds into convergence, just a little. I watched from behind my hair as people stopped by his desk to do that weird boy handshake stuff, bat their eyelashes (women mainly, but not exclusively) and even library staff acknowledged him with an air of deference. None of his visitors gave me a second look. To my embarrassment, every now and again Joel caught me distractedly looking at his interactions with his numerous admirers. He said not a word when he caught me; he just offered the occasional smirk.

Despite the floorshow right in front of me, I managed to achieve more than I expected. Joel always had good grades; I'd assumed these always came easily to him, like the rest of his life, but it seemed that, like the rest of us, he had to work hard to do well in class. So when his admirers weren't looking, Joel worked hard—really hard. Now, I wasn't competitive, but I wasn't letting a pretty boy like Joel out-study me. I took fewer breaks than usual, which may have had something to do with my view, but more than that, I wanted him to know I worked hard, too.

At lunchtime, one of his almost equally attractive friends came to over to ask him to grab a snack.

Unexpectedly, he asked me to join them and I hastily refused. I needed a break from study, but I also needed a break from being so close to him.

At just after seven I was ready to throw in the towel. Joel looked totally consumed by what he was doing—it looked complicated with graphs and numbers stuff. Without saying anything, I started packing up my stuff. As I closed my laptop, he looked up.

"Hey, are you going? I'll come with you." He looked exhausted.

"You stay. You look engrossed."

"No, I'm done. I'll walk you back." He collapsed back in his chair and ran his hands through his hair.

"Adam will be around, I imagine." Joel just looked at me and frowned.

Silently we gathered our stuff and headed out.

Following the pedestrian path back to the dorms, neither of us had uttered a word.

"So, you work hard?" I blurted. I wasn't as comfortable with the silence as Joel seemed to be.

Joel threw his head back and laughed. "Yes, I work hard. You sound shocked. Did you think I had my work done by someone else?"

"No. Sorry. No, I just thought it would have come easily to you or something."

He bent his head to my ear. "Nothing worth having comes easy, Ava."

I could feel the warmth in my cheeks. Was he flirting with me? I kept my eyes fixed on the path in front of me. I heard him laugh again. He was making fun of me. Great.

"Maybe that's true for most of us," I said.

"Who's that not true of?"

"All I'm saying is that life is easier for some people. The planets align for some but not others."

"Oh wow, you're one of those." He was laughing again.

"One of what? Don't laugh at me!" I stopped in the middle of the sidewalk.

"Come on," he said. He pulled my backpack off me and tossed it over his shoulder. "It's just girls have this fascination with astrology that I've never quite understood."

I could feel my temperature rising and my face contorted into a scowl.

"I'm not 'one of those,' as you put it." I could tell by his face that he knew I was mad as hell. "I wasn't talking about fucking astrology, about whether you'll get a better job because you are a Leo and not a fucking Virgo; I was talking about some people's lot in life being easier than others. It's a fact. Attractive people are more likely to be promoted at work, less likely to get depression, etc.

etc. There have been scientific studies about it. I'm not talking about fucking astrology."

Joel had stopped laughing but his smile was still there. He had a strange look on his face, as if he was saying something to me in his head but the words weren't coming out.

"What?!" I started walking.

In two of his very long strides he had caught up with me "Well, I ... It's just. You're right. I'm sorry. I misunderstood you."

"Ok."

"Ok."

"Ok." I giggled at our to and fro.

"Oh, and you're cute when you swear."

I swatted him on the arm.

"And you think I'm attractive. Nice."

I swatted him twice on the arm.

Back at the dorm, we bumped into Adam coming out of the block door.

"Hey, I just called you. We're off to the pub. Are you coming, Joel? Where have you two been? Come on, let's go."

I walked straight past them both and toward my room.

"Let me drop off Ava's bag and I'll follow you up." I heard Joel say as I kicked off my shoes and collapsed on my bed.

Joel knocked on the open door. "Are you decent or shall I come back later?"

"Thanks for carrying my books back."

"It was my pleasure. You're a great study partner, and you're very easy to wind up. It's a winning combination. Let's do it again sometime."

*Anytime*, I thought. I could be top of the class if I studied as intently as I did when Joel was around.

"Sure. I'm going to have to live in the library this term if I'm going to get my thesis done."

"Ok, I'll pick you up tomorrow."

Was he serious? "Ok."

"Ok." He grinned.

"Get out of here, loser." I giggled. He was pretty *and* funny. Bloody hell. He should share some of it with others. Why did it end up concentrated in just one guy?

---

True to his word, Joel picked me up and walked me to the library the next morning, and then walked me home that evening. The next day was the same. And just like that we were in each other's lives.

Our conversation was restricted to the walks to and from the library at first, but then we started to take lunch together and then the odd break. Pretty quickly, Joel was the person I spent the most time with out of all the friends I had at University, including the roommates

I lived with. More than that, he was the one I wanted to spend every waking moment with. As well as being great eye candy and making me laugh all the time, he was kind and thoughtful. Not just to me, but also to everyone he came across.

After that second day together in the library, I never bothered pretending to look for a desk on the first floor. I just went to our desk on the third floor. Of course, library study was interrupted by lectures and tutorials, but the first day that Joel and I went to the library separately, I wandered up to our desk and found a jacket on the chair opposite and a couple of books on the desk. My heart sank. He had a new desk mate.

"Hey, Ava," Joel said in a loud whisper.

"Hey." I faked a smile.

"How were lectures?"

"Good. Hard but good."

"Ok. You'd better sit down and study, then." God, I was interrupting him. How embarrassing.

"Yes, thanks Dad. I'm going to find a free desk."

"But I saved your spot." He'd saved me a seat. *He'd saved me a seat!* I really shouldn't have been so excited.

"Ok, thanks."

"Ok, you're welcome." He grinned his gorgeous grin at me.

"Ok, you loser." I couldn't help but grin back.

I pulled out my papers and laptop and got to work.

About an hour into things, my concentration was beginning to waver and my imagination started to wander across the desk. I wondered what he was like in lectures. Did he sit at the front with his hand up all the time, or was he at the back ignoring the lecturer and flirting with whatever girl was next to him? A scrunched up ball of paper hitting my keyboard pulled me back into reality. I looked up and Joel was grinning at me. He nodded his head in the direction of the bookshelves next to him.

"What?" I mouthed. Joel just nodded his head more vigorously. I strained my head but I could see anything. "What?" I mouthed again. "Come here," he mouthed back. I pushed my chair away from my desk and walked around our table toward him with my back to where he was nodding. What was he pointing to? Why was he being so cagey? He patted his desk and I leaned against his desk, my fingers gripping the wood either side of me. "What?" I mouthed again. He made a come here motion with his finger so I bent forward. Wow, he smelled good.

"Some people have more of a physical approach to studying than we do. Look to your right," Joel whispered.

As subtly as I could I turned my head and through the books I saw a very amorous couple who clearly thought they were better hidden than they were. They were kissing fervently, as if any moment they would be pulled apart and would never see each other again, their hands desperately running across each other's bodies, feeling each other's contours through their clothes. I couldn't pull my eyes away.

"You like to watch," Joel whispered. It wasn't a question.

He was so close to me that my skin prickled at his breath on my neck. In that moment, all I wanted was for Joel to kiss me like the guy I was watching was kissing his girl. My heart pounded and I was conscious of my skin tightening across my body.

"Oh my," I finally managed. "I guess it's a good way to blow off steam for them. Like, stress relief or something." I was scrambling for words.

"Wanna give it a try?" My head flicked back to Joel, whose eyes were twinkling at me.

"Don't you twinkle at me, Joel Wentworth." I faked a dose of haughtiness and went back to my seat.

"What? I'm just thinking about your stress levels."

"Ok, well thanks for the offer."

"Ok, well anytime." He raised his eyebrows and gave me that ridiculously handsome grin.

*Oh my* was right. I put my head down and did a great impression of someone studying extraordinarily hard. There was no ambiguity. Joel was flirting with me, and furthermore, I was enjoying him flirting with me. I had to remind myself that Joel couldn't help but flirt. He was genetically programmed to spread his charm and good looks around. I had to become impervious to his charms. It wasn't personal; it was just Joel.

---

*Present*

Now Joel was coming back. No doubt he hadn't lost any of his charm or good looks. I had spent the last eight years working hard to put my career front and center in my life, dodging any personal complications. I could control my career—the harder I worked, the more success I had. It balanced out the fact that I didn't have anyone special in my life. Of course, I'd tried; in the beginning, I'd been on a few dates. But my heart wasn't in it. I wanted Joel; I was in love with Joel, and no one else quite measured up. Adam provided my male company and came along to black tie events and dinners when I needed a plus one. I managed to piece together a reality that worked for me. It wasn't that I wasn't in love—I was. It was just that my love just wasn't in my life. Love hadn't been enough.

The thought of coming face to face with Joel brought the realization that my reality was twisted. It was eight years since I had had any contact with him, but I still thought of Joel as being with me because he was with me in my head and in my heart. I still had conversations with him in my head. I still smiled when I saw people

PDAing because I knew it would make Joel smile. I still followed his progress avidly, either from snippets from Adam or Matt or whatever my Google alert threw out. It was as if we were having a long distance relationship, but I was the only participant.

On July 10, 2006, Joel left for New York and I'd never seen him again. Never even spoken to him. I don't know if I'd expected him to come back before now. I suppose I had. I had assumed there would be some sort of resolution between us. Either he would come back, forgive me, declare that he couldn't be without me, and we would live happily ever after—or I would fall out of love with him. Neither happened, but I still kept waiting.

Of course, he had come back to London to visit, on work trips from what I could make out, but I'd always managed to be busy or away, and because no one knew about Joel and me, no one said anything. Now he would be back for good and I wouldn't be able to dodge him. My brain, which I'd managed to trick into thinking I was happy, thinking I could live with a one-sided long-distance relationship, was faced with reality. Shit. I needed Jules's help. I needed to date, get a boyfriend. Something.

Panic flooded through me, and when I was panicked, there was only one thing to do. Take positive action. I was good in a crisis and I was going to have to be.

"Jules, hi. So, I need your help."

"Anything. What I can do for you?"

"So, you know you're on those Internet dating sites."

"Oh. My. God. I've finally broken you, haven't I?" Jules screamed. She was always begging me to start Internet dating. "You know it's the only way to meet someone in London. This is going to be great."

"I haven't even said anything yet."

"I can hear the resignation in your voice."

"Ok, so will you help me put myself online, or whatever I have to do?"

"I so will. Tomorrow night. You bring the wine, I'll bring my laptop. This is going to be so much fun."

"Fine, whatever. Don't tell anyone. Don't tell Adam." I didn't want Adam to know because I didn't want him to tell Joel. I didn't want Joel to think that I was some sad spinster that couldn't get a date.

"Because you two are having a secret affair?"

"Because he will tease the shit out of me. Please Jules." I was whining. I irritated myself when I whined.

"Fine. Whatever. No need to get your knickers in a twist."

I put down the phone and immediately felt sick. Christ. I was going to have to get over him before he got over here.

Made in the USA
Charleston, SC
01 March 2015